Dear Dad

A Novel by
George Delmarmo

CCB Publishing
British Columbia, Canada

Dear Dad

Copyright ©2015 by George Delmarmo
ISBN-13 978-1-77143-213-9
First Edition

Library and Archives Canada Cataloguing in Publication
Delmarmo, George, 1936-, author
Dear Dad / by George Delmarmo. -- First edition.
Issued in print and electronic formats.
ISBN 978-1-77143-213-9 (pbk.).--ISBN 978-1-77143-214-6 (pdf)
Additional cataloguing data available from Library and Archives Canada

Contact the author George Delmarmo at: Hogfarmer@aol.com

Publisher: CCB Publishing
              British Columbia, Canada
              www.ccbpublishing.com

Contents

Prologue v

Chapter One 1

Chapter Two 9

Chapter Three 11

Chapter Four 18

Chapter Five 21

Chapter Six 28

Chapter Seven 33

Chapter Eight 54

Chapter Nine 63

Chapter Ten 71

Chapter Eleven 80

Chapter Twelve 93

Chapter Thirteen 108

Chapter Fourteen 125

Chapter Fifteen 140

Chapter Sixteen 154

Chapter Seventeen 182

Chapter Eighteen 196

Chapter Nineteen 203

Chapter Twenty 216

Epilogue 221

About the Author 224

Books by George Delmarmo 225

Characters

- George, author
- Commodore, storeowner
- Sue Ann, daughter of Dr. Stein, mother of Trina and Eric, George's daughter
- Dr. Joann Stern, Sue Ann's mother, Trina's grandmother, George's doctor
- Russ, George's friend
- Eric, Sue Ann's son…died
- Trina, Sue Ann's daughter
- Chief of Police
- Two Deputies: Ike and Mike
- Mrs. Lila Henderson, boarding house operator
- Lewis, Trina's first boyfriend
- Tisha, cleaning lady
- Chad, editor of paper
- Steven, Trina's boyfriend, husband
- Ruth, Chairlady
- Peter, juror
- Mildred, Lady Officer
- Eugene and Mary: Psychiatrist and his wife
- Hilda, State Attorney
- Nancy, Russ' computer lady

Prologue

This story is about me. In my golden years, I learned about a child I never knew I had. The child was not the result of a torrid, passionate, love affair. I never knew what had happened or that anything did happen. Some fifty years after the event was the first time I even realized that something did happen.

The event affected many people's lives in ways that seem bizarre at best. Living through the events was more unbelievable, but after the deed was done, the question of what to do about it became paramount. The question of what I should do to save my reputation compared to what is legal and not legal got all mixed up. What effect it had on me has to be measured next to the effects it had on others. Like a pebble that is dropped in a pool of water, no one knows for sure where the ripples will spread or what will happen when they mix with other events. The cause and effect of one deed has (in this case) created problems in my lifetime and will also cause problems in other people's lives for generations to come. There just is no end to the mischief one misguided event will have.

In my case I saw the effects on three generations of my family, and I cannot even guess what future effects it will have. After reading the book, contact me and let me hear what you would have done differently.

Chapter One

"Dear Dad" are two words that strike fear into my heart. I rechecked who had sent me the email, and it was from someone whose name I did not recognize. I didn't know whether to keep reading or just to delete the message. Of course, my curiosity won the battle.

The message continued with, "You don't know me, but you sure knew my mother; her name was Dr. Joann Stern. Please contact me at my email address, so we can arrange a mutually agreeable time and place to meet, Daddy.

Your loving daughter --Sue Ann Stern

I fell back in my chair and drifted off into space for the message had just erased fifty years of my life as I thought back to the first time I had met Dr. Joann Stern.

I had gone to my doctor for a checkup. After he ran a series of tests, he recommended that I go see a specialist, as my sugar level was higher than it should be. At first I said "no", but when he added, "You are the most magnificent specimen I have ever examined; that is the only reason you are not dead." That phrase got my undivided attention. He continued, "The only person who can hurt you is yourself. If you ignore your current symptoms, they will get worse, and let's just say that it is easier to prevent something than it is to cure it. My nurse will give you the name and address of a doctor to see; of course, the decision is yours."

With those words, he left the room. As I put my clothes back in proper order, a nurse walked in with a slip of paper with Dr. Stern's name and phone number on it and then promptly left. I finished getting dressed and left the office. As I walked to my car, I convinced myself that I had no symptoms and going to see another doctor would just be a waste of my time. As I drove home, I decided that I was through with doctors because all they were...were fear merchants. I was convinced that they were put on earth just to scare unsuspecting people like me.

As the week wore on, my opinion changed slightly for there was a history of high blood sugar in my family, so without telling anyone, I called the number and made an appointment to see Dr. Stern during the following week.

As the days went by, I talked myself in and out of keeping the appointment. I was determined not to go--right up to the time I walked into the waiting room of the good doctor's office. I was given forms to fill out, and by the time I was done, a nurse came in and led me to a small examining room. As the nurse left, she announced in a condescending tone, "The doctor will be right with you. Please be seated."

I looked around the little room and saw a metal folding chair, an examining table with a paper sheet on it that pulled down from a roll of paper secured at the top, two cabinets with various sized drawers in them, and a series of light switches on the wall. There were charts decorating the walls that showed different parts of the body with brightly colored veins running from one organ to another. I was convinced that they were there to scare the patients but as was explained to me later by Dr. Stern, "These charts are a great help in explaining to our patients their conditions."

Being in the room became more unnerving. I stood in the middle of it; I sat down on the chair; I got up and sat on the examination table for a while and then got up and was just about to leave when the door swung open and in walked a woman wearing a white coat. As soon as she entered the room, she started talking, "Please excuse me for keeping you waiting; I just had an emergency call."

Her words just drifted off into space somewhere. I was in awe of this lady, standing in front of me. She was of slight build with no distinguishing features, but still I was in complete awe of her. Her hair was a mousy brown that fit around her head in a helter-skelter fashion. As she spoke, a wisp of a smile floated across her face that made her whole face take on an angelic hue. As she spoke, her eyes glistened, which added emphasis to what she was saying. Her perfume was just a wisp, but it was enough to make me know she was wearing something; however, I could not distinguish what it was. She had on a white pants suit under her coat, which was visible as her open coat fluttered about her. I must have looked ridiculous, standing in front of her, for the room suddenly got much smaller as the door shut. We were no more than a foot apart; she was talking away, and I was just standing as though in a trance, for, in fact I was in one.

The air in the room became dense, and I was having difficulty breathing. I felt her gently touching my arm and realized she wanted me to sit on the examination table.

"George…George, I have looked over your chart and I …" Again her words drifted off as a nurse walked in with a machine to take my blood pressure. When that was done, I finally heard the words… "I am sorry I didn't introduce myself; I am Doctor Stern. You were sent to me by your doctor because…." The words became undistinguishable again. My face must have flushed as I realized I was acting like …I couldn't even describe how I was acting.

"Are you alright?" As she spoke, her face lit up with a smile. "Didn't you know I was a woman?"

"I guessed that when you walked in the room; I am very observant."

It was her turn to blush as she half shouted out, "I didn't mean that! What I meant was, did you know that your doctor recommended that…"

I just smiled and interrupted her. "Let's just say we are both here, and we might as well make the best of it."

"I took notice that you didn't answer the question about your occupation. I should know this, for I have to make a

3

judgment as to how much stress you have in your daily activities. Do you have a problem with the question?"

"I didn't want to say anything in front of your nurses or staff, since there is no confidential relationship with them."

"You sound like a lawyer."

"I am. Can we let it go at that?"

"We can, but you will have to make the determination as to when I should know more." As she spoke, she flipped her head from side to side and flashed a smile.

"Now you sound like a doctor...blame the patient for everything."

Our first meeting ended with her prescribing some pills and an additional blood test. When she extended her hand to shake mine as she said goodbye, I could not bring myself to shake it. She looked at me as if to say, "I understand", and she exited the room, leaving me alone to absorb the experience that I had just gone through.

Our future visits all followed the same routine: I arrived at her office; I was led into an examining room; we talked; she read the results of the latest blood test; and she told me when to come back, which usually was within two weeks. The only thing that did change, as I now look back, was the time we spent talking together in the examination room. She told me about herself and her husband. They came from an area outside Virginia Beach. They had gone through school together and, upon graduating, had received full scholarships to medical school. Her husband became a surgeon and she a hematologist. They came to New Jersey so that her husband could hone his surgical skills. She took a job in the hospital in her field of study. They didn't have any children but were planning to have one in the future.

All her family was still in the Virginia Beach area, and every other week, she made the six-hour drive to go see them for a day or two. Sometimes, her husband came, but most of the time, she traveled alone, for his schedule didn't allow much free time. She did most of the talking, and I was an ardent listener. Finally I heard, "Your condition has improved, and you can stop taking the pills I gave you. It isn't often that I get to say those words. Come back in a week so I can check to see what effect not taking the pills has. As far as I can see, stress is what caused your sugar level to rise."

"Well, it seems all I have to do is sit on the beach all day and let the rest of the world go by." We both laughed as I got up and left. As I was walking out the door, I had a strange sensation, for I didn't want to face the reality of not seeing her anymore.

The week dragged on except for a job contract I was offered in Venezuela. As I pondered whether or not I should take the assignment, I could feel the tension rising in me. I started to get the same uneasy feeling I'd gotten, which was the reason I'd gone to my doctor for a checkup in the first place. I was reminded of what Dr. Stern had told me, "Stress is your greatest enemy."

The time for my appointment finally arrived, and as I drove to her office, I kept asking myself if I should seek her advice? Was I in the wrong line of work? I resolved that now would be the time to tell her what I did for a living. When I arrived at the office, everything went as usual. The nurse came, and I was escorted into the examining room. As I stood in the middle of the room, I felt a strange feeling come over me. Suddenly the air in the room became very heavy, and I found myself gasping for air. I became very annoyed with myself, for I could see there was nothing different from all the other times I had been there, waiting for the doctor.

The door opened, and it hit me because I was standing with my back to it and much too close to it.

"I'm sorry."

Her voice became a sudden comfort to me while at the same

time, it made the air in the room very heavy again. Something was different and I didn't know what. I sat on the table as she approached me. She started telling me the results of the test she had me take during the week. She started to say something, and I interrupted her.

"I've been offered an assignment in South America, and my main concern is whether or not my body will let me down."

Now, as I thought back to that meeting fifty years earlier, I could still feel the tension that had built up in me. I suddenly remembered a clicking sound I heard as she shut the door. She was not wearing the usual pants-suit ensemble but a dress. She took out some little flashlight instrument and told me she wanted to look into my eyes. That was new, for she had never done that before.

"You know, you never told me what you do."

"I'm a mercenary"

"Are you joking? A mercenary? That kind of occupation could cause stress."

She said the words in a flippant tone that made me feel very uneasy.

"You're joking, of course. No, I guess you're not...I don't know. Well, that's just great." By now she was standing right in front of me. She reached over and shut off the lights in the room. She turned on the flashlight device to look into my eyes, and suddenly I wasn't there. I was like a fly on the wall, looking down on a scene from a movie. Her arm went around me and she dropped the light. It fell, but it didn't make any noise as it hit the floor. The two people were caught up in an embrace, and like two coordinated dancers, they became one in a room where there was no air and both people were gasping for breath. The doctor was on the table.

As quickly as the scene started, that is how quickly it ended. I was me again, still in shock as to what had just happened, and the doctor turned the light back on and, without saying a word, tried to turn the door knob. She turned the lock (I suddenly realized that she had locked the door), opened the door, and left; closing the door behind her. I was standing in the middle of the room, perspiring profusely and still gasping as I rearranged my clothes. Finally, I sat down on the table and calmed myself. Slowly, my breathing became normal, and I was able to leave the little room and the scene of the act that had given me a tremendous feeling of guilt. I did not feel as though I had made any great conquest or any of the other feelings my friends would brag about. No, I felt as though I had disgraced myself and the people who had faith in me. That guilty feeling stayed with me for a long time; in fact, even fifty years later, it was still with me. As the scene played over in my mind, it suddenly dawned on me that she'd had no problem dressing or undressing; I realized that she could not have had on any undergarments. She had set me up. Here I was thinking I was a macho man, but I now realized I was just a pawn in the hands of …I didn't know how to describe Dr. Stern.

In the days that followed our indiscretion, I halfheartedly tried to contact the doctor but was told she was not in, and finally, I was told she had left the employ of the hospital but that they would be happy to assign me to someone else. That was fifty years ago, and now someone who was calling me "Daddy" was contacting me.

In the week that followed, I tried to put the whole experience and the email out of my mind. The harder I tried, the more I was driven to respond to the email and visit my daughter…the one I'd never known I had. As a precaution, I sent a copy of the email to Russ and asked him to do a write-up for me. In the old days, Russ had worked on many cases with me. He had the uncanny ability to dig down deeper and find out more about something or somebody than any other person I knew. The yoke of oldness was starting to show on him as well, but after he read the email, he responded back with, "I shall take up my pennant as off to battle I go...Windmills beware." Russ was a wee bit of a wag, but he was the best man I knew for the job at hand, and more importantly, he was completely trustworthy.

Chapter Two

The next morning I went to my computer and reviewed the trip from my home in New Jersey to a little town on the coastline that went from Virginia to North Carolina. I had remembered at one of my meetings with Dr. Stern that she had mentioned that she was from that area. She told me about the ferry that went from the mainland to an island off the coast of North Carolina. I researched the doctor's name and read that she had died and left one daughter, Sue Ann. With this knowledge I started out two days later to drive to the area. There was a town there named The Cove.

From home, the route led me down the thruway to the ferry at Cape May. It was the 50th anniversary of the ferry's existence. Once on the other side in Lewes, Delaware, I continued south down the peninsula from Delaware into Maryland. Driving down the old highway was both relaxing and peaceful, as the scenery had not changed much from what I remembered seeing some fifty years prior while driving to the South. As I followed the winding highway, I was grateful with my decision to take the coastal route rather than the interstate highway, where the road just roars down on its travelers. Suddenly, while rounding a curve, I had to jam on my brakes, for up ahead was a large farm machine, lumbering down the highway. This shock reminded me that on a highway, my daydreaming would have to wait.

After a while I was able to get around the machine that was blocking the highway and relaxed as once again I could sit back and enjoy the rolling countryside as I wended my way past the fields. Occasionally I could see a farm tractor working in the fields and was very glad that it wasn't blocking the road. As I relaxed, my mind wandered, recalling all the meetings I'd had with Dr. Stern. They appeared before me as a slide show, each meeting lasting longer. At each meeting the doctor told me more about herself and about her life before we met. At each meeting she made a concerted effort to find out more about me. As I kept recalling the meetings, I became more enraged with myself for not seeing what the doctor was doing. As I rounded the curve, I was again reminded that this was a main road, for ahead was a farm tractor, towing a large machine. As I jammed on my brakes, the car skidded off the road, but I was able to stop it before it went into a large drainage ditch that ran alongside of the road. Luckily, I was able to move the car back onto the roadway and continue driving. The incident, although only lasting a few minutes, made me resolve to forget the doctor until I had reached my destination for the night, Virginia Beach. That night I dined in the hotel and went to bed, for after the second glass of wine, I suddenly realized how tired I was.

Chapter Three

The Cove was located about an hour and a half from my hotel. As I looked out the window of my room, which was on the fifth floor of the hotel, I could see my car in the hotel parking lot. Somehow it didn't look right, but I dismissed my notion that something was wrong and went back to my packing, for I had resolved that I would leave the hotel and get lodging closer to The Cove or even in the town itself. When I went to the desk, I was handed an envelope that contained the write-up I had ordered. I resolved that I would wait until I reached The Cove to read it. I checked out of the room and went into the parking lot. As I neared my car, I saw that the car was very low to the ground. As I reached it, I saw the reason it was so low: someone had stolen the wheels…tires and rims. I looked again in disbelief because I could not believe the scene before me; all four wheels were gone. I went back into the hotel to report the theft, and the clerk, without expressing any emotion at all and in a matter-of-fact manner, called the police.

When the police arrived, they told me that I would have to file a complaint at headquarters. I was still in shock from the thought of the missing tires, but what bothered me more was everyone's matter-of-fact attitude. In an annoyed tone I asked, "Does this sort of thing happen often?"

The reply from the sergeant who had just arrived on the scene was, "Yea, lately it has. We don't know why, but…well, who knows. When you buy a fancy car like a Lexus, I guess you have to expect these things. Here's the address of the station house; you have to go there to sign a complaint."

As the sergeant spoke, he handed me a card with an address on it. His car radio summoned him, and he left. One of the officers still on the scene came over and said, "You have to file a complaint if you want to report the theft to your insurance company." His radio summoned him, and he left.

I looked around the empty lot. I felt like a fool, just standing there. I wondered if the theft was an omen of what was to come, but I decided not to go back to bed and to continue with my plan to go to The Cove. I went back into the hotel and was allowed to use one of the house phones to call the local Lexus dealer. They were very sympathetic as they took down the information about the car. The lady on the phone, after excusing herself for a few minutes, announced, "We have rims and tires in stock, and a repairman will be with you shortly."

Within an hour a repairman was in the parking lot. He looked at the car and made the comment, "Whoever did this certainly knew what he was doing. You can see where he put the jack to lift the car up, and after he took the wheels off, he put blocks under the car so he could get his jack out."

I watched as the new wheels were put on. Soon I was on my way to the police station to file a report of the theft. I was thankful that I was able to drive there on my four new tires and wheels, even though I doubted whether they were new or just the old ones cleaned up. Filing the report took about an hour, and while in the station, I called the insurance company to file a claim. Finally, I was on my way. I was also amazed by the speed and efficacy with which everything was done.

The drive to The Cove took about two hours. As I pulled into town, I was awe struck by the quaintness of the scene. It was a perfect setting for a watercolor artist. The town was built around a natural harbor. There were numerous docks for small boats to tie up. Since it was October, there were a lot of boats in the dry dock storage area with an equal number of boats still tied up at their moorings. In the center of the horseshoe-shaped area was a general store/coffee house/restaurant. The proprietor was a weather-beaten gentleman with a white beard, moustache, and head of hair that was all blended together. He was short of build and looked as though he was as high as he was wide. He walked around his domain ready to share his knowledge about everything and anything. There was a sign on the outside of the building which read, "Come in and browse; U might find something you like...I liked it; that is why I bought it."

The shop carried everything from seashells to old books and records. There was a little clothing area that among other seafaring garments had a full array of tee shirts and sweatshirts with "The Cove" printed on them.

In another section of the store was a counter that had a coffee urn with an assortment of cakes with a sign, "Help yourself, I trust U." There was also an area where one could sit down and order a light lunch from a limited menu. There was a waitress in that area that stood on duty, ready to help anyone who wanted service along with a smile.

Overlooking everything was the white-haired owner who was known as "The Commodore."

The main street of the town went around the harbor. All of the buildings faced the main street. The courthouse was located on the far end of town, along with the town hall, library, and meeting hall; which was also the town auditorium, wherein all of the town activities were held.

Sue Ann lived a mile from the courthouse, and no matter how inclement the weather, she could be seen riding her bike with its little bell, which was used to attract attention, and a little basket which carried her pocketbook as well as whatever else she might need. As she rode through town, she either waved or tinkled her little bell as she acknowledged someone's presence. Since everyone knew her, the rides were always a constant, noteworthy event. The comments that went along with her passing ranged from, "She makes quite a sight riding her little bike" to "Here comes the bitch on her broom."

Sue Ann was a divorcee. Like her mother she had married her high school sweetheart. They went to college together, and when they graduated they were married. They both continued their education; he became a doctor and she a mother of twins, a boy and a girl, as she attended law school. She earned every award there was to win and was considered by everyone to be the brightest person in the town. After graduating, she received a clerkship with the local judge, and upon his death two years later, she became the youngest and prettiest judge in the state. Even though she was the youngest, she was held in the highest regard by her fellow jurists, as well as by the townspeople themselves.

Tragedy struck one day in the form of a freak boating accident. The boating accident occurred when two boats collided and blew up, killing her son and injuring three other people. No one could explain why or how it happened but only that her son was killed. The death of her boy put a strain on her marriage, and within two years she was divorced. Many said that her husband blamed her: that she should have been minding their children rather than being married to the law. After the divorce, she was known as the gay divorcee who knew everything about other people's business but wasn't smart enough to mind her own. When her daughter was twenty-one, she insisted upon getting her own apartment and very soon was known as the town pump, a title her mother didn't enjoy but was powerless to change.

On the entrance to the town from the main highway leading to The Cove was a little restaurant that had a more extensive menu than the coffee shop in town and also a patio dining area that overlooked the town and the harbor. It was at this restaurant that I stopped on my way into The Cove. I enjoyed a light late lunch before entering the town and confronting Sue Ann.

As I sat on the outside patio, baking in the unusually sunny afternoon, I finally had the nerve to open the report that Russ had sent to me. With shaking hands I opened the folder. The very first thing that caught my eye was printed in large letters:

"Many a man rocks his child
and rocks his child alone.
But there are many a man
rocking another man's child
when he thinks he's rocking his own."

"That, my friend, summarizes this report. Dr. Stein found out her husband couldn't have children, and it looks like you were elected, Daddy."

Russ was a self-taught detective/spy/researcher. He was the type of person that once anyone met him, they liked him. He could cite verse and chapter of any mystery novel or mystery movie. He knew all the methods of finding out information whether they were legal or not so legal. If someone wanted to find out something and he couldn't do it himself, he knew someone who could and, more importantly, he knew how to make him do his bidding. I first met him when he ran a restaurant in New York, located by the Aqueduct Race track. It was referred to and known as "Noah's Ark", meaning you went in twos or you didn't go. It was the favorite watering hole for some of the less savory characters of New York. When I first met Russ, we immediately became very good friends. When Russ found out what I did, he wanted to be included in my life. As we got to know each other better, I gave him some projects, and Russ always came through the test with flying colors. While working for me on a job in Connecticut, Russ met the only female judge in the state, and the two became inseparable. They were married, and I was the best man. Through his wife, Russ greatly increased his ability to find out things and quickly had a very thriving business of supplying information to an assortment of people. At one point he found out that a country club was having trouble running their food concession, which included a dining room and reception hall. Russ took over and the country club became the place to be. He quickly became a very successful restaurant operator, but his first love was still being a high-priced snoop, which he was better than ever at. He produced a fine product, and I was confident that the report I now was reading would be no exception.

The report continued: "After the doctor left the hospital where she worked when you met her, she returned home. Her husband was still doing an internship as a surgeon up North for another two months before he came home to stay. Everyone happily received the announcement that she was pregnant. In due course she had a little girl, whom they named Sue Ann. She was a very bright child, and everyone assumed that she too would become a doctor like her parents, but I guess your genes kicked in, and she became a lawyer. In any event, trouble arose in the happy home of Dr. Stein and her husband when he found out that Sue Ann wasn't his child. I could not find out how the secret was discovered, but it so unnerved her husband that one night he kicked the hell out of her. Sue Ann called the police. No charges were pressed and the whole matter was swept under a great, big, thick rug. Joann got a divorce, but her husband still contributed to Sue Ann's support. In fact, he picked up the full tab for her wedding, as well as her law-school education. She graduated with top honors. He died soon after her graduation from law school; she was his sole beneficiary, but she didn't get much."

"Joann died soon after her husband, but she left her money, again not much, to Sue Ann's children. She had twins: a boy whom they named Erick and a girl they named Trina. I couldn't find out how they got those names, but I didn't think that was too important. I guess doctors don't make too much down South. Erick died in an accident; no one knows too much about that, but Sue Ann's husband blamed her and that was the reason why they got a divorce, I think. Erick's money went to Sue Ann, which she put in a trust that Trina will get when she's thirty-five. This made Trina mad, and that is when she moved into her own apartment and, wow, what a life style she set up."

"There is a rumor that I couldn't confirm that Joann had a diary of sorts wherein you were mentioned (just a rumor), and that is why Sue Ann wants to talk to you. Good luck because I could not find out why. I think, my friend, that she just wants some sort of closure in her life, for she is a beautiful intelligent woman whom nobody wants; that has got to be a bitch to live with."

I put the report down and was so caught up in my thoughts that I didn't hear the waitress' asking if I wanted anything else. Finally her words stunned me as I looked at her with an annoyed look on my face as I asked, "What do you want?"

"I was just wondering if there was anything else I could get you. I'm sorry if I disturbed you."

"No, not at all. Please, just bring me my bill." The waitress handed it to me. I left a larger-than-usual tip for being so rude.

Chapter Four

I got up from the table and drove the short distance from the restaurant to the center of town I was able to park by the general store, and as I got out of my car, I came face to face with the town's chief of police, who was just passing by. We nodded to each other, and the chief continued walking down the street.

The chief was a roly-poly type man with his belly hanging over his belt. He wore a wide brim hat and a pair of sunglasses that covered half his face. He looked to be in his fifties, but it was hard to tell as he shuffled his way down the street. He was about six feet tall, but because he was hunched over, he looked smaller. I was about to walk down the street when I heard the tinkling of a bell, and I looked up and saw Sue Ann. She had to be Sue Ann, for she looked like the re-incarnation of Joann. I just froze in my tracks, for the sight of her erased fifty years off my life and took all of the wind out of my lungs. My mouth went bone dry as I stood on the sidewalk and watched "Joann/Sue Ann" go by. I mentally had to shake myself back to reality that whom I was seeing was not Joann and might have not even been Sue Ann. The sudden realization that I would soon be meeting my daughter and my granddaughter suddenly made me feel weak in the knees. I started to question the sensibility of getting involved in something that was going to make me feel very uncomfortable, to say the least. I finally resolved that I was there and would see the ordeal through before I made up my mind about what I should do. The thought of what I could do never entered my mind; I knew that there would be an answer to the riddle I found myself in. As I walked through the town, I realized that I had to find a place to stay. I walked back to the general store, for I just knew that the Commodore would have the answer as to where I could stay. As

I had predicted, he held his finger up as he announced, "I've got just the spot. Widow Henderson has a cute little three-room suite that her husband built for his children to stay in; it is empty and I know she could use the money. Let me call her right now and see if she would be okay with a stranger's boarding with her for a few nights." The Commodore turned and faced me with a strange look on his face as he asked, "You are a person of good moral character, aren't you?"

"I like to think so," I replied as I felt my face flush from embarrassment.

The Commodore made the call, and within minutes I was on my way, following the directions he'd given me to the home of Mrs. Henderson. The house was located about a half mile from the general store, which meant it was halfway between the general store and Sue Ann's house. By the time I got to the house, Mrs. Henderson was outside, waiting for me. She walked over to the car and greeted me with a big smile as she shouted out, "You can call me Lila. That's not my real name, but I like it much better than being called 'the recent widow, Mrs. Henderson'."

The house was a one-story ranch with an extension built on the side. The extension had its own entrance, but there was also a connecting door to the main house. There were three rooms: a bedroom, kitchen, and living room. The bathroom had a small shower in it. I looked at it and was visibly pleased with it. I smiled and said, "I'll take it." We negotiated the price, and I moved in. As I was unpacking, I suddenly felt very tired. I got undressed and just went to bed. Sleep came easy.

In the morning as I was taking a shower, I heard Lila yell, "I've made breakfast…come and join me."

I saw that the connecting door to the house was open, so I walked into the main house and followed the scent of freshly brewed coffee, which led me into a dining room. "You didn't have to do this…"

Before I could finish the sentence, Lila replied, "Do you know how many times I've had an opportunity to have breakfast with someone...and a good-looking gentleman at that." She served breakfast and never stopped talking. I could see that she was definitely the town crier and historian all rolled up into one. When she finally started talking about their judge Sue Ann, I sat up in the chair.

Lila continued with, "It is a sin that such a pretty smart woman like that can't find anyone who appreciates her. I think it is because she scares most people. Her own daughter has very little to do with her. She rides around on her little bike, ringing that damn bell like she owns the town. She goes past my house, both coming and going, and she always rings that damn bell of hers. I don't know whether to pity her or what. She was supposed to be appointed to some big court, but she never was." Lila just kept talking, jumping from one topic to another so many times that I lost track of what she was talking about. I was also deep in my own thoughts of when and where I was going to introduce myself to my daughter and granddaughter. Those two words made me finish my coffee and leave the room while Lila was still jabbering on.

Chapter Five

I went to my room where I made the final adjustment to my appearance. I was still trying to decide how I should approach the meeting with Sue Ann and where it should be held. As I left my room, I first drove out towards Sue Ann's house. In all of her talking, Lila had mentioned that it was on a bluff, overlooking the bay. It was one of the prettiest homes in the area. Lila had also added, "Why shouldn't it be--she has only herself to support. The blue and white mansion still doesn't help her get anyone. It will probably be her mausoleum." The last part of her remark had her laughing so hard that she had to pause to catch her breath. As I drove down the road, the house did stand out, not only because of its position but also the paint job. On the mailbox was the name "Sue Ann Stein" and under that "Judge Stein." The house was isolated, but just the sight of it made me decide that I would not be too comfortable there. I turned the car around and drove directly to the courthouse. I could see a bike parked on the side of the building under a little overhang. I parked the car, and with grim determination, I walked up the stairs and into the courthouse.

There was only one courtroom, and Sue Ann was holding court. I walked into the courtroom and sat in the last row. From the moment I walked into the courtroom, Sue Ann became visibly nervous. Her change of demeanor made everyone in the courtroom turn and stare at me. The bailiff wasn't sure what to do, for I was not doing anything to cause a disturbance, but my mere presence created one. Sue Ann concluded the case by saying that she was not ruling on the matter that day. "I will notify everyone when we will re-convene. I want more time to read the papers and consider this matter."

With those words she abruptly got up and left the

courtroom, leaving everyone in the room wondering what had just happened. As everyone filed out of the courtroom, they all hesitated for a moment as they passed me, but no one said a word. It was the nosiest silence.

The judge's chambers were located in the rear of the courtroom. I got up and walked to the door that the judge had exited by. The bailiff walked over, and while raising his hand (indicating that he wanted me to stop) he said, "May I help you, sir?"

I stopped for a moment and decided that now was neither the time nor the place to have my first encounter with my newfound daughter. "No," I replied as I turned and walked out of the building. I suddenly felt the need for a cup of coffee served by the Commodore.

Within minutes of my arrival at the general store, the chief of police showed up along with his two deputies. Both deputies looked as though that had just gotten out of the military. They looked as though they were in top physical shape, and both had military-type haircuts. Their uniforms were neatly pressed, and when they walked into the restaurant area of the store, they each took up a position on opposite sides of the room, allowing the chief to be the center of attraction.

The Commodore walked over and bought me a cup of coffee and as an aside he remarked, "You sure are drawing a crowd, but I don't know if you're good for business since you are the only one buying anything." After the Commodore spoke, he went back to his position by the walk-up window to take care of a customer.

There was an uncanny tension in the room. The deputies were shifting their weight from one foot to another as they both waited for something to happen.

"We don't get many visitors this time of year." The words uttered by the chief shattered the stillness of the room but did little to ease the tension that was building.

I just smiled as I asked, "Do you know where the men's room is?"

The chief, with an annoyed look on his face, pointed to the rear of the dining area. I nodded and got up and left the table without saying anything. When I reappeared, nothing in the room had changed. It was as though everyone was frozen in the position they'd been in before I left. Silently, I walked over to the Commodore and paid his bill and left. I had now resolved that I was going to face Sue Ann and find out what the email was all about. I walked to the rear entrance to the courthouse. As I walked in, there was a small hallway that led to a door that was labeled, "Judge's Chamber." I knocked and from within I heard, "Yes, who is it?"

I walked into the room and before me I saw "Joann." Time had reverted back to the first time I had ever met her: the same wisp of hair that floated across her face and the same warm, disarming smile that just put me at ease. I had to blink and shake my head to remind myself that it was not Joann I was looking at.

"Sit down, Dad; I think we have a lot to talk about." The words came out like a command rather than an invitation. "You created quite a stir in my little town; the police are ready to call for a swat team. You look just like your picture on your books."

I felt a little uncomfortable, for it was obvious that Sue Ann was still trying to be a judge rather than a woman, meeting her father for the first time. The nervousness in her voice made me resolve to let her talk herself out, for it was obvious to me that she had a speech she wanted to make, and I best let her have her say.

"You know your affair with my mother caused my parents to get a divorce. After she died, I found out about you for the first time. I was cleaning out my mother's things when I found a diary of sorts, and in it I saw your name. She referred to you as a patient, but then she made a note: he's the one. I went through her old treatment records and found yours, not in the regular file but in a separate part of her papers. There was also a note written sometime later about a book you wrote, "Two Point Eight Seconds." Was that the trip you had to go on when you asked her if your body would hinder you in any way? She made a note of that also. I researched the treatment records and the timing involved and came to the conclusion that…" At this point Sue Ann started to cry. The door to her chamber opened, and the bailiff stormed in with his gun drawn. Sue Ann screamed, "No…please just leave. I'm fine…please just go."

As soon as the bailiff left, Sue Ann continued with tears' streaming down her face, "How long did your affair go on? I read the book as well as a few others, and in one of them you wrote about visiting a doctor before you took on an assignment. The doctor you referred to was my mother. Were you lovers for long? What about her husband? What about your wife? What about all the people's lives you had an impact on? Didn't you care?"

Sue Ann had to stop talking, for she was now gasping for air. I was slumped over in the chair and in a quiet voice responded, "There was no love affair. I never knew about you. What happened was all your mother's doing."

"Well, you had to be there! Do you know the odds of having a child…" "You want me to believe that you were together once and that's all it took? This isn't some novel you're writing; this is my life. My parents were divorced. I grew up not sure how I came into being, and now you want me to believe you didn't know how or when anything happened." Sue Ann sat down in her chair with her face buried in her hands and quietly sobbed. I sat in the chair, not knowing what to do, but I felt silence was the best cure for what was going on.

Silently, I got up and walked out the back door of the courthouse. I walked towards the general store, oblivious to the fact that the chief and his two deputies were standing outside.

As I walked past them, they followed at a distance as I made my way to the store. The Commodore made the observation, "Here comes the Pied Piper with his entourage. He sure is good for business."

I had a sandwich for lunch. What I didn't realize was that my granddaughter (who worked at the store as a waitress, chef, and whatever else was needed) was serving it. As I sat and had my lunch, I was trying to think of what to do next. I took out my phone and called Russ.

"Oh, master, how can I serve you now? I know you want to know if she is really yours. Well, I already ran a DNA test and she is yours. Remember, old friend, "the mailman came the first of May; the policeman came the very next day; nine months later there was hell to pay! DNA can say who shot that shot--the blue or the gray." By the time Russ finished his little poem, he was laughing so hard that he had to put the phone down to regain his composure. "Was that what you wanted to ask?"

"How did you get that information?" I whispered into the phone.

"Aha ha, remember our deal; you don't ask how, so I won't have to lie since my only purpose on earth is to do or die." Again Russ had to put the phone down, for he was laughing too hard to continue talking. Finally, Russ was able to continue talking. "What now?" he shouted into the phone.

"Can you come down here? I am having a rough time dealing with this situation."

"I shall be there at first light. Just give me the address." I complied and that ended the conversation. I just spent the rest of the day wandering around the town while being constantly shadowed by the chief or one of his deputies whom I dubbed Ike and Mike…Mike was the taller one.

After I left, Sue Ann took a long time to compose herself. She told her secretary to cancel everything for the rest of day; she was going home. The ride home on her bike took forever.

People that she passed wondered why she didn't ring her little bell. One person remarked, "She must be having a bad-hair day." When she got home, she changed into her most comfortable housedress. She went over to her little bar, which when closed looked like a breakfront, and opened the door. She made herself a double Manhattan and went out and sat on the patio that overlooked the harbor and bay. On her way out, she grabbed a comforter that she kept by the door. As soon as she sat down, she started to cry. She willed herself to stop, but she couldn't stop the tears' welling in her eyes.

"Why did I do it?" the sound of her own voice startled her. Her mind was whirling with thoughts of everything she should be doing rather than sitting on her patio, trying to remember all the details of the meeting she'd just had with... she stopped short of using the word "father." "George may be my biological father, but the man who raised me and was always there when I needed him was my real father, and he's dead," she shouted out. As much as she didn't want to admit it, she finally realized that George was as much a victim as she was. "Why did Mom do it?" That question kept whirling through her mind. Her mom wanted to have a child to justify to herself that she was a whole woman was the only answer that seemed to satisfy her. Mom just didn't care about the effect that her satisfying her desires would have on everyone else. Sue Ann was sipping her drink as she kept punishing herself, trying to figure out her mother's rational. "What about me?" she asked herself. She became enraged at her own action of emailing George. "All I had to do was keep quiet, and everything would have just died a natural death. Now I have that poor man involved, and he's just as much a victim as my daughter and me. The question now is what should I do to undo my stupid move of notifying him. Why did I?" The next thought that jumped into her mind was the interest everyone had as to the reason George had come to her office. She knew her bailiff was the best keyhole listener in the business and that he had the biggest mouth in the town. He was referred to as Face Book. As she was thinking where they should meet again, her attention was drawn to a speed boater that was speeding in the harbor. This brought to mind her twenty-three-foot cabin cruiser. She rarely used it, and every time she got a repair bill, she resolved to sell or sink it. Now she thought of it as her savior; it was a perfect spot to meet. With the problem of a place for a second meeting solved, she slumped down in the chair, letting the empty glass fall to the floor. She pulled the comforter that she had brought out with her up around her neck and let the effects of the drink and her lack of sleep over the past few nights take over. However, her last conscious thought was, "What is George going to do?"

Chapter Six

The sun rose and by nine o'clock, Russ was knocking on the front door of the house, even though I had told him to come to the side entrance that led to my suite of rooms. Lila answered the door and was greeted with, "Good morning, good lady. I feel I am entering heaven, except I doubt if heaven has any angel as lovely as you. Is my friend George about? I pray not, for he could only diminish this perfect meeting."

Lila stepped back from the door, completely overwhelmed by the greeting she'd just received. In a stuttering fashion, she responded, "Would you like a cup of coffee while I call him?" As she spoke, she walked towards the kitchen with Russ, following. When she went to get the coffee pot, Russ stepped forward, "Oh, no, dear lady, it is unseemly for you to serve me. Sit down, for from this day hence, I shall be your obedient servant. Feel free to call upon me for anything. I have searched for someone like you my whole life and now...to be here with you...don't spoil this moment by calling that grump of grumps, George."

I heard the commotion and Russ' voice, so I quickly finished getting dressed and entered the house through the connecting door, which not to my surprise was left unlocked. "Russ, I am glad you came. May I introduce our landlady, Lila? Lila, this is my associate Russ. He will be staying with me." As I spoke, I walked over to Lila and pressed some money into her hand and shook hands with Russ, who had just finished pouring himself a cup of coffee. Lila got up and left the room as she said, "I know you two want some privacy."

"You know, Russ, I don't know what to do. Sue Ann is a fine lady...but?"

"My dear friend, George, make sense! If she is such a fine

lady, why would she bother you now? You are getting too involved in this problem. I know it's personal, but as I have heard you say many times, if someone comes into my office with a smoking gun, I can't make the smoke go away or the gun. All I can do is deal with it intelligently. Well, my friend, someone has a smoking gun pointed right at you, so deal with it. I can see three possibilities and only three; first, acknowledge she's yours; second, deny she's yours; but, of course, the problem with that is that you will live the rest of your life waiting for the other shoe to drop or, even worse, she shows up at your funeral and introduces herself as your daughter; and third, you kill her and take your chances with the legal system of the state. First, we grab her and get her to tell us how and where she first heard of you and get from her any papers or records she has, and after that we eliminate dear Sue Ann. You better face it, my friend; you have added a new dimension to her life--one she never had before."

By the expression on Russ' face, I could see he wasn't kidding. "Well, let's leave that possibility for last; there must be some other cards we can play first."

"Sure there are, but the longer you wait, the more people are going to find out what is going on. I will bet you that everyone in town is discussing you right now. They'll want to know who you are and why you are here. My friends told me that the chief has already run a check on you and your car. By now, they have done the same thing with me. We can act like tourists, but how long do you think that is going to last? Oh by the way did you have something to eat at the general store?"

Before I could respond, Russ continued, "Well, the cute little waitress is your granddaughter. How long do you think it is going to be before she finds out who you are? Sue Ann sent you that email because she wants something. I don't know what, but the longer you wait to resolve this problem, the more it's going to cost and the harder it's going to be to blow away the smoke and bury the gun."

Russ got up and walked to the door as he said, "Well, if we are going to act the tourist part, let's act as tourists and take a walk around town. We can rent a boat and sail around the harbor. We can even buy sweatshirts that say "The Cove" on them. Of course, on your shirt we will add 'Chump Samson'."

The two men left the house and walked down the main street towards the general store. They were alerted to the oncoming traffic by the tinkling of a bell located on a bike. Russ took one look and immediately remarked, "Old friend, would you mind if I go out with your daughter? I mean, after all you could always come and live with us."

I did not answer. We entered the general store and went to sit on the restaurant side. The waitress came over with a pot of coffee and two cups as she said, "You two look like you could use some."

"Boy, George, you sure make cute kids. Do you think I'm too old for her?"

"Knock it off, will you?" was the only response I gave.

Breakfast was done and we walked down to the pier. There was a celebration of some sort going on in the town for the school's band was getting ready to march. Russ started a conversation with one of the twirlers and soon found that his ability to twirl a baton was gone. Frustrated, he handed back the baton while I just smiled.

From behind him I heard, "Your friend seems annoyed with himself. Before he takes out his anger on me, can you and I have a conversation if I promise I will not become irrational again?"

"Of course," was my immediate reply.

As Sue Ann and I walked away from the crowd, Russ just waved his hand, indicating he was going to the general store.

Sue Ann and I walked towards the pier where she had her boat moored. There was a strange silence as we approached her boat. She handed me a package as she pulled the boat closer and boarded it. Once we were both aboard, we went into the cabin. She sat on one side with me on the other. As we faced each other, she took a deep breath and with tears running down her face, she spoke in a barely audible tone. "I realize now that I should have never contacted you. It seems you were an unwilling participant in an unspeakable situation. Why my mother did something like she did is beyond my comprehension, but maybe we are not supposed to know everything our parents do. My daughter blames me for my divorce and, as she says, losing her father. No matter how I try to understand what happened, the only explanation I can imagine is that my mother somehow found out that her husband couldn't have children. She wanted to have that experience, and she chose you. I don't know how you should feel, but obviously you don't think it was any kind of honor."

Sue Ann had to pause to catch her breath, for she was crying too hard to breathe. I was staring at her, for I could not believe what I was hearing. I felt sorry for what my daughter was going through, but at the same time, I could not feel any sympathy for her. The strange feeling I was experiencing was maddening. It was obvious to me that she was finding some rationale for her mother's behavior, while I still felt a deep hurt and could not find any sympathy in my heart for her or her mother. I realized that, no matter what she said, I still had a bastard child and grandchild that I wanted no part of.

After Sue Ann composed herself, she continued, "I don't know what to do, but the only resolution I can offer is this. I made this package, and in it are the notes my mother made and her old medical files about you. I also included all my notes of what steps I took to locate you. Please take them along with my apology for even bringing this sordid situation to your attention. I have told no one about this, especially not my daughter, and shall keep my silence. When we part company, it will be the last time you will hear from me, and hopefully, it will be the last time you will hear about this matter. Goodbye." With those words Sue Ann got up, bent over and kissed me, and left the boat.

I sat for a few moments, still trying to comprehend all that I'd just heard. I finally got up and exited the boat. I walked down to the store to meet Russ. He was standing outside, talking to the Commodore. What was strange was that Russ was standing in front of his car. He had obviously gone to Lila's and gotten ready to go home. Across the street from him was Ike, trying very hard to look disinterested in what was happening. Russ left the Commodore's side and walked towards me. As he approached, he started with, "I know she is sorry for starting this whole thing and begs your forgiveness…right? Do you believe her? Well, Samson, since you now have had your hair cut, I shall leave you. Call me if you need me."

Before I could say anything, Russ got in his car and waved to the deputy as he drove out of town. I stood in front of the store and watched until I could no longer see the taillights of Russ' car. I stood there as though in a trance. The waitress came outside to see the Commodore for a moment, and after showing him something, she ran back inside. I stood motionless, for I could not bring myself to believe or trust everything I'd heard. I turned and started walking back to Lila's to pack my car and leave.

The tinkling of a bell finally broke my trance, and I was left with my dilemma. What to do… what to do?

Chapter Seven

The drive home was much longer than driving to The Cove because on the way home, I tried my best not to think about what I had to ultimately decide--what to do. By drifting back and forth mentally about what I should do, I was able to have brief periods of tranquility by concentrating on my driving. The roar of an eighteen-wheeler's going past me was a God-sent diversion. I could not bring myself to decide anything, for I was too afraid of the possibilities that I had to choose from. Mentally, I quickly made a list of people I felt I could trust and who might be able to help me. My list boiled down to one person: my friend who was a priest. We had known each other for many years. I knew I could trust him; then I remembered that he had died. My list was at zero. But the idea of talking to a priest stayed with me; to find one I had confidence in would be a search I felt I would have to take. The perfect spot to relate the story would be in a confessional booth. The confidentiality of the topic would be assured, and I could remain anonymous. The drive home was shortened tremendously once I had reached a resolution. A priest...young or old was the next question that came to mind, but I quickly dismissed the problem by resolving to go to two: one of each. Finally, I arrived home secure in my decision and my assurance that I would find an answer that I could live with… maybe.

The next morning I drove around the area where I lived, and with the help of my navigator located many churches, which I reduced to two. They were on opposite sides of town. I went into the first one and, after reading the bulletin, chose a priest I would "confess" to. I made note of the hours of confession and, afterwards, drove to the other church I had selected, which was on the far side of town. I followed the same procedure and drove away with the names of the priest and the hours he would be hearing confessions. My plan, which I considered brilliant, had a major flaw, which I was to find out later; there was no guarantee as to which priest would be hearing confessions. Still I felt secure in my decision. As soon as I got home, I made a brief outline of what I was going to say, for I wanted to be sure that I told the same story to each one.

Every day when I opened my email, I prayed that I would not get another "Dear Dad" missive. Finally, the day came for my first confession. As I walked to the church, I felt like everyone in the entire area was watching me. As a young man, going to confession was a snap. Where else could I go and get the slate wiped clean by saying a few prayers. I thought it was great. Of course, the sins I was talking about didn't measure up to the one I had built up in my mind. I rationalized that to commit a sin, a person had to have an evil intent. I had none; therefore, I had no intent to do wrong, so I had not sinned. Why was I subjecting myself to the ordeal of a confessional booth when I had done nothing wrong? I kept walking, for I knew if I stopped, I would never start walking again. I purposely waited until I was the last one. After everyone left the area, I walked in. There was a curtain that slid over the opening to the rest of the church. The booth was very small, but I chuckled to myself, for I soon realized I was a lot smaller when I first went to confession. Trying to kneel was impossible, so I sat cattycorner, trying to shift my bulk so it didn't hurt as much. While I was busy trying to find a more comfortable position, the little door, dividing the priest from me, slid open. The noise it made was deafening.

Through the screen I could see the outline of a man. I was mute. I moved my mouth, but nothing came out. I could not say the traditional opening phrase," Bless me, Father, for I have sinned." Thankfully, he spoke first. "Sir, I am done hearing confessions for the day and, frankly, if I don't get out of this box, I will go mad. May I suggest I meet you outside the church in five minutes, and we can go for a cup of coffee at the corner store? The coffee is good, and they have fabulous pastries. They make them right there."

Silently, I got out of the booth and calmly walked out of the church. Some little kid I passed on the way out made the observation to his friend, "Boy, he didn't take long." I stood on the church steps, and in a few minutes, the priest showed up. He looked like a fighter with a crooked nose and all. He looked to be in his late twenties, but I rationalized to myself that the older I got, the younger everyone else looked. He was about my height and about half my weight. It was obvious that he was working out. He walked over to me with a disarming smile and said, "I've got a feeling you want someone to talk to rather than someone to confess to."

I just nodded and our strange duo walked together down to the corner bakery/coffee shop. Along the way, every third person was saying hello to the priest or waving to him. "You must be very popular in your church." After I said the words, I felt stupid for saying anything, but I knew I had to say something, for the tension in me was just building up. As it did, I was becoming infuriated with myself for even being there. "What could this guy tell me? I knew I had experienced more things than he ever would. The turmoil in me started to show, but he calmed me down by saying," Sometimes just talking to a stranger who isn't going to be judgmental helps. Even if it doesn't, you will still be a winner, for the coffee and cake here are great."

We walked into the store, and the operator immediately acknowledged the priest's appearance. The priest motioned towards the back table, and we were immediately seated there. The priest ordered, "Coffee and whatever you just made."

I followed with, "I'll have the same."

"Well, as soon as you feel comfortable, you start the

conversation. I am a very good listener."

I waited until the coffee and cake were served. I took out my little note sheet, and I started telling the story of my encounter with Joann and Sue Ann. I spoke non-stop, for I was in fear that if I did stop, I would never continue. I was a man on a mission, and at that point, I felt like a very weak man. When I was done, the waitress who had been observing us (but was kind enough to stay out of earshot) came over and took my cup away as she said, "I'll get you a new cup; this one must be cold."

While I spoke, the priest listened without interruption, but every so often his facial expressions changed at what he was hearing. He waited for me to sip my new coffee and take a small bite of the cake before he commented, "They told me in the seminary that I would hear many different things in confession. I know this story has got to be one of the …well I don't know what. You know, of course, I have to respond in the way I was taught and that would be to acknowledge the existence of your up-to-now unknown family and to bring everyone together and hope that it will not destroy your current relationships with your current family. A person now exists that didn't exist before. She also has produced a child; they exist, and there is nothing you can do about that."

After he said those words, he hesitated for a moment. I mean that under God's law and the laws of the state, I am afraid that there is no other answer. No matter what, at some time the truth will come out, and you will have to admit that she is your daughter; that result is inevitable. The guilt you feel is self-imposed. We all carry our own standards with us, and it is that standard that you have violated, and that is why you feel guilty. As priests, we ask that you confess your own guilt, not that which other men place on you, for what is crime today may change tomorrow. I can only advise that you will be better off if you make this fact known, rather than have your friends and family find out from strangers. Truthfully, I don't know of any other way. If you want, give me your name and address, and if I come up with anything else, I will contact you." In a stuttering fashion he added, "That's all I can do."

I got up and left some money on the table and walked out. I just couldn't think of anything to say, nor did I want to say anything. At that moment I knew that I was grasping at straws, and as Russ had warned, the longer a secret is around, more people will know about it. I'd just told another person. I know he will tell someone else. This confession idea was stupid; forget the other priest; silence is my best ally. I will have to live with this guilt; but the problem is--what am I guilty of?

I drove back to my office and listened to my messages, and one of them was from Sue Ann. She sounded very distraught, for she had a hard time talking while crying. 'George, I am sorry to call you but please call me. I don't know what to do, and you must realize how hard it was for me to call you, but...please call me tonight at my home. The number is..." and she left a phone number.

As I waited for the proper time to call, I swore I would not respond. I resolved that at best I would just be getting deeper into something I wanted no part of. I could not believe the voice saying "Hello", for I had no memory of even dialing the number. In a quiet voice I said, "This is George." That was all I could say before Sue Ann blurted out, "Thank you for calling. My daughter, who is your granddaughter that you don't want to acknowledge, is going to marry a local hoodlum, and I don't know how I can stop it. If I say anything, she will marry him just to spite me. She is making a terrible mistake. He is involved in a money-laundering scheme and ...please do something."

I tried not to get emotionally involved, for I was still mad about her reference to her daughter as my granddaughter...the one I didn't acknowledge...but I could not help but feel sorry for the person I heard on the phone. Before I could restrain myself, I heard my own voice saying, "Now calm down, for I can hardly understand you. How do you know he…what's his name?… is involved in anything like money laundering?"

"A friend of mine that I graduated from law school with…at one time we were considered an item…called me and told me that my daughter's boyfriend, his name is Lewis, was brought in by the FBI for questioning about how he got financing for a project he is developing. I can't go into more detail than that, but he bought an engagement ring today and …you've got to stop this."

"Well, can you give me more than just his name and…" Before I could finish, she replied, "I've sent you a letter wherein I've put all the information I could find out about him. Of course, there is no way that my friend or I can in any way be connected to this…"

I just interrupted her, for I could hear that she was becoming very emotional again. "All right, I'll look at it and see if I can do…"

She responded in a loud voice, "I've read all of your books, and I know you can; the only question is will you? I'm sorry; I shouldn't have said that. I guess above all I am a mother first, and I will not let Lewis hurt my daughter; she's only twenty-one and he is thirty-two. When I tried to talk to my daughter, she kept yelling at me that I don't know anything about love or making a marriage work." At this point Sue Ann just started crying so hard that she couldn't speak.

"Hang up the phone. After I take a look at what you've sent me, I will call you and tell you what I can do. Now please…"

The phone went dead, and I sat in my chair, looking at it and still trying to believe that I was feeling sorry for someone I was not too happy about knowing. I tried to put the whole incident out of my mind but to no avail. I got very little sleep. I met the mailman walking up the steps and had the envelope from Sue Ann open before I got to my desk. In it was a biography of the man she wanted me to stop from marrying her daughter and photos of him and what looked like fed's or gangsters…I didn't know which. I sat down and immediately called Russ.

"Oh, my day is now complete. Master, how can I serve you today? Speak and your words shall be my guiding light." Russ always had a unique way of greeting people. It was his inquiring mind that made him a good researcher and his effervescing personality that made him a success in the restaurant business. I always felt like he was two people crowded into one body.

"As usual you are right. She called me; some character by the name of Lewis is courting her daughter, and she is absolutely against the union. I am sending you a bio of the guy. See what you can find out about him. I'd like your ideas on what we can do about it or if we should…or I mean what I can do about it, if anything…"

There was a strange silence that came over the phone, and although it lasted only a few seconds, it felt as though it was an eternity. A very somber voice responded," My friend, do you really want to do anything? That lady is the worse person on earth to start giving advice about affairs of the heart! She stayed in school for as long as she could and she married another bookworm. The first set back they have, he leaves her. I didn't dig into it, but he had something else going on, and the loss of his son was an excuse to dump her. Their union was doomed from the very first: she's rich; she's beautiful; she's the queen bee of her world, and no one wants her--not as a woman and not as an attorney. The only path open to her is to keep being a judge; she should just stay in her ivory hell but, as usual, I shall do your bidding."

I sent the information I had on Lewis up to Russ and sat down with Russ' words ringing in my ears. All night, what he'd said kept going through my mind, for I could not fault him for anything he'd said. I kept trying to step back from the whole situation and project myself into the role of an honest-to-God grandfather. I kept asking myself what I would do if I were truly confronted with this problem. In today's world what can any parent do about whom their children marry? Disown them? You never see them again. Is not seeing them worse than seeing them and hating the thing that you're viewing? With sheer determination I dismissed the whole idea and tried to sleep as though sleep were some kind of shield to surround myself in. The shield didn't work, for as soon as I stopped all the wheels from spinning and settled down to a peaceful night, I was rudely awakened by a new thought: the latest one was Russ' laughter after I told him I'd gone to see a priest.

When morning came, I felt as though I hadn't slept at all. The phone's ringing was my first indication of a new day dawning, one that I wasn't particularly looking forward to. My hand shook as I lifted the receiver, for I knew it would be Russ. What a wonderful way to start what I could envision as a miserable day.

"I worked all night, but it seems as if Sue Ann is right. The dear boy, Lewis is the front for …well, never mind who…but they are definitely not people you would call friends. The poor jerk is being taken for a ride and doesn't even know it. He goes to a bank of their choosing and borrows money. The money he gets comes from the bank. What he doesn't know is that the local drug cartel is guaranteeing the loan; that is the only way he gets it. He repays the loan and pays a portion of the profits to the cartel. It's clean; they keep reinvesting, and the whole money scheme becomes one big mess so after a while, no one can tell what is what. That is what he was questioned about. The word I got is that Lewis is scared stiff. If you act fast, I don't think it will take much to tell him to leave town quietly and quickly."

The news knocked me back into my chair. I couldn't tell Sue Ann what I just heard for her own safety. Her daughter would be better off staying away from him as well. "Oh, by the way, when you came to The Cove, you left in a big hurry. How come?' That question was on my mind, and I felt now was a good time to ask.

"Now, Georgie baby, thou should mind thy own business, least you hear something thou would not like to hear," was the glib answer from my friend.

"Okay, when can you be here? Do you want to drive or should I rent a plane?"

"Get a plane. I'll be there tomorrow morning. Call me and I'll meet you at the airport."

As soon as I hung up, I called a friend of mine who owned an airplane. He told me not to worry; he would fly us down in his new plane because he was just itching to try it out. He told me where to meet him the following morning. I relayed the information to Russ and spent the rest of the day getting ready to leave. I called Sue Ann and told her not to worry; I would be there the next day to settle things for her.

"Well, can you tell me anything about what is going on or what you are going to do about Lewis?" Her words sounded more like a plea rather than an order.

"No, just go about your business. I'll call you when I think it's appropriate to meet with you. You called me and asked me to help, so you'll just have to trust me and an associate of mine."

"Do you mean that man Russ who was with you last time?"

I didn't appreciate her interruption; I didn't remember introducing Russ to her. "How do you know about Russ?"

"Lila hasn't stopped talking about him. She tells the same story, yet each time it sounds better. Even our chief of police and his deputies were impressed by him."

"Yes, he'll be with me, and what I want you to do is keep track of Lewis. We would like to meet with him in the afternoon."

"Should I tell Lila to expect you? Will you be staying

41

over?"

"We will stay in Virginia Beach if we do...not in The Cove."

The next morning we met at the airport, and our unlikely trio with overnight bags got in the plane, and within a few minutes, we were soaring over New Jersey. Russ sat next to the pilot so he could act as co-pilot, while I sat in the back and acted as navigator. We followed the parkway to the ferry and crossed over into Delaware. We had decided to follow the same roadway we drove over the last time when I had gone to Virginia Beach. It was a strange sensation to watch the same scenery from above, rather than on the same level. The scariest part was flying over the bay bridge tunnel. The flight took a couple of hours, but I was glad when I felt the wheels touch the ground and I could at last take a deep breath. While we were in the air, Russ had called the airport and told them to have a rental car waiting for us.

Our pilot stayed with the plane while Russ and I drove to The Cove to meet with Lewis. He lived about a mile from Sue Ann, further down the coast. His house was of a modern design. It was painted in a blue/gray that made it blend into the scenery. Sue Ann had made an appointment for us to see him. He truly was scared, for he did not leave the house all day. Trina, Sue Ann's daughter, at her mother's request, had kept her distance from him, for she too had started to hear rumors. She didn't believe them and she would stand by him, but she stayed away. Anyway, an old boyfriend of hers from her college days was in town, and she felt she should entertain him.

Russ and I parked the car and walked up to the front door of the house. The doorbell was the tune-playing sort that went on forever. A voice came over the speaker, inviting us in. As we walked in, we were overwhelmed, for the entire wall of the house facing the water was made of glass. There was very little furniture in the room for everything was built into the walls. If one pressed a button, a portion of the wall moved, and behind it was a bar. Press another one and a very modern kitchen appeared with all chrome fixtures. There was a large fireplace that took up another wall, and off to one side was a magnificent spiral staircase that went up to the second floor, where I imagined the bedrooms were.

To one side was a glass, dining-room table, which could seat fourteen people. The chairs were made of solid mahogany. By the kitchen counter was a small counter with high stools, where we were motioned to sit. He immediately offered us some refreshments while pointing to a side room, which was the bathroom. I was truly impressed with the house.

Lewis was busy preparing something and just engaged in a nervous chatter. Finally, I'd had enough, and while Russ went to the bathroom, I said, "Lewis, you don't know me, but..."

"What did that bitch tell you about me? She must have told you I was Jack the Ripper and Mr. Hyde all wrapped into one."

While he spoke, he kept rubbing his hands together. His knuckles were well developed; I was waiting for him to break boards at any moment. He was thirty something but in top physical shape. As he spoke, I looked around, expecting to see a mini gym, but none was in sight.

"Lewis, I came here to help you. You're in with bad people, and they are just using you as a front man. When the trouble comes, and as you have already seen, it is on its way, they will leave you to the wolves. You appeared for testimony in front..."

"That was supposed to be confidential. That is why I went to..."

His smug attitude was now gone, and he forgot about preparing whatever he was working on. I now had his full attention. "If you don't know that by now your buddies have the transcript with pictures of everything you said, you are really naïve."

"So what!" he screamed. "What are they going to do-- send

two gorillas like you to handle me? Just let them try!"

Russ, who had gone to the bathroom, was walking towards the counter. Lewis had gone shopping and had bought a melon. It was about six inches round. Russ walked over to the bag and took it out. He placed it on the counter and looked at Lewis as he said, "They will not send two; they will send one like me. He will come in here and have dinner with you. He will have a drink or two, and when you are relaxed, he will walk to the middle of the room…"

Russ was an excellent man with a knife. His favorite trick was to put a target on a wall and walk about twenty feet from it; suddenly, in one fluid motion, he'd pull out a stiletto, open it, and throw it at the bull's eye he had set up. He swore he never practiced the stunt; it came to him naturally. No one believed him, but he stuck to his story.

I watched as he set the scene up, and when he was in the center of the room about twenty feet from the melon, he swung around and opened up the knife and threw it all in one fluid motion. When the knife hit the melon, it made a noise different than any noise I had ever heard. Lewis's lower jaw dropped as he watched the event. The knife went half way into the melon and took it right off the counter. It hit the floor with a smashing sound. Lewis, judging by the expression on his face, was deeply impressed. His arrogant attitude changed; he bowed his head and in a whisper that was barely audible said, "What should I do?"

"Leave! How hard is it for you to … if you left right now…I mean the house and all…"

He replied, "Easy! I don't own this house or anything in it. It was set up for me by…well, you know whom. The only things I own are my clothes and the two suitcases I packed them in when I moved here from Chicago. I could go back there; my uncle never wanted me to leave. I can call him. I can pack right away. I can be out of here in twenty minutes. The ring…I got a ring from the local store; they ordered it for me because they don't carry that size in inventory."

I stood up and said, "Go pack! I will give the ring back. There is an airplane at the little airport near the town. I'll call the pilot and tell him to fly you out of here. I don't know where a bigger airport is, but he will; go back to Chicago or wherever."

In a cold dead silence, Lewis was on his way. Russ called the airport and worked out that part of his trip for him. He turned to me as he asked, "What about us? What do we do?"

"We will be tourists for the night. You call Lila and tell her to expect us. Tell her to get her party clothes on, and we will take her and Sue Ann to dinner. I'll tell Sue Ann to ask her daughter and her old boyfriend to join us…that should make for a nice dinner.

Lewis came down the steps and headed for his car. As he went out the door, he said, "I'll call Trina. I don't really have to do anything; when I wanted to give her the ring, she said "no"; she wanted to leave everything the way it was. I called the airport and told them I would leave the car there."

"What about the car?" Russ shouted after him.

"I'll leave it at the airport; it's not mine; they own it."

Russ and I stood in the doorway and watched as his taillights faded into the night. Russ announced, "Come, dear boy, we have earned our grub and grog for the night."

"Russ, I don't think it was a good idea that he called from the house. I'll bet his friends have the phone tapped."

Russ just laughed as he said, "That's why you have so much gray hair; you worry too much. Be like me…be happy…be gay…for this may be your very last day."

As Russ and I were getting ready to go to dinner, the idea that we had just gotten rid of Lewis, Trina's boyfriend, but were getting ready to go to dinner with Trina's "boyfriend" bothered me. I called out to Russ, who was also getting ready, "How many boyfriends does Trina have? We got rid of one, and she has another ready to go. Do you know anything about him?"

"Well, you know I don't like to gossip, but when I was researching Lewis, I heard about Steve. She and Steve were an item throughout high school. Of course, you know that rumors have a way of being true. Steve didn't want to make a commitment, so Trina went out with Lewis. It is rumored that she only did that to make Steve jealous."

"What does Steve do?"

"From what I could gather from the few facts I got was that his father, for some reason, bought a nice fishing boat, one that could be used commercially. He must have known something was going on with his wife, for when he died...suddenly...she was going out hot and heavy with someone else. The father left the boat to Steve; there was an insurance policy that paid off the boat when he died. There also was another policy that went directly to Steve. The wife was going to contest them, but for some reason, she dropped the case. That meant that Steve got the boat and some cash. Now, again I repeat, it is mostly gossip; he and Trina had a misunderstanding, and Lewis came into the picture. Steve came back to town and was a good customer at the store, and Trina held Lewis at bay. Ain't life wonderful?"

"Russ, before I die, are you ever going to tell me how you find out these things?"

"George, my man, it's a combination of hearing a fact...hearing some gossip...adding logic...and you have a reason why people do things."

The doorbell rang in the main part of the house, and I could hear Lila answering the door. I heard her say something, but I could not make out what she was saying. I heard Russ calling to her as he went into the main part of the house. When he came to get me so we could go to dinner, he was carrying two small bouquets of flowers. Before I could say anything, he announced, "I knew you would want to, so I took the liberty of

46

ordering flowers for the ladies. I know how you like to do nice things like that." I remembered the ring Lewis had given me; I didn't know where to put it, so I just brought it with me.

When the three of us got in the car to go to the restaurant, Lila was just beaming as she said, "George, that was so nice of you. I don't know too many men who would even think of doing something like that. Thank you. I know the other ladies will be thrilled, too." Russ quickly added as he put the car in gear, "He's just a sweetheart." As soon as we arrived, Russ gave Sue Ann and Trina their flowers; they were both thrilled.

The restaurant was a quaint place. It was much bigger than what it looked like from the outside. It looked as though it was a house and the owner kept adding rooms on as his business increased. The decor was early American, which meant that whatever he found for sale at a flea market or a house sale was bought and added to the decor of the place. This included the table and chairs that had no overall continuity except that they were table and chairs. Sue Ann had called ahead for reservations, so as soon as we walked in, we were brought to the largest of the rooms and shown our table grouping. It looked like someone's old dining room set.

On stage there was a three-piece band that night, which was ready, willing, and able to fill all requests. Within a few minutes Sue Ann, Trina, and her boyfriend arrived, and our group settled down to the business of ordering dinner. Sue Ann moved her chair closer to mine because she wanted to hear about Lewis. I just said, "He's gone, so don't worry about him. He gave me the ring he wanted to give your daughter."

Before I could finish the sentence, a large group of people came in, and Sue Ann said, "There's the jeweler now. Give it to me and I will return it to her. I have a feeling she is worried about it. It is the largest one she has ever handled."

I gave her the ring, and she promptly walked over to a lady on the far side of the room and judging from the expression on her face, she was very glad to get it back. She looked at me and nodded, and I nodded back.

The trio started playing, and the whole room took on a festive aura. When the traveling mike came to our table, Russ brought the house down with his rendition of "My Way." His rendition included many words and phrases that the composer never thought of, but everyone enjoyed his rendition. The drinks and food kept flowing, and Russ made a point of dancing with everyone at our table and the table next to us. Lila was not thrilled with his actions.

Russ took note of Trina's boyfriend's attire. He made it a point of coming over to me to point out its deficiencies. "For a young man, where did he get that get up? He looks like he shops at the Sister of The Poor haberdasher store. "

"Russ, shut up. That is the way they live down here. Can't you just settle down and be a nice warm person instead of a...I don't know what. Go dance with Lila; she wasn't too thrilled with your dancing with everyone else." Russ complied, and the look on Lila's face when he swept her up into his arms was well worth seeing.

"You really seem to have fit into our little town." I didn't have to look up to know that the chief had joined our group. He was standing behind me on my right side, which put him between Sue Ann and myself. His protruding belly was acting as a wedge between us. He kept talking but I just ignored him. Sue Ann started a conversation, but I chose not to hear what she was saying. Russ made the most germane comment when he said, "Do you go to bed with that outfit on? "He was referring to the chief's uniform, which the chief still had on. Although I felt the statement was inappropriate and damn rude, I couldn't help but laugh.

"I am on duty tonight. I thought I would come by and make sure everything was okay here." His words were said as though he was throwing darts. It was sad that he tried to banter words with Russ, for Russ immediately responded with, "Without the hat and sun glasses, I didn't know." Everyone at our table and the two adjoining tables just laughed. Other comments were shouted out and, thankfully, the band started playing a lively tune, and many couples, including Trina and her boyfriend, filled the dance floor. The chief left.

Sue Ann leaned over and nudged me as she said, "That wasn't very nice; you know I have to work with him after you and your friend Russ leave. He has been the law and order in this town for many years now. He started out as a deputy, and as the others on the force left for greener pastures, he stayed on. Some members of the council said it was because no one else wanted him. The council realized that our town was just a stepping-stone for young officers, but we really don't need a super cop. He keeps the drunks quiet and the tourists in check, so the town's people generally feel safe. He has no one, so he is on duty all the time, for he has nowhere else to go or anyone to go with. He is invited to all the parties, regardless of the reason for the party, and his mere presence keeps everyone in line."

When she was done talking, I paused for a few minutes before I said in a quiet tone, "I didn't invite him. I didn't want him here. What did you want me to do, just tell him to get the hell out? I thought it was very rude of him to join our group, but I guess you're right. Just keep him away from me. Come on; as long as you don't do anything too tricky, we can dance."

She looked surprised but quickly got up, and we walked to the dance floor. Once there she said, "According to your book *When God Ain't Lookin'*, I thought you would be a great dancer. I am working my way through all of them. They were delivered yesterday. I didn't realize my father was so prolific."

As she spoke, she could feel me tense up. I did not respond verbally to the father remark but rather kept moving in time to the music until, finally, it stopped. We went back to the table in a strange sort of silence. She quietly said, "I'm sorry. I won't say that again."

The evening ended on a high note, and everyone kissed each other good night as Russ took my credit card and signed my name to the bill. We drove back to Lila's and settled in for the night. Russ' last statement was, "The dear chief followed us home. I'm glad you drove because I know he would have pulled me over and given me a ticket for DWI."

In the morning a gentle roar awakened me. At first I could not identify what it was, but when Russ jumped up, he announced, "Someone is using a vacuum cleaner." Over the din of it, we heard Lila's voice…"Breakfast is ready." We walked into the main house and Russ first spied Tisha. She was much shorter than I was and was dressed in a loose sweatshirt and cotton pants. She went to a bucket containing her cleaning supplies, and when she bent over to get something out, the word "PINK" was printed across her seat. Russ looked at me, and by his expression I knew he was set to say something witty, so before he did, I interjected, "Breakfast is served…cool it." Lila introduced us to Tisha, and as we were saying hello, Russ added, "That must be short for Patricia. Why you would want to shorten a beautiful name like that is more than I can understand."

Tisha smiled and flipped her head from side to side as a wisp of a smile came across her face. She spoke in a very soft tone, which made it hard for me to understand her. She had to repeat everything she said for me to hear her. Russ and she carried on a conversation, but I was out of earshot. I motioned to Russ for us to leave, and the last words I heard him say was, "Are you conservative or…"

Before he could finish his statement, she responded, "Conservative."

He said, "Damn," as we walked back into our suite and got ready to leave.

"I think we better call the rental company and tell them we

are going to drive the car back to Jersey." As I spoke, Russ nodded his head in agreement, and as I was about to call, my phone rang; it was Sue Ann. "George, Lewis was killed in an accident out at the airport... the one you landed at. There was an explosion of some sort, and a small plane with its pilot and Lewis blew up. No one knows what happened." Sue Ann was speaking so loudly that Russ heard everything she said.

I looked at Russ, but from the expression on his face, I knew he had already read my mind. "That chief is going to be looking for me." Russ sounded very nervous as he spoke and moved around on the seat. "He didn't appreciate my humor the other night. This is all he'll need to detain me for questioning. Drive me to the train or bus station, and I'll go home that way."

I asked Sue Ann which was closer, a bus depot or train station, and she gave me directions to the bus depot. I drove Russ there and waited with him until the next bus that was going north. Luckily, there was one leaving in a half hour. I stood in the station until the bus with my friend on board was out of sight. I was not sure what I should do or where I should go, so I drove to the airport to find out what I could about the accident. I knew the chief would know by now that Russ and I flew in on it, and with all probability he would know that Lewis was going to fly out on it. The airport manager would have told him. In any event, I wanted to know what had happened to the pilot; after all, he was my friend...not a good one... but someone I could call upon for a favor. I felt very badly that the last favor I asked cost him his life.

The airport was overflowing with local and state police. Also the aviation board was there, trying to piece together what had happened. Standing on the side were three men from the FBI. I was amazed how similar they looked. The owner of the airport also pointed them out to me. He was highly agitated as he spoke to me. "No one knows what happened. The plane just exploded! Nothing like this has ever happened to me before.

Thank God no one else was injured or any other planes were damaged. I don't know if my insurance would cover something like that." He kept rambling on, but I just turned him off. There was a representative from the car rental agency, so I asked if he would give me a ride back into town; I would turn the car in as long as I was there, and he agreed. As we were leaving, I could see the chief, standing on the side and looking very irritated, for he was just being pushed aside as all the other agencies were doing their work. He definitely did not like being put in a subservient position. He was more the type who would pound on a desk and pronounce, "This is my town...this is my airport...I run things here... no one is going to tell me what to do."

I asked the driver from the rental agency to bring me to the general store. I was positive that by now the Commodore would know what had happened or at least what the rumors were. He was definitely the type who would have his finger on the pulse of the town. Also, I didn't know what else to do. I didn't want to leave without finding out if Russ or I would be implicated in any way. I also could not figure out why Lewis didn't fly out the night before when he was supposed to. I kept asking myself why he waited until this morning; he should have been long gone. The only other person who would have known Lewis was leaving was the jeweler, but she didn't find out until that night at the restaurant. There were just too many unanswered questions for me to leave. I was so engrossed that I didn't even realize that the Commodore was standing beside me. When he spoke, I was startled.

"I ordered you coffee and our midmorning special; you look like you could use some nourishment." As he said the words, he immediately sat down and, without any prompting from me, told me everything he had heard about the incident out at the airport. The only new thing I heard was when Lewis went to the airport, there was something wrong with the plane and to be on the safe side, the pilot wanted it checked before they left. They went to the local bar by the airport, had dinner, slept in the airport, and left in the morning; that is when the plane blew up.

That story made no sense; my friend was very meticulous; there is no way he would allow anyone to touch his plane. There was just one more thing that compelled me to hang around awhile. My phone rang and it was Sue Ann.

"I heard you had left Lila's and you are now in town. You turned the car in, so you are in need of a room and wheels."

"You sure have a good spy system. Do you get minute-to-minute updates on my whereabouts and activities? I'm impressed." I sat in my chair and just shook my head in disbelief. Before I could say anything else, she said: "Why don't you stay at my home; there is plenty of room, and you can use my car while you are here. Don't worry what people will say; they will talk any way. Will you stay?"

"Only if you let me use your bike when you're not using it."

"That is out of the question, but I will get you one of your own. Walk down to the courthouse when you are ready. I will go home now and get my car, and you can take me back to get my bike." After she said the last phrase, I could hear her laughing before she hung up.

Since I had decided to stay, I called home and told my housekeeper to pack some clothes for me and mail them down to me.

"How many is some?" she asked.

"Two weeks' worth."

"Where should I send them?" I didn't know Sue Ann's address, so I gave her the address of the store in care of me.

Chapter Eight

The general store became the pivotal point for all stories about "The Incident" as the accident at the airport was referred to. Everyone who came in first reported what they had just heard; they would add their interpretation of what they had learned and end up with their conclusions. The consensus was that there was foul play and that there was a murderer in The Cove. Another version was that there was a murderer in The Cove, but he left and his friend was still here. The Commodore would be the recipient of all the gossip, and as soon as he heard it, he would immediately repeat it to me. I tried not to react to anything that was being said, but as the stories increased, it was harder not to scream.

The Commodore would listen to all before making up his version and promptly tell it to me. I would "ooh" and "ah" at the right times, which he used as an acknowledgement and continue. Of course, the one question everyone asked was, "Where is Russ…? George is here, but Russ isn't." One version had Russ being blown up with the plane. I liked that one the best. Finally, I had heard enough and walked down to the courthouse to meet with Sue Ann.

When I walked into the courthouse, she was just finishing up a case and motioned for me to go to her chambers. As I walked in, there was Tisha; she also worked for the county.

Sue Ann asked, "You know Tisha?"

I nodded. Tisha turned, and when she saw me, she also nodded. Sue Ann continued, "Being around the court house made everyone look up to her as being an authority on what was happening. When she denies knowing anything, her friends become enraged, for they want to know more, and she won't tell. It makes her very popular around town."

We left the courthouse and drove to her home. As we walked in the front door, I was truly impressed by the home and all the decorations in it. Everywhere I looked, there was a science. The fireplace commanded my attention as we walked into the living room. It was a gas fireplace that was fueled by propane gas. When I asked Sue Ann about it, she was surprised that I knew. "How can you tell?"

"If it were real, there would be dirt somewhere." She just laughed and complimented me on my powers of observation. Next to the opening to the fire chamber was an elaborate iron set that would be used to turn the logs and fix the fire if it were a wood-burning one. In front of the fireplace was a coffee table with curved legs and an etched glass top. Three matching sofas surrounded it. Each item was unique and yet matched each other by color and design. The setting looked like it should have been in a movie rather than in someone's home. There was a doorway that led outside to a patio that overlooked the harbor and bay. There was a glass table with four chairs and a lounge. As I looked around, I could feel that what I was looking at was a sterile sight; it lacked the intangible warmth of a home with love in it.

On the other side of the patio was a small cottage that acted as a guesthouse. It was a one-room affair that was designed like a typical motel room with a king-sized bed. I put my small travel bag inside. When I came out to the patio, Sue Ann had made us a drink, and we sat down to enjoy the evening. She started to tell me her school days experiences, but I stopped her. "Please, I really don't want to hear about your childhood. I should have never agreed to stay here. I better go to bed."

"Would you rather talk about the incident at the airport? Would that sort of story be more to your liking?" As she spoke, tears were flowing down her face. Thankfully, the doorbell rang. Sue Ann got up and answered the door; it was the chief. They were talking for a while before they came out to the patio.

The chief walked out onto the patio, and as soon as he stepped on it, he inquired in an authoritative tone, "Where is Russ?"

I was annoyed at the attitude he was taking, so with the same tone I responded, "None of your business."

"I want to question him!"

"He has no obligation to talk to you, and as his attorney, I would advise him not to talk to you."

The chief was visibly upset with my response. He kept shifting his weight from side to side as he was searching for something profound to say. He continued, "There has been a crime committed."

I interrupted him by saying, "You have evidence of a crime? Pray tell, what is it?"

I cannot discuss an ongoing investigation with anyone." He said the words as though he had just gotten done rehearsing them. He was talking in a monotone, which made him sound even more ridiculous. "Well, if you can't discuss it, there is nothing more for us to say."

"You know your friend has a very strange way about him. How come he left town?"

"Who said he did?"

"Well, where is he?"

"I can't discuss the whereabouts of any of my clients without their permission and especially in this case, when I don't even know why you're asking."

While we were talking, Sue Ann was obvious by her absence. I looked around, but she was nowhere to be seen. The chief kept talking, but I just ignored him. I got up and went into the house, but I still didn't see her. The chief followed me in, still talking away. I went to the front door, and as I opened it, Sue Ann walked in.

"Was I missed? I went to put the car away. Would you gentlemen like coffee?"

"No," I said, "the chief was just leaving." I held the door open as the chief walked out of the house, mumbling to himself. As he passed me, he said in an aside, "I'm going to get that friend of yours."

"We come as a package deal; you get him and you get me; be careful what you say, least you get more than you ask for." Before he could respond, I closed the door and went back out to the patio and bid Sue Ann "Good Night." I went to my room and by the time I got undressed, I was ready for sleep. I snuggled into the comfortable bed and soon I was fast asleep.

In the morning I realized that I didn't have that many clothes to choose from, so I did the best I could with the clothes I had and made a mental note that I would go down to the general store and buy some seafaring items. As I opened the door to come out on to the patio, I heard Sue Ann say goodbye and, "The coffee is on the stove; the keys to the car are on the counter, and there is bread for toast...bye...I'll talk to you later." Her announcements done, she closed the door.

I went to the coffee machine just as Tisha was walking in the door. "I forgot some of my supplies here; I will be leaving right away." She went into a closet and came out with a small basket of cleaning supplies. "If you want, I will get the coffee for you. Do you want me to make breakfast for you? I will be back later to clean this house, so you can just leave everything in the sink, and I'll take care of it."

"No, that's okay. I'll do it myself." With those words she left. I was anxious to get to the store to find out what was happening about the "Incident." I had my coffee as I finished getting dressed, got the car, and headed for the store. The Commodore greeted me with a few updates before I could even walk around the store to buy a new outfit. Since the Commodore and I were about the same size, it made my job easier, for he picked out a complete outfit for me. He allowed me to go into his private rooms to get changed. When I emerged, I fit right in with the locals…at least clothing wise.

I sat down at one of the tables, and Trina came over to serve me. "My friend and I want to thank you for the other night; we really had a good time. Your friend Russ is something else; here's our local paper to read while I get you our breakfast special."

The headlines referred to the incident but little else about it. There just wasn't enough information to write anything about it. The major article was about Sue Ann. The reporter described her as an independent, intellectual giant that the town should be proud to have. When I got done reading it, I didn't know whether or not to be proud or to pity her, for there was no one in The Cove that could measure up to her. The last part of the article was," She rides through town, looking after her flock, and the familiar ding-a-ling is a comfort to all." I really thought that was childish, but I knew I should keep my big city ideas to myself.

As my breakfast was being served, a man came over to my table and introduced himself as the manager of the paper. He looked to be in his early fifties with a two-day-old beard. He had an old sports jacket on with a faded sport shirt and faded dungarees. As I looked at him, I could just imagine what Russ would be saying. Before I could say anything, he was sitting down with me and starting to explain why there was so little written about the incident. He said, "There are a lot of rumors and conjectures but no real hard facts to write about. Our local chief is being brushed aside, which is driving him nuts, and the other agencies won't tell me anything."

I didn't respond because I just wanted him to leave. He must have sensed that I didn't want him near me, so he got up, and as he walked away, he said, "I guess you'll be leaving like your friend Russ?" I did not respond at all. With all that was going on, I still had not resolved what I was going to do about Sue Ann. I didn't think she had told her daughter Trina about me, so the only problem I had was Sue Ann. I was going over everything in my mind and trying to figure out when I should go home when I realized I had no way to get home except by train or bus. I resolved that I didn't want to fly.

"Well, I see you are still with us." As I looked up, the chief was standing before me in his full uniform: hat, glasses, and all. "You know we have a nice quiet town here, and I get paid to keep it that way. It is usually a dull job, but then you and Russ show up and that all changed. We are starting to get a lot of strangers in town, many of which I have never seen before. I have to ask myself how you are tied in to all of this activity. I mean, you and your friend fly in, and a resident of our town is blown up, and Russ is nowhere to be found. These things are…"

While he was talking, I got up and went to the men's room. When I came out, he was standing by my table with his two deputies. I walked between them, paid my bill, and started to leave when he again started talking, "It seems every time I'm near you, you have to use the bathroom. I don't understand that."

I paid my bill and as I turned to leave, I looked him in the eye and said, "That is because you scare the shit out of me." The Commodore who, as usual, was close at hand, just roared. I paid no attention and just left.

I drove out to the airport, but it was all roped off, and no one was allowed to enter. I turned the car around and drove back to Sue Ann's house. On the way there, I stopped off at the bus depot and picked up a bus schedule for a bus that was going north. I brought it with me so I could study it and make my plans for leaving. I'd solved the question of how I was going to leave; now the only thing I had to decide was when. Of course, the Sue Ann issue was a constant burden to me, for no matter what else I did or thought about, what to do about my problem was on my mind, always nagging at me. I realized that the problem wasn't going to go away, and it wasn't going to solve itself.

The outside patio looked very inviting, and the comforter that was on the chair next to the door seemed to be calling to me. There was a slight breeze off the bay, which added to my need of a blanket to keep the chill out of my bones. I went outside, got in the lounger, not worrying about how I would get out of it, and just let the day and the surroundings overcome me.

"You seem to fit right in here. Why don't you stay for a while? You have your own room; everyone in town is dying to meet you. I was already asked to bring you to the tea; each week a different lady has a tea at her house. It is a very casual affair, but it does bring us together and makes for a pleasant few hours. It seems you and the new manager of the newspaper are the two most-sought-after people in the town. Of course, if you can get Russ to come back, they would all love that?"

Sue Ann's speech woke me up, especially the part about bringing Russ back. 'I would be afraid to bring Russ around for I know that chief of yours just can't wait to bring some sort of charge against him."

"Well, if he has done something wrong, why shouldn't he?"

"Because Russ doesn't like that sort of thing and would think nothing of taking his head clean off. Your chief has a way of irritating me and especially Russ. What is it with him? If you have any influence over him, you better tell him to cool it. I am positive he won't listen, but try anyway. Oh, before I forget, Tisha was here this morning. She has her own key; anyway, she had forgotten some supplies here. She said she would be back, but she didn't say any specific time."

"Yes she has her own key. You're in The Cove; we trust people here. She and I have a special arrangement; she does my house when she has some free time; she says I'm her "filler" work. As to your friend, do you really think your friend can come into our town and intimidate our chief?"

By the tone of her voice, I could tell that she was getting

annoyed at the conversation. After all, this was her town and her chief; before I could stop myself; I responded, "I know he can."

"Is he the same person you refer to in your books?"

"Yes."

"In your books, or at least the ones I have read so far, he doesn't come across as a particularly aggressive person."

"That is because 'in the business' he is referred to as a 'man down under'. You never see him; he just has things happen out of sight and earshot of everyone else."

"Do you mean like blowing up planes?" Her last remark was said with a cutting tone to it.

"No, that's too crude for him. How can you control the harm that could be done by doing an act like that; no, Russ is much more subtle and direct." I thought for a moment and added, "Do you think he had anything to do with the incident? I can assure you he did not; he was in bed sleeping."

"How can you be so sure?" Her voice took on a more commanding tone. I got the feeling that she wanted to question me more about the incident but I didn't want to lead her on. She might ask the right questions, and I might give the wrong answers. After all, she was my brilliant daughter. I couldn't tell whether that thought filled me with pride or disgust; therefore, I decided to end the topic. In hopes of doing just that, I added, "Russ was drinking; if he wanted to do something, he would never drink; also, if he wanted to do something like that, he would make sure he got the chief also. Why would he leave the one person who could give him some grief around? It would make no sense."

My explanations seemed to satisfy Sue Ann; as she started to go to her room, she yelled back over her shoulder, "I told Trina and her friend that we would take them to dinner tonight. I hope that was alright?"

"Of course, let me go shave with my new razor that the Commodore said I needed and should buy."

Sue Ann went to her room and I went to mine; her last words to me were, "In a half hour, okay?" I didn't respond.

At the appointed hour, we met in the hallway. It seemed to me that no matter what, she still looked like a judge holding court. I could not understand it, for she was very fashionably dressed with a flowing dress, low high heels, bangle bracelets and rings, but I still felt intimidated. I smiled inwardly and resolved it was her hair. It was piled on top of her head exactly as it had been the first day that I had seen her. I concluded I was just being stupid. "My, you look very nice; in fact, you look like a butterfly just out of its cocoon."

She stopped and looked at me as she responded with a bit if sarcasm. "You mean I'm as pretty as my mother?"

By the expression on my face, she saw I didn't care for that remark, so she immediately added, "I'm sorry...really I am. Come on, Trina and her boyfriend will be waiting for us."

When we got to the restaurant, we were seated in a different room. The host said, "Your daughter didn't want to sit with the band. I hope that's okay with you?"

Sue Ann and I both nodded our approval and were lead to our table, which was located on the quiet side of the restaurant. The night was filled with light chatter. Trina's boyfriend must have heard Russ' condemnation of his last outfit, for tonight he was wearing shoes instead of sneakers, pressed pants instead of jeans, a sport shirt that looked as though it was recently pressed, and a sport jacket, and everything matched. Trina looked like a clone of her mother except that her hair was done up in some kind of twist with a large clip holding it together.

The night ended and we all went our separate ways.

Chapter Nine

The next morning started off with a storm cloud coming in over the bay. It shrouded the entire town in a milky white, wet substance. Some called it a cloud; some thought it was fog, and some just realized it was a wet miserable morning. I heard all three descriptions on my way to the store for the early morning special the Commodore offered. It was so cheap it didn't pay to eat at home. The other big advantage was that the Commodore brought me up to date on any news that I might have missed. If there was nothing new, he restated what he'd said already. Either way, it was an entertainment that I liked and looked forward to.

The incident at the airport still held center stage, but the latest news was about the new look the editor-in-chief was giving the newspaper. His name was Chad. He had come to my table the day before and was annoyed at the way I'd treated him. The Commodore assured me that he had explained my rudeness away and that I had nothing to worry about from Chad. His article about Sue Ann was well received by most people. At that point I wondered if the Commodore conducted a poll on everything that happened in town and the world. His voice sounded so authoritative that I believed everything he said. In an aside, he suddenly whispered, "The chief is still looking for your friend Russ. He tells everyone, especially me, to keep a sharp eye out for him and to call the station with any news or sightings.

The chief isn't here yet because there was going to be a big meeting out at the airport that he wanted to attend. The aviation board was going to present their findings as to what made the plane blow. A group of the investigators were here around dinnertime and sat at the table in the back, and they were all excited because the aviation board investigators usually don't make their report public. I don't know what they meant by that, for if they don't make the report public then why make a report?"

Finally the Commodore was called away by a customer who needed help to find something. I was happy for the reprieve. As soon as he walked away, I suddenly heard, "I hope you are going to come to our luncheon/tea time today? It is the first one we are trying. I'm on the committee; in fact, I am the chairlady, and we tried a brunch once, but that didn't go over so well; in fact, we lost money on it. The reason it didn't do well was because most of our group have too many things to do in the morning; that is why we thought an affair around tea time would be better, but we wanted to give more than tea and little sandwiches so that is why we are calling it a luncheon/tea time. I hope you will come? It is being held in the town auditorium; that is the building down at the end of the center of town. We asked our judge Sue Ann to at least stop in. The town council members promised they would come, but they want to come for nothing. I don't think that's fair, but the rest of the ladies on the committee voted me down. Will you come?"

I was so overcome by the deluge of words that I shouted, "Yes, in fact, give me two tickets. I'll bring the Commodore as my date."

The Commodore, upon hearing his name, came over and said, "I can't come; I have to…"

Trina interrupted him with, "Go! I can take care of things while you're gone. We are usually slow after the lunch crowd, and anyway, if I have a problem, you are only five minutes away. I know all the ladies will be thrilled if you two go."

From the other side of the room, Chad shouted out, "I'm going to cover the affair, and if you are there, it will be a free plug for your store. I know the ladies can't wait until they get their hands on you."

The chairlady who had done all the talking nudged me as she whispered, "His wife died three years ago; it's no good that he is all alone. All he does is stay in this store. You know he sleeps in the back; he never leaves day or night. That's no good for a widower to be by himself like that. Are you widowed?"

I just nodded my head, "Yes."

"Good, you can …Oh, I'm so sorry! I didn't mean…"

"That's okay; I have the same problem as the Commodore. You tell all the ladies we will be there."

Chad added, "I'm going to bring my camera, so warn everyone." The chairlady sold me my tickets and she was on her way.

I didn't know if I was happy or sad that I was fitting into the fabric of the community so well. I suddenly felt very old.

The Commodore suddenly changed his persona from the old Commodore to a man who was going out on the town. He announced with a tone of finality, "I'll get a trim." The few customers in the store, without any prompting, applauded. Trina quickly said, "I'll call him to get you an appointment." A lady customer added, "Men don't make appointments like ladies do when they go to a hair dresser; they just show up."

With a look of grim determination, the Commodore grabbed my arm as said, "Come on; you need a trim, too." The barbershop was an easy walk to a side street away from the harbor. There were two barbers. One was busy, but the other was standing and looking out the window. As soon as the Commodore walked in, the barber dusted off the chair and, like a matador, took the apron that they tie around the neck of the customer and led the Commodore to the chair. He quickly tied the protective apron around the Commodore's neck, waited until he settled himself in the chair, and without waiting for instructions as to what he was supposed to do, started snipping away. The scissors sounded like something mechanical as the barber started at the top of the Commodore's head and proceeded down one side of his face, around the chin, and up the other side. With an artistic gleam in his eye, he gave symmetry to a wild formation of hair that now looked tamed. He stepped back to admire his work before he set about snipping a little here and there as he finished his masterpiece. While he was finishing up, the other barber just trimmed my hair and was visibly annoyed that his partner got to work on the Commodore. As I was getting out of the chair, he motioned towards the Commodore as he said, "I could have done that."

I had to admit that the Commodore looked very distinguished. He looked like the picture of a man I would put on a commercial to sell a fine bottle of wine. We walked out of the shop and back towards the store. As he walked in, the very same customers that were there when we left were still there, and with their "Ooh's" and "Ah's" and slight applause, they showed their admiration and approval.

I walked around the harbor while I waited for the time when we were to go to the luncheon/tea. As much as I wanted to, I could not get the reason I was in The Cove out of my mind. Here I was, in a perfect little community with the residents' waiting to include me in their group, and all I could think of was how to kill the one person they looked up to, even if they didn't like her. No matter how I tried, I could not bring myself to accept her as my daughter. Those words just made me shiver. The clanging of the bell that hung on the back porch of the store, thankfully, got me out of my gloomy frame of mind. The Commodore was waving to me; it was time to go. I reversed my direction and walked back to the store. The Commodore walked out with a sport jacket on, carrying one over his arm. "Here," he said as he handed it to me, "I know it will fit you." It did.

As we were ready to leave, Trina came running over, "George, a big box came for you. Where should I have the bus boy put it?"

I thought for a moment before I responded with, "Have him

66

put it in your mother's car. I'll deal with it later."

The dynamic duo, as the customers dubbed us, had everyone's attention as we walked down the street to the auditorium. The Commodore broke the strange silence with, "I feel as though I am a lamb being led to slaughter; the worst part is that I go gladly."

"How did you get the title of Commodore? What is your real name?"

"Alistair Mack. Everyone liked to call me "Al" or "Big Al", but one day, someone came into the store and asked if I was the harbor commodore and that name sounded classier. From that day forth, everyone called me Commodore, and I liked it."

As he finished talking, we were at the table where we had to turn in our tickets. The Chairlady greeted us and immediately introduced us to two other women, who had labels on designating them as "Hostesses." "Now if you want to meet anyone in particular, just ask us, and we will do the introductions."

"I feel like I am at a high-school dance with hostesses and all," the Commodore said as he was being led away to a table. I followed, and when we were seated, I responded with, "Would you rather be greeted by St. Peter?" We both laughed as we were being introduced to everyone and food and drink was being brought to us.

I looked up as I said, "Wait! Aren't we supposed to walk around and serve ourselves?"

One of the hostesses replied, "Yes, but since it's your first time at one of our functions, we want the two of you to feel welcome."

I felt as though I was introduced to everyone twice. There were about forty people there, but the introductions never stopped. When the town council cut short their weekly meeting so they could attend, the chairlady made it a point to stand next to me as she said, "I have to pay for those free loaders; that just annoys me to no end."

Everything came to an abrupt halt when Sue Ann walked in. The only thing that was missing was the banging of a gong. Everyone made it a point to greet her and thank her for coming. I felt a guilt come over me as I shuddered to think that the only way I could accept this lady was to kill her. The thought just unnerved me. I said a silent prayer that I would think of a different way out of my dilemma. The priest's words, "Someday you will have to acknowledge her" just weighed heavily on my mind. That phrase, in conjunction with Russ' prediction that, "You'll never get rid of her; you have just added a new dimension to her life that she never had before" just had me in a terrible spin that blocked everything else out. Sue Ann's calling me just proved him right. I guess his being right was what was bothering me the most.

The party wore on and it was becoming more difficult for me to keep a happy face on as the two predictions that had been made were wearing on me. I tried to nod and laugh at the right time, but after a while, I just wore myself out. At one point I just wanted to scream, but I didn't know what good that would do. I was becoming two people, and there wasn't enough room in my one body for both of me. Finally, through the turmoil within me, I heard the Commodore's voice saying, "Well, come on, George; I have to get back to the store. The early dinner crowd will be coming in, or at least, I hope they will. But you don't have to leave."

It took all of my strength to smile, stand up, and say, "Oh no, I go with the one I came with." The two of us shook hands with the other guests when that was appropriate, kissed when we should have, and said "yes" to all invitations, regardless of the occasion. In this state of organized confusion, Sue Ann took my arm and led me out. The Commodore just made his own exit and left me to the wolves. There were a few comments about my leaving with the judge, but I ignored them. I was too thankful that she held my arm as we left. Although I had consumed no alcoholic beverage, I felt intoxicated. The strange feeling had me depending on the judge's arm much more than I would have liked. Her words: "Are you okay to drive home?" brought me back to reality.

"Oh, yeah, I am just not used to all that attention." I shrugged my shoulders stood up straight and said, "I'll go get the car; you ride your bike, and we will meet on the patio."

Sue Ann laughed a little, and with that she went for her bike. I walked down to the store and got the car. As I walked past the store, the Commodore stuck his head out. I waved as I went by, saying, "I'll see you tomorrow, you traitor." I got in the car and backed out onto the street. I started to go forward, and there she was; my hands gripped the wheel tightly. I started to step on the accelerator when I heard a siren. It was the chief just waving, "Hello." I pulled to the curb for a minute to regain my composure. I couldn't believe that for a fleeting second, I was going to run her over and say it was an accident. I broke out in a sweat as I realized I was thinking of murdering my own child; that thought alone just completely un-nerved me. For the first time, I truly felt I was mentally capable of doing such an act...the one act I was becoming surer of...the one act I knew was the answer to my problem. With an unsteady hand, I drove home--my daughter's home.

As soon as I got home, I took the box of clothes out of the car and put it in my room. I opened it and took out the contents and hung them up or put them in drawers, whichever was appropriate. I put the box on the side, for I knew I was going to need it to take my clothes home. That being done, I walked out onto the patio.

Even the cooling breeze off the bay did not completely erase the thoughts I had from my mind. My daughter...that word was working its way into my thoughts far more often than I wanted it to...made us Manhattans, and we sat outside in the cooling breeze and reminisced about the party and everyone's reaction to the transformed Commodore.

"I guess there was no reason for my being there. The Commodore stole the show; he had to be the most talked about person there!'

"Oh, no, your friend Russ was still number one. You will have to figure out a way of bringing him back. Everyone, even those who never met him, wanted to know his marital status; I just kept telling everyone I didn't know."

The doorbell rang, and in walked Trina with two early-bird special dinners from the store, compliments of the Commodore. She added, "He wanted me to say thank you for showing him there was truly life after death."

Trina joined us as we moved the party inside. She lit the fireplace and put on a pot of coffee as she told us the versions of the party she had heard. Every so often she would ask, "Did that really happen? Next time they want to have a band." Finally, Trina left to go to her own apartment, I to my room, and Sue Ann to hers. As she walked up the stairs, she turned and said, "If you want something to think about as you wait for the sandman to come, Trina told me Steven wants her to move in with him."

"Who's he?"

"You had dinner with him twice; it's Trina's boyfriend." In an annoyed tone, she added, "Don't you remember anything? And I don't want you and Russ to go talk to him. Good night! I'll see you in the morning."

Russ' words rang true again: "There just was no way I was going to get rid of her." The lights were shut off, and the day... except for the old and new thoughts still spinning in my mind ...came to an end.

Chapter Ten

The morning, for some reason, came crashing in on me. I blamed it on the Manhattans from the night before. My night's rest came in the form of short naps, after which I would wake up with Steve and Trina on my mind or the return of Russ or my "daughter" problem. Tisha came in and I told her, "Wait and I'll get out of your way. I gave her some money to straighten my room out and make the bed. She didn't say a word but just nodded her head and smiled. I finished getting dressed and went to the store, for I wanted to get my early morning briefing from the Commodore. As soon as I sat down, he brought over the early-morning special and a cup of coffee for himself, which I interpreted as an omen that it was going to be a long report. I was not disappointed.

He started off with, "It was a bomb of some sort. They don't know what kind, but it was put in the gas tank, they think, and it was set to go off as soon as the plane went down the runway. It doesn't make sense to me because how would it know when to go off? I figured it must have had a mercury switch in it so that when the plane titled back for the takeoff, that's what set it off."

He continued his analysis of how the bomb was detonated, repeating himself many times. I just sat quietly and nodded my head occasionally. Finally, he left to do something useful, and Trina quickly replaced him.

"May I talk to you?" Before I could answer, she was sitting at my table, fidgeting with her hair. "My boyfriend, Steven, you know him from when we had dinner the other night, well, he wants me to move in with him. We used to go together during high school and college, but when we were in college, we could only see each other on breaks from school. I met Lewis, and he wanted to get married right away. I knew my mother didn't like him, well anyway, you know what happened to him. Now Steve is asking me…well I mean he wants me to move in, and after a while, we will get married. What do you think? I mean, I know you don't know him that well. His father just died and left him a fifty-foot trawler, you know a boat…. Well, that is where we would live; he wants to be a fisherman. I mean…"

"Wait," I said, "You're losing me. You're asking the wrong person. By today's standards I am a dinosaur. In my days of courting, it was not the right thing to do to ask a girl to move in with you. I lived with my parents until I got married, and so did my wife-to-be. Today, hopping in and out of houses and beds seems to be the thing to do. Either the two of you are willing to make a commitment to each other to try to build a life or forget it. What do you gain by moving in with him? You save a few bucks on rent? I'm sorry; I know it may seem weird to you, but I think you're making a big mistake. Also when you are riding around on the boat, how do you expect to live? What about a family? What about all the other things that make up a steady relationship? One day he'll leave you on the pier or you'll abandon ship; you deserve better than that. "

Trina was startled by my answer. It was obvious to me from the expression on her face that she did not expect the answer I'd given her.

"Well, look at my mother. She went for the white gown, shoes, and rice thing; and my father left her anyway."

"Yeah, look at her. Do you really think she enjoys sitting on that perch of hers while the rest of the world goes by? The bed is a lonely place, and a house without love is not a home; I'm positive you have heard that before. Trina, it all boils down to what you and Steven want out of life; no one can answer that question for you."

"I wish my grandmother was still alive. She…"

Whatever else she said, I didn't hear, for at the sound of "grandmother", I went deaf. How could I possibly tell her about her dear grandmother?

"I don't know what happened between her and my grandfather; the story I heard was that he went nuts. He would beat her and…" Her voice trailed off, which made me happy, for I really didn't want to hear anything else. All I could see before me was the product of two broken homes, which based upon what I knew meant the odds were stacked against her to have a happy home. I felt very sorry for her, but I decided that I best be still, for I still hadn't solved my own problems.

I don't know if she was still talking when I turned her off, but the next words I heard were, "I have to make my mind up because Steven has an opportunity to get involved with some fishing fleet or something like that, and he has to leave soon."

I looked up at her and just shook my head as I blurted out, "It doesn't take long to arrange the white dress, old shoes, and rice thing." I suddenly felt very stupid for saying what I did, but words once said cannot be brought back. They have a way of staying out there forever. Thankfully, some people from the airport came in and Trina's services were need. The Commodore came from nowhere; he wanted to hear what the airport people had to say.

From main attraction to an old man at the front table was my plight. Somehow, no matter what else I did, the water had a certain attraction for me. I left the store and walked down to the pier. There was a boat taking on fuel, and the captain of the vessel was beckoning to me. As I got closer, I recognized Steve. "Come on; get aboard. I had to have some work done on the boat, and I want to test it out. I just want to go to the point and back. It will only take about two hours."

To myself I said, *If we don't get stuck.* I got on board, and soon the refilling was done, and we pulled away, heading for the point at the end of the bay. We went up to the flying bridge, and Steven gave me some rain gear because on the bridge, it gets cold. "We can go below if it gets too cold for you."

73

"Oh, no, this is great. There is nothing like the salty air blowing in your face."

"Trina told me that in one of your books, you went through the Canadian locks and through the Erie Canal. Did you really do that or was it just some creative writing?"

"No, I did it, but of course I was much younger."

We rode for a while, but I could just sense that Steve had something on his mind. He just looked nervous to me. He looked like he wanted to say something; he would change his mind, and the process would start over again. The wind was picking up and our craft was starting to be bounced around. Steve's whole persona changed, as it was obvious he was becoming concerned on how his craft was being bounced around. It fascinated me how much the boat had shrunk from the time we left the dock. We were surrounded by water, and the waves were starting to break over the bow. It splashed over the deck, and the spray that hit us was getting heavier. The rain gear gave me some protection but not nearly enough as we went further out into the bay. As we neared the point, it really got rough. Steve was having his hands full, keeping the bow of the boat facing the wind and waves. "I better not try to turn around just yet, lest we get swamped."

I shouted over the waves, "I agree. Why don't you throttle back? The boat will ride easier." He hesitated for a moment and finally took my advice. The boat slid over the waves rather than banging through them. This greatly reduced the amount of spray we were being hit with and made for a much smoother ride.

Steve turned to face me, and I thought he was going to thank me for the advice, but instead he said, "Trina texted me. She wanted to know why I just wanted for her to move in with me instead of my marrying her and starting a life together. That's what I wanted to do, but she was the one who said 'no.' Now that she's talked to you, she's changed her mind. What happened to Lewis? I told her not to listen to that nut! I know he had more money and a nicer house than I could ever afford, but well, I don't know. That was some ring he bought her! All the money I have I'll need if I want to get into this fishing group. I'll get those things for her, but I can't right now. Now she wants to get married in a church. I never knew she even went to church."

"How do you know she spoke to me?" As soon as I asked the question, I knew it was stupid because one thing about The Cove, no matter who did what, everyone knew about it.

"She told me...I'm going to turn around now; the boat feels good to me." As soon as he said the words, he spun the wheel, and the boat answered the helm, and we were headed back toward the dock. The seas had subsided some, so the ride back was much smoother. When he got to the dock, I helped him tie the vessel up and took off the rain gear; as it turned out, it had been of little use, for I was sopping wet. I headed for home...wet clothes and all. I was grateful that I had received my own clothes from my housekeeper.

"As I was walking along, I heard the familiar bell. I paused and Sue Ann pulled up next to me. "I don't know what you said to my daughter, but she is now talking about marrying Steven. I still think she's too young, but I like him much better than that other guy. She asked me to ask you if you would walk her down the aisle; she never liked her father, and I told her she could just make believe her grandfather was escorting her."

Before I could say anything, Sue Ann was speeding away from me. I didn't know whether I felt proud or just annoyed at Sue Ann for using the "grandfather" word, but I was wet and tired from walking, and I still had a half of a mile to go. When I got home, I took a quick shower and went to bed. I went there, not because I was tired, but to hide from life, for I felt I was being dragged into a place I didn't want to be...Grandpa George.

When I got up, Sue Ann was dancing around for two

reasons, which she quickly told me as soon as she saw me. "Chad asked me out to dinner, and I'm going to be the mother of the bride. There are only three days in a woman's life worth talking about: the day she is married, the day she has her children, and the day she is the mother of the bride."

"What about when you become a grandmother...?"

"Not so much, for that means you're getting old. Why don't you call Ruth and take her out to dinner? I know she would love that. Who knows? She may even ask you to come to her house. Well, it's up to you; here's the number."

With that, she put a piece of paper on the coffee table and did a little twirl before she ran up the steps to get ready for her date. I argued with myself about calling Ruth but finally gave in with the profound statement, "Why not?" I also remembered I had to go get the car, for it was still down by the store. I looked up the stairs, and I could hear Sue Ann getting ready, so I quietly went outside, got on the bike, and rode down to the car. I put the bike in the trunk and very slowly drove home. I waited a few moments before I called Ruth. As predicted, she was thrilled. We set the time...she gave me directions to her house...and my evening was planned. I went back to my room because I did not want to be around when Chad was picking up Sue Ann. She had told me what time he was coming for her, so I'd purposely told Ruth a later time. However, when I thought about it, I realized it had been a stupid move, for there was only one place to eat in town, but I resolved that I would get a table in a different room. That done, I waited until I heard Sue Ann leave before I ventured out to get Ruth. When I got to her house, she was all a glow and wearing her very best go-out-to-dinner clothes.

When we arrived at the restaurant, I asked for a seat in the smallest room. Ruth became highly agitated. "If you are ashamed to be seen with me, I can go home."

"What are you talking about?" I didn't know what to say. I

felt like a fool telling her I didn't want to meet Sue Ann and Chad. The hostess heard her complaint and my searching for an answer took us to a larger room. In the corner was Sue Ann. We sat down and Ruth started with an apology.

"I'm sorry, but being asked to go out for dinner may not be a big deal where you come from, but this is the first time I've been asked out since I moved here. Being here with you will make me a celebrity. Look, Sue Ann is here. I've never been invited to any place she goes." As she was speaking, I could see her searching the room for other people she knew. Unfortunately, it was a slow night.

I made it through the night, and finally it was time to take Ruth home. When we got to her house, she insisted I come in for a few minutes. After what happened at the restaurant, I'd felt I better go in. I should have suspected something was up when she didn't want any coffee or dessert at the restaurant. She had made three different desserts and had a pot of coffee ready to be plugged in. It took me an hour before I finally convinced her that I had to go home. It took another fifteen minutes to convince her I didn't want to take anything with me. I was going to shake her hand when I left, but before I knew it, she was kissing me.

Sue Ann was already home when I got there. She yelled down, "Well, did my daddy have a good time?" I could hear her laughing as I walked to my room.

The next morning I was still washing the sleep from my eyes when I heard Tisha starting the vacuum cleaner. I got dressed and came out of my room, just as she was about to clean the coffee table. "Isn't it nice that Steven and Trina are going to get married?" She said those words and never even looked up from her work. "Last night… well anyway, everyone is very excited about it." Again she did not let her talking interfere with her work.

I didn't respond at all. I quickened my pace, for the

Commodore would be busting something if I didn't get to his store so he could bring me up to date. I walked out the door and drove to the store. He came over to me, carrying the breakfast special and coffee for the two of us. As soon as he sat down, I asked, "Is there any new news about the incident?"

His response was, "Who cares? Steven asked Trina to marry him last night and she said 'yes'. He could only afford a small ring, but he's a good kid; he'll do better. Last night she went to his boat, and that was when he asked her. A group of his friends were at a costume party, and when they found out Steven and Trina were not there, they decided to surprise them. When they got to the boat dressed as pirates, they found the couple in an awkward position; that is when he told them about their plans. Ain't it great?"

I knew then that between the Commodore and Tisha, the whole world would soon know. I was right. The Commodore continued with, "They are planning to be married right away, for they will be leaving on his boat so he could join the fishing fleet that is just being formed. It is a cooperative, so each member will be receiving the profits from the company with the slogan, "From the sea to your table." Trina is going to be working in the office on land, while Steven goes fishing. Trina's girlfriend will be taking over for her here at the restaurant."

From behind me I heard, "I'm going to be the Maid of Honor. We are going to drive to Norfolk tonight for our dresses. Steven's best friend is going to be the best man. The town council said they can use the auditorium for their reception, or at least Ruth said that she will ask them, and everyone knows that what Ruth wants, Ruth gets."

I looked at the big clock behind the counter, and it read 10:05. I was amazed at the rate news traveled in the town.

The cook came out to talk to the Commodore and when he heard what was happening, he quickly added, "I like Trina; she was always nice to me. We can have a wedding like they had in the *Godfather* movie with all kinds of sandwiches. I'll make them." When he went back to his kitchen, the Commodore leaned over to me and said, "He saw the picture, and since then, it went right to his head. He knows everything about it. He is forever quoting chapter and verse from it, but we love him."

Chapter Eleven

The next day the whole town came alive. I was amazed how the sleepy little town known as The Cove became a beehive of activity, as everyone wanted to do something for the new couple. There was the task of decorating the auditorium. Ruth kept running around the store, saying that for a few hundred dollars, she could make the place a wonderland; that is, of course, after the council gave her permission. I donated the money after I made her swear that she would not tell anyone I did. She kept the secret for ten minutes after she was informed by one of the town council who came into the store and with a loud clear voice proclaimed: "The town council felt that having a wedding reception there for the daughter of one of its most prominent citizens would promote harmony in the town, so we voted unanimously to grant permission to the decorating committee to use the hall. However, we will not allocate any money for decorations or for cleanup. The decorating committee is responsible for that."

One person yelled out, "What did he say?"

Another responded, "We can use the auditorium for the wedding."

"What wedding?" was the next catcall.

"Trina and Steven are getting married," was the response from another person.

"Where are we getting the money from?" another anonymous caller yelled.

"No problem," Ruth responded, "George gave it to me."

A strange silence fell over the store. It was broken by someone's yelling, "George... George, who's he?" "Russ' friend," was the answer given by yet another.

The store was the meeting place for all donations of things, such as money and help, for what everyone expected to be the biggest event to happen in the town. A table was set up in the auditorium to substitute for the place at the store. Someone put me in charge. I immediately set up a register to keep track of who gave what so that the new couple could send them thank you cards. Another comment that was heard was, "What happened to Lewis?"

There was a quick response from one of the decorators, "Oh, Russ blew him up." After I set things up, I relinquished my job to one of Ruth's assistants and was glad to get away from the hubbub of the auditorium.

The store, which had become the nosiest and busiest place in town, settled back down to a general store/coffee shop/ restaurant. I went there, and on my way I heard the tinkling of a bell as Sue Ann pulled up behind me. "Oh, I could just cry. People I know have given me over eight hundred dollars to pay for the food, and they have also volunteered to help. It seems they all saw *The Godfather*, and the backyard reception they had with the sandwiches and all, and they want to top that. I want to go see the cook and the Commodore to get them to be in charge of the refreshments. Aren't people wonderful?"

It was a sight to behold when Sue Ann asked the Commodore and the chef to be in charge of the refreshments. The Commodore nodded his acceptance, and the chef just glowed as he started explaining the different salads and garnishes he would make. I sat down at a table, while the new waitress bought me over the luncheon special with a small soda. "A large soda costs more," she said as she walked away.

That night a caravan was being formed to drive to Norfolk to go dress shopping. No one knew who was being invited, and no one seemed to care, for everybody was going. Sue Ann was overwhelmed by the enthusiastic response to her daughter's wedding. She came over to me, "I am sorry that my mother isn't here to see this. Do you see that whatever you two did turned out so well?"

From nowhere, a man walked up to Sue Ann, for she was crying, and he put his arms around her and tried to comfort her. I just stood by and watched, for I didn't know who he was. Sue Ann regained her composure as she said, "This is my son-of-a-bitch ex-husband."

We just stood staring at each other for what seemed an eternity when Trina walked up and grabbed my arm as she said, "He is going to walk me down the aisle. I didn't know if your whore girlfriend would let you, so I asked him, and he said 'yes'."

The man was visibly wounded by those words as he put his head down and walked away. Sue Ann and Trina wound up in each other's arms, and then they came over to me and made me part of their group. I cried as I realized I'd wanted to kill both of them, and there they were, clinging to me at what had to be a low point of their lives. Somehow, I wished I had more strength as I stood there, trying to console both of them. I said to myself, "I've got to find a better way."

With the whole town getting involved in the wedding, the investigator still working on the incident were greatly hampered in his investigation. He came to the store and sat with the Commodore, talking about the lack of community interest in finding those involved in such a brazen crime. "Can you explain that to me?" the investigator lamented.

The Commodore in a matter-of-fact tone replied, "Easy...no one really cared for Lewis. He was an arrogant person, and when he started courting Trina, that really turned everyone off. No one here knew the pilot, so what was the big loss?"

I sat and watched as the investigator squirmed in his chair as he was visibly searching for something to say. "But a horrible crime has been committed. What kind of people are you?"

"The kind that like to be left alone. But more than that, I don't think anyone knows anything, and they sure as hell don't like the way you have just pushed our chief aside and have tried to take over our town. So they didn't see anything and haven't heard anything and really just don't want to get involved. Now you'll have to excuse me; I've got a business to run."

The Commodore walked away and left me with the investigator. I felt very uncomfortable, for I knew he was going to ask about Russ, and I didn't want to get involved either; in addition, I didn't know anything. Thankfully, Ruth walked in. I got up and went with her to meet with the chef as we planned out what kind of sandwiches we should make for the affair. As I walked over to Ruth, I could see the chief in his usual spot, leaning up against a car in his full outfit, which included his hat, sunglasses, his belly hanging over his belt, and his arms folded on top of it. He reminded me of a lost soul.

As the big day neared, the excitement in the town intensified. The seamstress in town came to the store to complain how busy she was. She would complain to anyone with a willing ear. After the third time of listening to her, I tried to hide, but she would seek me out. Of course, the bride's dress came first, but after that, she would always add, "And, George, wait until you see Ruth in her outfit."

The tailor would follow the Commodore around, for he was altering a tuxedo to fit him. "Why don't you be still and give the guy a break; he just wants you to look handsome."

"I'm not getting married," he would growl at me. Why do I have to wear one of those things?"

I would smile as I responded, "Because I don't want to be the only one at the wedding wearing one."

The day finally came, and every woman in town started crying early. The crying started with Sue Ann and continued to include Tisha, who'd made it a point to clean Sue Ann's house every day. It also amazed me how many articles of clothing and jewelry was exchanged for the occasion. It seemed that I was told of every exchange. Also, the lead gossip story was why I was doing the job that Trina's father should be doing. I was amazed that no one asked me but would mention the fact that I was escorting Trina down the aisle and not her father in a loud enough voice and in close enough proximity that I would hear the comment. I would ignore the speaker and pretend that I didn't hear them. That ploy really annoyed them. The fact that I wouldn't take part in the discussion was the main reason I think that the topic was brought up.

The next big dilemma was a runner for the bride to walk in on. The chef was consulted, but he announced, "There was none shown at the wedding of the *Godfather's* daughter, so one is not needed." That seemed to satisfy everyone.

The priest's garb took center stage…black suit or frock; the suit won out.

The song that would be played when she would walk in was the next item of main concern; someone donated a recording of the wedding march, which raised some concern. It was replaced by another song from some opera that no one ever heard of, but the substitution stopped the wagging tongues. Again I was surprised that all these items would be discussed within my earshot, but I was never part of the discussion. I assumed they didn't want my input, and I wasn't about to give any.

At last the big day arrived; there were so many volunteers at the store to help with the food that some were turned away. Ruth acted as the coordinator, and she genuinely had the voice and the personality for the job. I was seated with the Commodore, quietly having the early-bird-special breakfast.

Ruth's voice came booming over the din caused by all the people. "We have enough people to help with the food; those of you that we can't use here, please go to the auditorium and help there. If they don't need you, go home and get ready. The affair starts at noon sharp." The crowd thinned out.

"I must be going nuts," the Commodore said, "for I swear I can hear the barber clicking his scissors."

"That's because he loves you," I added. I said goodbye and was heading for the door when Ruth yelled out, "George is leaving, so load up his car, and he will deliver some of the food to the party."

I did as ordered before I went home and found Sue Ann had the house in shambles, as she was looking for one thing or another. Trina was dressed and ready to go; she looked beautiful as all brides do. I quickly got dressed and the three of us headed for the auditorium. Ruth decided to have the ceremony there rather than having everyone going back and forth to the church. I had been seated in the store when she discussed the problem with the priest.

We pulled up to the front door just as the maid of honor arrived with her father. The Commodore saw us coming, so he ran inside with the town council. All was set. It started to rain. It was a slight mist, but I though Sue Ann was going to scream. She ran between the drips, and I helped Trina get out of the car and walk to the front door. I was carrying the train so it wouldn't get soiled. There was a little vestibule before entering the main room. It was decorated with white netting of some sort with paper flowers pinned to it. The creativity of the décor absolutely astounded me. The maid of honor walked in and was greeted with the usual gasp of breath and comments of "How beautiful." Her mother, who was a good friend of Ruth, had to be helped to a chair because she was crying so hard. When the maid of honor reached the priest, and the best man and the groom were assembled, the song was changed to the one chosen for the bride's entry. We stepped into the room, and instantly, a round of applause rose up from the crowd. All I could think of as a reason for it was that everyone had been bottling up his/her emotions for the whole week, and the applause, although not usually heard, was a release of all that emotion. It ended as fast as it started. I, with the bride to be, walked the long walk from the door to the priest. When we reached the priest and I helped pull her veil back, she leaned over and said in a tone I could barely hear but which the maid of honor (judging from her facial expression) clearly heard said, 'Thank You, Granddad.'" She kissed me, and I went to my seat next to Sue Ann, who had just lost all control of her emotions. I finally had to push her down on the chair least she fell. The ceremony continued without incident.

At the end of the ceremony, the priest announced that everyone should come up to the makeshift altar to congratulate the new couple, for it was raining too hard to go outside, and after all, everyone would have to come back in for the reception anyway. Ruth nodded her approval. Immediately a line was formed so everyone could file past the newlyweds.

The band started playing as the dance floor was cleared and the announcement "The bar is open…the food is to the right… everyone should come and get it" was made. When the reception line finally ended, the seamstress went up to the bride and helped her unfasten the train, and the bride displayed a beautiful pants suit. That move was a better show than the ceremony.

Everyone started moving around first to see what everyone else was wearing and to partake of the refreshments offered. "We didn't have to buy any wine or whisky; everyone brought the bottles they had at home and never open." I didn't say anything as I thought of how many bottles I could have contributed. The biggest shock to me came when Tisha walked over and asked me to dance. I didn't even recognize her.

Ruth walked to the outside door and stood there for a moment, looking out into the rain. She beckoned me over. When I got near, she said, "I'm going to invite the chief and his deputies over; I mean, everyone else is here…"

"You don't have to sell me. We have plenty of everything, and after all, he is an integral part of the town. Call him…what can he say no…use your sexy voice. I know you can entice him and his crew to join us."

She took out her phone, and within a short time one deputy walked in, then the other, and finally the chief himself showed up. The three of them were quickly made part of the festivities by a concerted effort of the young ladies at the affair. I could not believe my eyes when the Commodore led the Congo line. He didn't do it for long, but he made quite a sight during the time he was the leader.

The topic at the party switched from the newlyweds to the rain. It wasn't stopping. In fact, it was quickly becoming a deluge. The wind was picking up, and at one point blew open the doors to the auditorium. Someone announced that there would be a full moon that night and that the wind was coming in from the ocean. I wasn't quite sure what that meant, but one of the fishermen who worked out of the area explained, "We are inland, and when the wind blows off of the ocean, the water has nowhere to go except up. The lower part of The Cove floods, and with the rain, that flooding will be higher than usual. The height of the water will play hell with the boats at anchor and who knows what else."

"What can you do?" I asked in a concerned tone.

"Not much but we better check on our moorings," my newfound friend told me.

A rescue group quickly assembled at the door. None of them were dressed to go outside in bad weather and certainly not for the weather that was waiting for them. The groom was going to lead the group, for his boat was bigger than any other in the harbor. The deputies who'd worn rain gear to come to the party volunteered to go as well. The chief was convinced that he was a little too old to go." Ruth said, "We love you, but this is a young man's job."

The Commodore was also in the group, for his store was on high ground, but it wasn't that high, and the stronger the wind got, the more nervous he was getting. I grabbed his arm as I said, "Come on; if you're that intent upon drowning, let's go." It was a rag-tag but well-dressed rescue group that left the auditorium and headed for the waterfront. The Commodore and I had to stop a few times to catch our breath on the way to the store. He'd closed it down while the affair was on, but he wasn't too sure how weatherproof the windows were. Our first job when we got to the store was to close the shutters on all of the windows that had shutters. The job was not easily done when working in sopping-wet clothing and a strong wind, as it would have otherwise been. It took both of us to close them. He had a large sheet of plywood that he had made to slide in front of the doors that led from the restaurant to the patio dining area. The table and chairs were already blown into a pile, so there wasn't much that could be done about that. We finished doing what we could do on the outside and then went inside to inspect everything and to start the portable gas-driven electric generator so that the store had power to keep the lights burning and the refrigerators operational. "This was one of my better purchases," he said as he flipped the switch and the generator roared into service.

Luckily when the chief came to the party, he had driven there with the police van rather than the car. He tooted the horn as he went by, ferrying the ladies home. All the Commodore and I could do was to look down at the pier and watch as the rescue group went about securing what they could on the pier. The governor was on the television and had declared the area a disaster area, which meant help was on its way, but until it got there, we were on our own.

Some of the boats had already broken their mooring lines and were being thrown up on shore. One boat... a twenty-one footer... was thrown right on top of a mooring pole. The pole broke right through the middle of it. Thankfully, the groom's boat, for some reason, stayed out of harm's way as it rode the waves and didn't hit anything too hard.

The rescue group came to the store before going back to the party to help with the evacuation. One of the group went to the auditorium and got Sue Ann and the bride first and then came back to pick me up and took us home. I drove him back to the auditorium and went back to Sue Ann's house. She also had purchased a generator, and by time I got back, it was purring as it was supplying electricity for the house. However, it wasn't big enough to supply electricity for all of the appliances. Sue Ann took out the list of do's and don'ts the electrician had given her when he installed the unit. The list stated which appliances had to be turned off while others were running. The electric coffee pot and toaster were definitely a no-no.

The bride and the mother of the bride changed into something more appropriate, while I went to my room to do the same. The furniture on the patio had already been blown into a pile, but as far as I could see, nothing was broken. All we could now do was have a cocktail and wait for the storm to blow itself out. That process took most of the night.

We were all startled when the doorbell rang. I went to the door, and Steven was being helped in by his friend. While trying to re-more the boat, a line had wrapped itself around Steven's arm and had given it a hard yank. Steve had paid it no mind, for he was very concerned about mooring his boat. When that was all done, he found that he had great difficulty in moving his arm without experiencing tremendous pain. His friends wanted to take him to the hospital, which was fifty some miles away, but he insisted that they bring him to his mother-in-law's house. Just using that new word brought a smile to everyone's face.

They were just dropping him off because they had to get to their own homes to see what good they could do, so my offer to bestow on them some hospitality was declined. The closest healthcare facility was a doc-in-the-box about five miles away. Sue Ann said, "I better call first; they are probably swamped, and for that matter so will the hospital. I know an intern who appeared before me on a DWI; I'll call him. After the break I gave him, he owes me."

"Was that a judge I heard?" I said as a smile came to my face."

"No, that was a mother's concern."

"But he's not your kid."

"He's my son-in-law and a new one at that." Her remark was just what was needed to relieve the tension that was building in the room.

She was on the phone, and in a few minutes she was saying, "No, there is no blood; he can move the arm, but it hurts. No, he still has his color. I don't think he is going to pass out; well, that's great. I thought the prescription was only told as a joke." She hung the phone up and turned to face us as we sat there waiting to hear the prognosis.

"He said it doesn't sound broken or that he's in any grave danger. We should just watch him, give him two aspirins, and bring him to the hospital in the morning for x-rays.

I couldn't help myself as I said, "Well, Steve, look at it this way: when your friends ask how you spent your wedding night, you can tell them you were under careful observation by your mother –in-law."

Everyone laughed, but it was plain to see that he was not having an easy time of it. He winced every time he moved. Sue Ann gave him two aspirin and said in a judge-like tone: "Don't go to your apartment or your boat; just stay here. Trina, use your old room."

Trina was about to say something, but when she saw the painful look that came over Steve's face when he tried to lift the glass of water to take the pills, she just nodded her head "Yes."

I bid everyone good night and told Sue Ann as an aside, "If you need me, just yell." I said the words, but after the events of the day and helping the Commodore close up his store, I really did think I couldn't be of much help to anyone. I was awake as long as I was moving, but sitting down and having a drink had wiped me out. I made it to my room, got undressed, and fell into bed, still thinking about what I was going to do with my new-found family that I never knew I had.

The last comment I heard as I was starting toward my room was Trina's telling her mother." I guess everyone will be wondering why we got married so fast."

Sue Ann thought for a moment before she responded, "There are month counters at every wedding. Don't let it bother you."

With all these thoughts whirling around in my head, sleep was an elusive thing. What do I do if I become a great-grandfather? I would have to become the most sadistic mass murderer in history. At that moment I wished Joann were there. I would wring her neck for putting me in this position. I thought back to happier days before I got that email that started off "Dear Dad." I was retired and happily living in a retirement community, perfectly content to listen to other people's problems. Now I was in THE Cove, trying to figure out my own problems. I kept hoping that the damn sand man would come, but after a while I couldn't blame him. Why should he help a mass murderer to be?

In the morning after a quick breakfast, we put Steven into the car and headed for the hospital. On the way Sue Ann called the intern, and he was at the emergency entrance when I pulled up. By the time I parked the car and walked back to the emergency room, I was met by my passengers. Steven didn't break anything; it was only a sprain. There was nothing they could do other than put his arm in a sling and give him some painkillers. The doctor's parting words were, "It will just have to work itself out...goodbye."

We all walked back to the car, and I drove back to Sue Ann's house.

I dropped everyone off, and I drove down to the store. I was quickly served the "storm" special, and the Commodore came over just beaming. It was obvious that he had a story to tell. He sat down, and before I could say anything, he mentioned a man's name that I didn't know and continued with, "He just bought a forty-foot motor home and had it parked next to his house. He wasn't supposed to do that, for we have an ordinance against it, but the chief didn't say anything because he was loading it up, for he and his wife were going to go to Florida on their maiden trip this morning. They didn't want to miss out on the wedding. During the storm a branch broke off a tree and fell on the motor home. When it fell, it broke the gutter and drove the gutter into the motor home. Consequently, all the rain that fell on the roof of his house ran off the roof and into the gutter and right into his motor home. He didn't know about it until this morning when he opened the door to finish getting ready to leave and the water came cascading out on him. He had a foot of water in it. He was here this morning with his wife, for they have to wait for the insurance adjuster. I pity the two of them; I mean, a brand-new forty-foot motor home flooded."

Try as he might, he couldn't help himself from laughing. He ended his story with, "Those poor people." Many other stories were told, but that one won the prize.

Chapter Twelve

I stayed two more days before I packed my clothes in the box they came in and asked Sue Ann to take me to the bus station. I never mentioned the fact that Trina had called me Grandpa when I walked her down the aisle; it was Sue Ann who swore to me she never told Trina about me. "Trina told me she called you 'grandpa', but she said it as a term of respect, not because of anything I said."

I said goodbye as I got on the bus. Sue Ann's words were my constant companion all the way home. I didn't get any relief from them until I got home and received a call from Russ with his usual glib greeting. "Hey, man, what's up. I saw on the news that you got a little wet, but I knew no storm was going to touch my main man."

Russ kept me on the phone for over an hour. I had to tell him everything that had happened. When I got to the part about Trina's saying, "Thank you, Grandpa," he shouted as though he'd won a great battle. "I told you the longer you wait, the worst it's going to be."

"Sue Ann swore she never said a word to Trina about our relationship." As soon as I said the words, I knew what Russ' comeback would be, and he didn't disappoint me as he said in a louder voice than before, "You've got to be kidding. Only you would believe that…oh never mind…I'll call you next week for lunch or something. I know you are going to be very busy trying to invent lies to tell your kids. Good luck and if you want me to swear to your lies, you know the drill: you say them and I'll swear to them."

I hated it when he was right. I was supposed to have Sunday dinner with the portion of my family I knew about, a treat I was not too happy about, for I knew once a lie is told, it just gets bigger as the days go on. I felt ashamed of myself for I was doing what Russ had just accused me of, trying to invent a story that my kids and real grandchildren would believe.

I tried a few out on my audience-less room, "I went to look for a house as a summer... winter... investment." The last one had a good possibility. The Cove was a resort type area; it was a natural harbor; it was still in a rural part of the state, so land values were much cheaper than in our area. I was positive that if I slept on the idea, I could come up with a few more good reasons. If all else failed, I could always use the reason for not answering their questions: "It's none of your business." With these ideas in mind, I was feeling very low and also tired. A good night's sleep in my own bed would help me work everything out. I said the words but had great difficulty in believing them. Sleep did not come easily, but it did come finally.

The next morning I had to remind myself to get up and start the day on a positive note, resolved that as I got older, I had to do things like reminding myself to get up. Age has a way of wearing people down. Of course, I didn't think it would happen to me, but I was wrong. In the old days, there was talk of putting me in a straitjacket because I would never stop. But as I sat on the edge of the bed, I concluded that those days were definitely gone. As I analyzed my situation, the only problem I had was Sue Ann. All I had to do was forget about her and my problems were gone.

I went to my desk that I kept in my house and wrote up a scenario of a case. If a person came to me to write a will and, like most people, wanted his estate to be divided equally among his children, would that phrase be interpreted to mean those children he knows he has? If the will read "to my children" and the children were named, could a case be made that he forgot one? A judge could conclude that the intent of the deceased was clearly that he wanted to share his estate among his "children", and the child excluded would be included for purposes of distribution of his assets. If the will read "to my children", and all the children were named, and Sue Ann was left one dollar, would that cure the problem? The question raised would then be, "Who's Sue Ann?"

Maybe Sue Ann would keep her word and forget all about me. So far she hadn't; the minute something bad was going to happen and she didn't know what to do, as Russ had said, "She called in the first team," namely me, to the rescue.

In addition, I'd walked my granddaughter down the aisle. The thoughts of what had happened and what could happen just would not leave me. The simplistic answer that the priest gave was not to my liking, so that was out. I was caught in a maze; what I should do was not acceptable; therefore, I was back to what I could do. That thought gave me some relief from my dilemma, so all I had to do was figure out how, when, and where.

How to dispose of Sue Ann now occupied my thoughts. At least I had peace of mind. I laughed as I thought of the outdated phrase, "There was a light at the end of the tunnel."

The first thing I had to consider was that she was a judge and an important figure in the community. That limited my choices to accidental or an unsolved mystery. The plane's blowing up was one or the other, and so far it was in the unsolved mystery category, or was it? I called the Commodore, just to say hello. When he answered the phone, I felt he was genially glad to hear from me. "George, I missed our morning get together." I just kept quiet, for I knew if I just let him ramble on, he would eventually tell me something about what I wanted to hear.

He was true to form.

"I had to throw my tuxedo away. I didn't realize it at the time, but I had split the seams in a few places. Also the shiny material on it just crinkled up, and the tailor didn't think he could ever straighten it out, so I just threw it away. Steve and Trina left Sue Ann's house and moved into Trina's apartment. Ruth led a group of ladies over for a visit, and they helped her set the house up for two. Steve is coming along, but he still has a lot of pain. His friend straightened out the boat for him, which was a big help. Sue Ann thanked all the people who helped Trina and Steve, but I could see she was mad that no one had asked her opinion or for her help. She really is a piece of work."

I quietly listened, still hoping he would get to the incident without my having to mention it, for I had a feeling that the phone...his or mine...could be tapped. Finally, he said, "The investigators have now talked to everyone in town and have not come up with anything. They are packing up their stuff, and the case will be put in the unsolved mystery file of our local police. The chief is glad and can't wait for the group to leave. He really is mad, for they have left him out of the case, and now that they have beaten it to death, they are going to leave it to him. When I asked, 'Who says it wasn't just an accident?' no one answered. I think they are all nuts. Instead of just calling it an accident and letting the whole matter die down, they had to create a big to-do over nothing. But now they're leaving, and things should get back to normal. Well, I've got to go. Please stay in touch and come visit me again. If you don't want to stay at Sue Ann's, I've got a lot of room here for you. Thanks for calling and don't be a stranger."

My arm had gone numb from holding the phone, but I had heard what I wanted to hear. I put the phone down and went out for breakfast. I felt that I had accomplished something, and now all I had to do was create a mysterious happening.

I was just about to go out for a while when the phone rang. I had a quick debate with myself about whether I should answer it, but somehow curiosity always wins out. The minute I heard, "Hello," I knew it was Russ and that I would be in for one of his encyclicals.

"I just thought you would like an update as to the happenings in The Cove. They hired a new detective; she's a woman and what a woman! However, the good part is she has a lot of detective experience. She must be something else, for the chief went on a diet, and he's visiting the pistol range more than he ever has. I don't know what you're planning, but it better be good."

"I'm not planning anything. Anyway, how do you find out these things?"

"You keep me around because I'm good at looking or because I hear things. These messages come from out of space. I'm super sensitive, which--by the way-- makes me very hungry. Why don't you drive up tonight, and we can have dinner? There's a new show at the club I think you'll like. See you at seven?"

I thought for a minute and replied. "Why not? Seven it is."

"Good, you'll stay at the house…bye."

The drive from my house to Russ' place takes about two and a half hours, so I cleared up some more paper work, took a quick shower, changed my clothes, and I was off. During my drive to Russ' place, Sue Ann occupied my thoughts. I was convinced I had to do something, for she was driving me mad. Why did she have to start this thing with me? It was the why part of the problem that bothered me most. As I entered the circular driveway to the country club, there was Russ, directing traffic and shouting out orders to the valets to "Get moving…we don't make any money until we get them inside." Whatever Russ was, he was one heck of a boss. When it was my turn, with quick dispatch the valet took my car and a hostess showed me to a reserved table, where six other guests were seated. The hostess introduced me to everyone, took my drink order, and disappeared. By the time we all sat down, she was back with my drink and one for Russ, who was hurrying to the table. "If I don't keep on them," as he spoke, he waved his arms around in a wide arc, "nothing gets done." Everyone laughed, and dinner and the show began after Russ gave the high sign to the bandleader.

The show and our dinner seemed to move at the same pace so that when the singer was done, so were we. After dinner drinks were served as the band quietly played dance music and Russ got everyone's attention with, "George, these men are my "Skull group." They are all trustworthy and each has his own brand of genius. I have told them a fictional story, and each of them has a contribution to make as a possible solution." Russ sat back and pointed to one man whose name I forgot and said, "Why don't you start off."

"There are many solutions to the problem, but as I see it, only one sure proof method; namely, there can be no tail to the solution; by that I mean there can be no come back."

Another man added, "Death has a certain ring to it, but regardless of the method, there is always a possibility of some new discovery later on that may come back to haunt you."

Another man contributed, "You can't depend on witnesses to keep their mouths shut, since one of them may get his tail caught in a trap and decide to turn you in if given the right incentive."

Another cited the Gotti case, "They let a convicted murderer out for testimony against Gotti, a man who never even got a parking ticket in his whole life! Face it, our government doesn't play fair."

Another, "You need publicity."

Another, "You need a trial."

Russ stood up with a glass in his hand as he made a toast. "You need to win...here's to Double Jeopardy." He was the seventh and last contributor to speak. The rest of the evening went as planned, a group of old warriors re-hashing old war stories.

I went to Russ' office and slept until he woke me up to go to his house. I didn't understand why he did that, for I was perfectly comfortable where I was. His house was twenty minutes away. His wife was away at some conference, so he went upstairs to his bedroom, and I went to the cellar, which some years earlier had been made into an "overnight lodging" as he called it. In the morning we met in the kitchen, where toast and coffee was the menu of choice.

"My friend, you have done enough talking about your problem, so let's face it, it is time to plan our strategy. Until you unburden yourself of this nonsense, you're no fun. Let's start off with how. It has to be a way that leaves clues that point to you. You will need an inside person who points the chief in your direction. I don't know enough about the new detective, so I will do some more investigating and find out the best way to push her buttons. Do you remember the guy who said you need publicity?" I just shook my head, "No."

"Well, it seems he knows the owner of the local paper in The Cove. He will write some articles about demanding justice in the murder of the beloved judge...Sue Ann. You can believe me; he can make a brass monkey cry. Let's make a list of ways to kill a person--nothing too gory; shooting her would bespeak of robbery; stabbing her is easy, plenty of knives around, and it's news worthy."

"Russ, I am going home before you make me as nuts as you are. Discuss it with your friends; I'll call you next week."

"Do you think we can trust the Commodore? He's stupid but very influential in the town."

"Good bye, I'll talk to you next week." On that note I left for my drive home. Driving home was usually a pleasant experience, for I would mull over in my mind the fine time I would have had with Russ. The parties he had at the club were always very imaginative: everything from dancing bears to belly dancers. Once, he was going to have them dance together; the girls refused; the bears were all for it. However, on this drive the only thoughts that came to mind were those invoked by the Skull group. No matter how I tried to rationalize it, killing was a serious business. Why I had to deal with such matters in the late stages of my life was what weighed on me the most. Did Joann really mean to do me harm, or was it truly that the big wheel of chance had pointed at me. She had to know that someday her folly would be grievous to me. Why did she keep a diary with clues in it that would point to me? That part bothered me the most. Those thoughts (running through my mind) made me pull off the highway and drive towards the water. I must confess that at one point I realized that all I had to do was drive right into it and leave whatever problems to be solved by others. That thought didn't last too long for what reason I don't know, but I just parked the car by a little park by the water and walked along the shore in hopes that the wind that was picking up would not only clear my head but give me reprieve from the thoughts that were going through my head. I was so engrossed in my thinking that I walked right into a lady who was walking the other way. We both stopped within inches of each other. She was as startled as I was.

"I thought I was the only one who would be foolish enough to be walking today?" Her words were said with warmth that made me feel very foolish for being so worried about nothing. She was about my age with brilliantly colored gray hair. She was slender of build and had a coat wrapped tightly around her. She had a multi-colored scarf wrapped around her neck and head that clashed and yet complimented her hair and complexion.

"I'm sorry," I said as I stepped back. "I guess I wasn't looking where I was going. Do you come here often?" I don't know why I asked that question except I felt I should say something, for I had almost knock the poor lady over.

"No, not really," she replied, "it's just that sometimes the house closes in on me. It really doesn't do any good, for the problems at home are still there when I get back. I just kid myself that I'm going to find any answers out here."

"I wish you hadn't said that. I was hoping for some divine intervention, but I guess you're right. Anyway, it's nice to have the wind blow in your face for a while."

With those words the weather changed to a cold biting wind. It became overcast, and the ominous sky gave a gloomy look to everything. We both looked around for somewhere to go when rain started to fall. My car was about two blocks away, and the only other shelter was a gazebo that was in disrepair. We both moved towards it.

"I have been here before, but I never saw this. I have no idea what it is doing here; it is some protection but not much."

The wind picked up and was blowing the rain right through the shoddy structure. I was just wearing a sport jacket and shirt, which afforded me little protection from the elements. She looked at me and I at her, but neither one of us had anything to say, for we were two strangers caught in a storm under a gazebo that looked like it would collapse on us at any moment.

"Come," she said, "my daughter lives across the street." We both hurried across the street, both of us trying to dodge the raindrops as we went. Her daughter must have seen us, for as soon as we got to the steps, she opened the door to let us in. When she closed the door, she had to lean on it, for the wind had picked up and the rain was coming down much harder. 'Wait a minute," she said as she disappeared but was back in a second with towels for both of us.

We both dried ourselves off as my new friend suggested, "Why don't you take your jacket off; you can let it drip dry a little?"

I complied. I still had a chill; and it must have been obvious as she suggested to her daughter, "Could two cold and weary intruders have a cup of tea?"

Her daughter went into the other room as I followed this

strange woman into the dining room. She motioned to a chair and I sat down. I was having a hard time believing what was happening. A strange woman brings me into her daughter's house and is offering me tea. Who could I tell this incredible story to, for I myself could not believe it and I was living it.

The dining room was very nicely decorated with a mahogany table and six matching chairs. There was a breakfront and a serving stand that was made of some different kind of wood, but they fit together somewhat. The chandelier over the table was very plain looking and really didn't go with the rest of the room. The drapes on the window were old. The room looked like it was assembled with whatever was available. I was trying to think of something nice to say, but the only words that came out were, "Thank you for taking pity on me."

"My name is Rosemary and my daughter's name in Vivian."

When she hesitated I used the opportunity to say, "My name is George, and I want to thank you again. When I went on a walk, I didn't expect this."

She smiled as she replied, "Well, it just goes to show that you never know what's around the next corner."

Vivian came in with the tea and some little cookies of some sort, and the three of us sat together and enjoyed our tea mixed with some light conversation.

The weather cleared as quickly as it came upon us, and when a ray of sunlight came in through the window, I said, "Well, I better be on my way, and again I want to thank you for your hospitality. I was given back my jacket, which had dried off, and I was out the door and on my way to my car. As I was walking down the street, I could not believe how much better I felt. Meeting nice people just gave me a lift, both mentally and spiritually. I don't know why, but I just felt I could solve the Sue Ann thing; at the same time I fully realized I had to, for here I was still thinking about it and her. When I got into my car, I became annoyed at myself, for I'd forgotten to get the address of the house I was in. I turned the car around and drove down the street, but I could not figure out which one it was. Annoyed with myself I drove home, thankful for the brief interlude with Rosemary and Vivian.

Once home I resolved that I was going to clean everything up so the only thing I had to do was in The Cove. I went through the rest of the papers on my desk, which really only amounted to opening advertisements from companies and throwing them out or not even bothering to open the letters before throwing them out. The weekend came, and I went to my daughter's house and played "grandpa" for a day. The question of what I was up to on my last trip only came up once, and I answered it with, "The weather in Virginia isn't as severe as it is up here. Thankfully, that ended the topic. Sunday dinner over, I left and went home to pack for a two-week trip.

Sunday night in The Cove is very quiet, for the people who go for the weekend are gone, and the regular inhabitants are resting after their Sunday dinners. As I predicted, the Commodore called. His call started with, "Everyone is mad because they want to take a lighthouse down. I don't know if you went to see it, but it is out on the point. It doesn't work anymore, but it is a favorite spot to walk to. Many an engagement ring has been given there. In the old days when you could walk to the top, it was...it's a damn shame that some jerk wants to tear it down for a condo."

"It was what? You didn't finish the sentence."

"It was known as a lover's leap. You know, a real Romeo and Juliet story. It wasn't true, but so what...well, I don't think it was true."

"Just tell me the story or better yet wait, and I will come down tomorrow, and you can tell it to me when I'm there."

The Commodore yelled out, "Hey, Ruth, George is coming down tomorrow. Sure, we'll come to dinner...seven is perfect... see you then. George, are you still there? I just accepted a dinner invitation for tomorrow night. I'll clean up the spare room for you. Drive carefully."

Before I could say anything, the phone went dead. I just sat in my chair for a moment longer before I went to bed in anticipation of the drive I had to make the following day.

The drive down went without any problems. I pulled into town and went to the store. The greeting I got from the Commodore and Trina's replacement made me feel good. The tinkling of the bell in the background announced Sue Ann's arrival. After everyone exchanged a brief hello, I was allowed to go to my room and rest and freshen up for my dinner date that night. At the appropriate hour, I was dressed and ready to go. The Commodore was also all spruced up with his new sport jacket and shirt on, and we were ready to go. I didn't have the heart to tell him that he should have had the shirt pressed, for I could still see the creases in it from how it'd been packed. He was in a very jovial mood and had even bought two bottles of wine for the occasion. When we got to Ruth's house, Ruth had invited one of her lady friends to join us for dinner. The Commodore had a certain glow come over him.

Dinner was pleasant with everyone engaging in a light conversation; when it was time for coffee and everyone had settled down I said, "Are you now going to tell me about the lighthouse."

All three of them looked at each other with a strange look on their face.

"What did I say? I mean if it..."

"Oh, no," the Commodore said. "Well, no one knows for sure, but there was this young couple...fifteen or sixteen years old...and like all lovers' leap stories, they were forbidden to see each other. The lighthouse had just been built, and at that time when it was high tide, the water would come right up to the base of the lighthouse."

At this point of the story, Ruth's friend interrupted as she said, "The night was an especially stormy night, and the lighthouse keeper had left the door to the lighthouse unlocked. The young couple went into the house to the top floor and jumped. Their bodies were washed out to sea but found three or four days later." The entire town swore never to reveal what really did happen, and like most lovers' tales, it was just adopted as the truth, the whole truth, and nothing but the truth, so help me God. I understand that you are a lawyer, George; the last part was for our benefit."

The three of them laughed as I sat there staring at them. Finally I said, "In other words no one knows what happened, but the story is cute, so why not believe it? Is that what you're telling me?"

In unison they all said, "Yes." On that note the evening ended, and after promising that we would go for dinner again, we left. On the short drive back to the store, the Commodore was just bubbling over about the promise we'd all made to go out again. When we got to the store, between the drive I had made, the dinner, the wine, and the fact that I just didn't want to hear anything else from the Commodore; I excused myself and went to bed.

The following morning, after being served the early-morning special, I left the store and drove around to the other side of the harbor. I went to a high spot where I could see the courthouse and, more importantly, the backdoor. I sat down and using a straight stick to stand in for a rifle with a scope, I could see that a clear shot could be made from my position to the spot where Sue Ann would exit the building or where she would be when she arrived. If a silencer were used on the rifle, no one would even know from where the shot had come. It was a short walk from my vantage point to my car. There was only one road out, which was not ideal, but the plan had a lot of merit.

"The view from up here is really beautiful." The voice that came from nowhere was that of the new detective that Russ had told me about. I turned to face her and must admit that I wouldn't mind being arrested by her. I would even bring the handcuffs! Of course, I was reminded of the reality of my age and overall condition as I tried to stand up. Her long dyed hair made her look younger than the wrinkles on her face said she was. But age becomes a relative thing. She was younger than I and in a lot better shape. She was a little shorter than I, but with an obviously well sculptured body. She must spend a lot of time in the gym. Her nails were cut short, which made her hands look disproportionate to the rest of her body. The gun that was tucked in a holster strapped to her side just looked way too big for her. She had a smile that flashed across her face, which made her eyes twinkle. I resolved she was wearing contact lenses. She continued talking with, "Someday, I hope I can build a house up here."

"Why not now?" I asked as I started walking down from my vantage point. I made a mental note that she had seen me there, so if I were to use the plan, I would have to do something about her. When I got to the car, I took notice that the ground was soft and there were perfect tire marks, another problem to keep in mind.

"Well, I can't afford it on my salary." As she spoke, I just got the feeling that I better be careful as to what I said.

"What were you doing up here? This is private property?"

The question caught her off guard, but with a quick smile and a flip of her hair, she responded, "I'm supposed to ask you that; after all, I represent law and order. You must be the infamous George I've been hearing about, or are you Russ?"

Now that's not fair; you didn't tell me your name; after all, you're the trespasser, not me.'

"Well, okay, let's start over again. I'm Mildred and I am the cop on the scene."

"Well, Mildred, I'm George, the better looking of the Russ and George team. Now what were you doing up here?"

"I was just following you; my chief has a special interest in your whereabouts.'

"Well, Officer Mildred, I shall make a special effort to make my plans known to you. Do you have a cell phone, or should I just call your headquarters?"

"That will be fine," she said as I got in my car and left her standing on the side of the road next to her squad car. I could see she was using her car phone.

As I drove to town, I tried to calculate the distance from where I was stationed on the far side of the cove to the courthouse. It would have to be one great shot. I didn't think I could make it--maybe when I was younger, but not now. I hated to admit it, but Russ' idea of a knife would be much better and a surer way to know the job was done. As I was thinking over the plan, the familiar tinkle of the bell woke me from my trance.

Chapter Thirteen

"Do you intend to avoid me all the time you're here?" Sue Ann's words just had a way of sounding like a song. I could not believe that I had spent the morning trying to figure out how I was going to shoot her.

"If you're on your lunch break, let's eat; I'm starved."

She tilted her head to one side and smiled as she said, "Okay, but nothing big. I've noticed that when you're around, my food and liquor intake increases. We will go to the store for the lunch special: no drinks… no dessert…just lunch."

"Why do I get blamed for everything? Let's go." I took notice that Sue Ann's outfits were all one color. Today it was blue. Blue was in everything from the ribbon in her hair to her sneakers for riding her bike to the bracelet on her arm. I just could not believe why someone would not want a smart, beautiful creature like this. If she is so perfect, why do I want to kill her? It is because she is evil! Why else did she do the things she did to torment me? She is the devil personified. As I walked into the store with the devil at my side, the Commodore quickly found a table for us and put in our order for two specials. I made a vow to myself to one day look at the menu, for it seemed all I ever ate in his restaurant was the specials: breakfast, lunch or dinner.

"I'm glad you came back to our little town. Are you here for any special reason or…?"

She stopped in mid-sentence as Chad walked over and kissed her hello. "I just wanted to say hello, for I am on my way out to the lighthouse to take some pictures and put together a nostalgic story about it. I am going to include a bit about the jumpers. I've heard three versions of the story; I have to pick one. Hi, George, it's nice to see you again." With those words,

Chad left.

"Have you been seeing him in my absence?"

"No, not really. We've had dinner twice, but ...well you know...my being a judge and all, I think I scare most men away, and let's face it, I don't have many to choose from in this town."

"Why don't you move? Are you afraid of the competition from the women in the big cities?" My words really annoyed her.

She glared at me as she said, "I love my little town; I feel as though I make a contribution here; in the city I would live in an apartment without a view and would be trapped in a city that would roar down on me every day. I couldn't ride my bike; my daughter and son-in-law, along with my friends, would all be here."

Our lunch came and we ate in a morbid silence. Did you come back just to point out to me the things I am missing in my life? I would like to be closer to a cultural center, but I enjoy our local band and parades, and don't forget our local fairs and special events."

I put my hand up to stop her. "I came because they want to knock the lighthouse down, and the Commodore said you can't find a way to stop them. First of all, who is "them"? He wasn't sure. Who started all this?"

"You remember Lewis. Well, he was quietly buying up the property in different names and with a blind trust. Before we knew it, he had enough land to build his condos. I mean it's all perfectly legal. After his demise, which is still a big mystery, a gentleman showed up in town who had a mortgage on the parcels of land, and since Lewis had no will or any heirs (or anyone we could find); the mortgagor started foreclosing and submitted his plans for the destruction of the lighthouse and the construction of the condos. As far as I can see, everything is legal. The town council always wanted to have the lighthouse declared an historical monument, but they never got around to it. They really didn't want to spend the time or the money to do it, so now they are sorry."

"Has anyone looked into who these people are? Who would give a mortgage on vacant land and an old lighthouse? That doesn't sound like the kind of an investment a legitimate loan company would make."

"Oh, as far as I could find out, it's a group of private investors. We have a group of people who are willing to put up enough money to buy their interest—well, almost enough..."

"It sounds like you're on the one-yard line and need someone to score. Am I right?"

"This won't involve another accident, will it?"

"Do you really care?"

"I'm a judge for goodness sake."

"Right, but not God, judge and jury." I looked to see what reaction she would have to my last statement. Suddenly she disappeared before me, and I was talking to Joann. The same smile and facial expressions...the way she just moved around in the chair...the perfume...I had to blink several times to bring myself back to reality, and after I did, I was sorry that I did. For the first time, I questioned myself as to whether or not Joann had seduced me or if I was a willing participant in the affair. I had been secure in my beliefs before this moment in time, but now I wasn't so sure. I felt very cold as I sat and watched Sue Ann's lips move, but I was not able to hear or if I heard her, I could not comprehend what she was saying. I just sat motionless as though I was suspended in some sort of vacuum. Up was down and in was out; nothing made sense to me. What if I wanted what happened to happen? What if I was as much to blame as Joann? That thought alone just made me shiver. I wasn't any better than ...?

Sue Ann was leaning over to kiss me goodbye as she looked at her watch and scurried off to get her bike and race back to court.

Ruth and her friends witnessed Sue Ann's exit and quickly exchanged their version of her exit. One lady was the most demonstrative as she said, "That was one hell of a good bye. No wonder that bastard came back so soon. Ruth, you better forget George; he has hooked a bigger fish." The ladies all started to laugh. I just pretended I didn't hear them as I paid my bill and left. I went back down to the water and sat on a bench from which I could see the entire harbor and bay. After I sat for a while, I don't remember how long, I got up and decided to find out more about the loan company that held the mortgage. Since legal procedure hadn't been started yet, I went to the attorney that was supposed to handle the matter. I found out who he was since he had called the court and asked for an appointment with Sue Ann before he filed any papers. When Sue Ann had gotten back to her office, her secretary had given her the message, so she called me.

"I know this isn't exactly legal, but I know this man and well …"

"You're doing the right thing," I said. I then called the Commodore and asked him to make a call to the attorney and smooth the way for me.

"No sweat," the Commodore responded. "I know that old fool; he should have retired years ago. Go! I'll tell him you're on the way."

When I got to the attorney's office, he greeted me as though we were long-lost friends. I spoke to him for an hour and, based upon our conversation, resolved that no one would trust him with such a complex legal matter. He had his office about five miles from The Cove and freely admitted he never had done a foreclosure before.

"Do you know why they…whoever they are…came to you?"

He didn't verbally respond but just shook his head, "No."

"Lewis, you know who he was, was laundering money. They came to you so that when the government starts nosing around, you will take the fall, for the government will say that you (as the attorney) should have known."

The way he slumped in the chair looked as though I'd hit him. "What can I do? I'm too old to get mixed up in this mess."

First, you hire me as an assistant. Don't worry; you don't have to pay me. I'll contact your contact man and get you out of the middle."

"No, I want to be fair to you...fifty-fifty...okay?"

He stopped sweating when I said yes. "How do you ..."

Before I could finish the sentence he handed me a piece of paper with a number on it. "They told me to call if I had any questions."

"Call them now. Introduce me as the person who is going to handle the contract. I'll take over from there."

He did my bidding and had a look of relief on his face when he handed me the phone. I said, "Here is my phone number; I want to have a sit down. Call me with when and where." I turned to see my "boss" sitting at his desk, wringing his hands. "Don't worry; it's in my hands now. Did they give you any of the papers?"

Again he just shook his head, "No."

"When it is time, you will handle a simple closing on the sale of a mortgage from them to a charitable purchaser. Just relax; believe me; you're doing the right thing."

"You're George. The Commodore called me." He never finished the sentence as I walked out of the office. It occurred to me that it was the first time he'd called me George. On the way back to town, I called Russ and brought him up to date. "Be ready to move when I call you...that is if I need you."

I could hear Russ laughing as he said, "She's never getting rid of you. Face it; you have added another dimension to her life. Ain't daddies great."

Two peaceful days went by without incident. One day the Commodore took the afternoon off (or four hours of it) and took me on a tour of the nearby towns and harbors. No matter where we went, everyone knew the Commodore. At night I was invited over to the home of the chairman of the group that was trying to raise the money to buy the lighthouse and make it into a monument. They had raised eighty percent of the value of the mortgages on the property. The chairman said, "If the holders of the mortgages agree, we will pay it off as quickly as we can."

"Let me see what I can do, and I'll get back to you. In the meantime, just keep quiet about what we are doing. A lot of chatter is not what we want. I'll call you as soon as I am contacted."

Another night the Commodore and I took Ruth and her friend to dinner at a little café down the coast a ways. It was someone's house that they also used for quiet dinners. The Commodore just glowed when I told him, "This is wasted on us; we should have been here about ten years ago." The highlight of the evening was when Ruth said through clenched teeth, "Sue Ann must have missed you a lot; my friends told me she had lunch with you. I wasn't there when she said good bye ...Oh, never mind...you know, when she left you at the store the other day."

Her comment caught me so off guard that I didn't say anything. The following morning, as I was walking back from a walk down to the pier where I watched Steve wash his boat, my phone rang. The voice said, "Be on the far side of the harbor in an hour...see you." The phone went dead. I made my way back to the store, got my car, and drove to the other side of the harbor. There was a little parking area near where I'd been the other day when I took a rifle sighting. Right on time a worn pickup showed up, and a man got out and walked over to my car. "He'll see you," the man said as he motioned me to the truck.

113

I went over to the truck and got in. There was no cordial greeting or a shaking of hands, just a gruff voice saying, "How do you see the mortgage deal going down, and why should we do it?"

"The 'why' is that if you don't, the town's people will fight you tooth and nail; you'll probably win, but you will also get a lot of publicity, which I don't think you want. They have raised enough money to buy out three of the mortgages and to make a thirty percent payment on the fourth. They will pay the fourth one off as soon as possible. All you have to do is assign your rights, title, and interest over to them."

"Will you handle the deal? That attorney we contacted…I don't think he knows what he's doing."

"He will draw up the papers and hold the fourth mortgage until it is paid off. I will see to it that it is done properly. You can count on me to do that."

"You got a deal. Call the number you got when you're ready to close. I'll send over the mortgages to that attorney today and the signed assignment tomorrow. You have the checks there. Remember there are four different entities involved. Bye."

I left the truck and went back to my car. His driver went back to the truck, and they drove off. From the corner of my eye, I could see Mildred, sitting in the squad car, watching everything that was going on. It looked to me as though she had a camera, but I couldn't be sure. I left and went to the chairman's house and told him the news. He was thrilled.

"What do we do with the mortgages?"

"Nothing. You can do what repairs are necessary and since you will own three mortgages, if some heir pops up, he/she will have to pay you off, plus interest and late charges and anything else…"

"I understand. We can always deal with it at a later time. I will draw the checks when you want them and to your specifications."

The deal was the most guarded secret in town. That night Sue Ann invited me to her house for a victory drink. "You sure get things done; now don't say anything; it's a secret."

I just laughed as I commented, "Small towns will be small towns."

The deal went off exactly as planned. I called Russ and told him he would not be needed. The only annoying thing that was happening was that Mildred always seemed to be around. No matter where I went or whomever I was with, she made sure that I saw her or else she was the worse shadow I had ever met, which I didn't believe.

I started to talk about going home when the Commodore said, "Oh no, not now! You have to help me with the appreciation bash. Every year I have a big party; everyone is invited for an appreciation celebration. I only charge a nominal fee to cover the absolutely nominal cost, and everyone has a great time. Any money I get over my cost, we use toward a town decoration. You've seen the gold leaf sign as you come into town…that was last year's. I leave it up to our decoration committee to decide what to do with the excess money …party …party."

Word got out and the town came alive. Sue Ann came over to me as said, "You don't get this in a big city…"

I was going to say that is true but you also don't go to bed alone, but I thought better of it. I was in charge of ticket sales. My job, as told to me by everyone in town, was to make sure I approached everyone and sold them a ticket…no exceptions. Two ladies offered to buy Russ a ticket if he would come. When the chief heard that, he offered to pay for his own ticket. The airport incident was still bothering him, even though it was never proven conclusively that it was a bombing. I even called the man in the truck and offered to pay for his ticket. I found an envelope on my car with a hundred-dollar bill in it with a note, "For tickets for those who can't afford to come."

The party started right on time; it officially started when I, with majestic stride, walked to the ticket table and announced, "Let Appreciation night begin." Immediately, ticket holders who were anxious to get their favorite table for their group besieged me. The three-piece band that had been dubbed the Cove Three started to play. The food was piled high on the four tables in the rear, and to the side was another table that had beer, wine, and soda on it. Trina's replacement was the bar maid, but the job was too much for her. Ruth, with her big mouth, walked over and a line was formed and order took the place of chaos, and the service of beverages was done in an orderly fashion. The Commodore was everywhere. He helped for a while, went to serve food, and then wound up on the dance floor, organizing a limbo line. It took four of us to pick him up off the floor. Trina and Steve won the event. Everyone marveled at how quickly his arm had healed. He went over to the Commodore and asked permission to hand out flyers' advertising his "New Fishing Adventure." The Commodore grabbed the flyers from him; and he and I, whom he'd taken off ticket duty, handed them out.

The doctor showed up with a stethoscope around his neck and an oxygen bottle with the explanation, "Better safe than sorry." Sue Ann showed up in a loud swirled print dress that seemed to be moving, even when she wasn't. All tongues started wagging when I was the first she walked over to and kissed hello. The entrance of Mildred, wearing a form-fitting red dress was another highlight among many. The group that was standing by me immediately surmised that she was a lesbian after the judge. The other comment that deserves note was, "Where does she have her gun?" I walked away, shaking my head in disbelief. The doctor who had heard the same comments just looked at me as he said, "People are wonderful." I added, "And vicious," to which he commented, "You have too much gray hair to still believe in Santa Claus. "I didn't get the connection, but I attributed it to the new drink I had introduced at the party, "Apple Pie Sangria." It was the first item to run out; even all the apples that were in it were gone.

Lurking in the corner was the man from the pickup truck. I started to walk over to him, but he held up a finger and waved me off. I complied.

The chief walked in and took a position where he could see the entire room. He stood out because his belly wasn't hanging over his belt. The doctor nudged me as he said, "My special diet for senior citizens who don't know when to just say "no." I went to the other side of the room, for I knew what would be coming next.

Chad walked in with his camera, and everyone was suddenly busy combing their hair, straightening their clothes, and taking their eyeglasses off. The first picture he took was of the judge and then one of Mildred. After that, he worked his way around the room, snapping pictures of individuals and of groups. He took two of Steve and Trina, and after I handed him a flyer about their new business, he said, "I will definitely mention this in the write up." The couple smiled their approval. He made a special trip to the far corner of the room where Tisha was standing. She was wearing a flowery blouse and jeans. She turned bright red when he took her picture. He turned to me as he commented, "No one really sees the true beauty of this fine lady. She and she alone makes our town hall and courtroom sparkle. Tisha was blushing so hard that I thought she would pass out. I left the area.

Lila was walking around in vain, looking for Russ. I walked over to her and said, "I'm here; you can say hello to me." She threw her head back in a defiant fashion as she replied, "Not since you met the judge." She promptly turned and walked away. The Commodore, who had witnessed our meeting, laughingly said, "You sure know how to treat women; you have them swooning at your feet." His comment had him laughing so hard that he walked right into the lady he had taken to dinner with Ruth and me.

It was over. Just as fast as it started, it was over. There was no formal announcement, but all of a sudden people started to leave. The chief yelled out, "There are plenty of people here to drive, so don't drive if you have been drinking." The bandleader spoke over the mike, "Let your night end on a bang, the kind that doesn't hurt." Mildred even added her own comment, "A DWI costs money and points." I was amazed at how many people started to hand their keys to other people while others just said, "Come with me; I'll bring you back in the morning; you can leave it where it is until morning."

The next words heard were from Ruth, "Come on now; help clean up. It isn't fair we leave this mess for the Commodore." The younger members of the crowd started folding up the extra tables and chairs and put them back into the storeroom where they had been stored. Four young men grabbed brooms and swept the entire area. They pushed the garbage into piles, while others bagged it and put the bags in a pile for the trash man to take the next day. If the garbage man hadn't sampled so much of the Apple Pie Sangria, he would have gone home and brought the garbage truck back with him, but his condition dictated that it wait until morning. Someone made the suggestion, "Next year bring the damn truck with you."

I just stood in the middle of all the activity and watched in amazement with Sue Ann's whispering in my ear: "You don't see this in your big city." Reluctantly, I had to admit she was right.

One man yelled out, "What do I do with the leftover bread?"

Another screamed back, "Give it to the fish."

The man did, and within a few minutes, the area where he had thrown the bread was just bubbling from all the fish that had come for the unexpected treat.

The next scream heard by everyone was, "Oh my God, he

fell in." Everyone froze for a second, while one young lady was pointing at the dock screaming, "He's there...there he is." Everyone ran to where she was pointing. One man fell to his knees and reached down into the icy cold water and pulled a man up by his shirt. Two more men grabbed on, and within a few seconds, he was on the dock, shivering from his unexpected plunge into the ice-cold water. The doctor came over with a tablecloth that was used as a blanket, and the young man, who was very embarrassed, was led away to a waiting car to get warm and be driven home. The doctor was shouting, "Take a warm bath; if you get dizzy call me." The disaster averted, everyone looked at his girlfriend, who offered an explanation as to what had happened. With a sheepish look on her face she just said, "I pushed him." Nothing else was said, and the cleaning up activity continued until the Commodore announced: "Everything is ship shape; thank you all." On that note everyone headed home. Sue Ann walked over and kissed me good night, witnessed by Ruth who was the last to leave. The Commodore and I went about closing up the place. From behind the counter, he brought out a bottle of his private stock, and we had a goodnight toast. As we clinked our glasses he said, "Ain't my people wonderful; no wonder I don't want to move."

Between the physical activity, the Apple Pie Sangria, and the good night toast; I was asleep before my head hit the pillow.

"Just coffee," was my order in the morning.

The next day everyone walked around in a stupor and complained they'd eaten too much or they'd drunk too much. I was amazed the way one day was just rolling into the next with really no way of telling one from another. The part that scared me the most was that I was fitting right in and just rolling along with everyone else. I was annoyed at myself for not concentrating on the reason I was there: to kill someone. The thought just sent shivers down my spine. I kept telling myself it had to be done, for it wasn't fair to the rest of my family...my family...that now included Sue Ann and Trina, but not for long. I decided I would believe Sue Ann when she said she hadn't told Trina, so I just had to take care of Sue Ann. The more I said or even thought about her, her name became like a curse. I was so deep in my thoughts that I didn't hear Steve and Trina come up behind me. "Why don't you come out with us? We are just going to check the boat out. Come on; it will be fun; the Commodore is coming. Without anything else to be said, we went on the boat. Steve had to get fuel, and I, without thinking, told the boy pumping the fuel to fill it up. Steve had given him an order and went into the shop to get something; so he didn't hear what I said. He looked at me and followed my instructions. When I saw the total, I was awe struck. Steve almost passed out, and the Commodore just roared with laughter. I refused to react at all; I just took out my credit card and said, "Here you are, son." I considered it a wedding present to my granddaughter and her husband. I signed the card without saying a word. Trina kissed me, and Steven was still in shock, and I cursed myself for using that word again.

We left the gas dock, and with a gentle breeze at our back, we went out into the bay and headed for the ocean. The ship was handling well, or at least that is what the Commodore told me. Suddenly he jumped up: "Look, there's a great white; he must be lost." I looked at where he was pointing, and the dorsal fin was very obvious.

"Sit down, you nut, and let him go his way, and we will go ours. "

"Are you kidding? Catching one of them will go a long way towards advertising this boat and the skill of the skipper. Having one of them hanging from the pier will be printed in every fishing magazine on the east coast. Quick! Help me fix the pole and fishing chair. You sit in it, and do what I tell you."

Steve was down off the flying bridge and told Trina to take

his place. He took out a very stout pole for me to use and started to throw some terrible smelling stuff in the water. The Commodore put the hook through a big lure and threw it into the water. The line started to play out. All I could envision was the closing scenes from "Jaws."

Steve, in a high-pitched voice said, "I came out here to start chumming so that when I have customers I would have a starting place to fish from. I never thought I would attract a great white." He pointed at me as he said, "It's you...you brought me luck."

The Commodore was busy attaching the pole to the chair and strapping me into it. He was very excited as he started pushing me back and forth in the chair as he shouted, "Feed the line out until you feel him hit it...yank back to set the hook and just let him run a while. Keep rocking back and forth so you set the hook deeper into him."

"Wouldn't one of you be better at this?" I said the words with a plea in my voice, for I just didn't feel I was qualified for the job they'd given me. Also I was scared stiff.

"No! When you get it alongside the boat, it will take the two of us to land him...it will not be an easy task...it looks like a beauty." The Commodore was in charge. Steve, Trina and I were but pawns in the hands of the master. "Does she know port and starboard, or should I use left and right?"

"What are you talking about?" my voice was at a higher pitch, for I now fully realized that he wasn't fooling. The Commodore was going to get this shark, even though he only had a rag tag crew to help him.

"Do you have a gun on board? You better get it now. I don't know if a gaffing hook will be enough."

Steve went below and within seconds, he was back with a rifle.

I just kept quiet, for I didn't know what to say, and I knew no one was going to listen.

"Go right…that's it…try to keep the line right behind the boat; we won't want to cut or snag our own line."

Silently I added, "God forbid we should lose this fish."

"Now when the shark hits the line, it's going to jerk hard. That is when you have to pull back and then let him run. I'll tell you when to stop him." As he spoke, the Commodore was leaning over the rear of the boat, watching the line and straining to see if he could see the prize he so dearly wanted. Steve was standing at the ready with rifle in hand, waiting for his next instruction. Trina was doing a great job of keeping the line straight behind the boat.

Just as the Commodore had predicted, I felt a tremendous pull on the line. I rocked back in the chair, and the line went taut as it jumped out of the water. The Commodore started screaming, "Yank him again…let him run… throw water on the reel…you got him…you really got him." Steve ran over and poured water on the reel, which meant it went on me as well. "Keep rocking. Let him run and then pull him in…that's it keep it up…don't let him spit the hook out. Trina, keep him behind the boat…that's it; we've got him…Steve, can you see him… when you can shoot him…the hell with the idea of good sportsmanship, shoot him."

My arms, back, and legs were killing me. Although the pole and I were anchored to the chair, I still had to keep the pole straight and keep rocking so there was no slack in the line. Every time I rocked forward, I took some more turns on the line. The distance between the shark and the rear of the boat was getting shorter. I knew I just didn't have the strength to keep doing what I was doing too much longer. "Steve," I yelled, "I can't keep this up; my arms feel like they are going to fall off now."

The shark charged the boat. The Commodore with lightning swift hands took the slack in the line and wrapped it around the rear cleats of the boat. The line between me and the rear of the boat went slack, which allowed me to relax. The line between the shark and the boat remained taut. He yelled up to Trina, "increase your speed by two knots and hold it at that speed.' Trina complied and the line from the boat to the shark remained taut.

"Go up another few revolutions." Again Trina complied, and it was obvious the boat was pulling the shark, who was now about twenty feet behind the boat. He was much closer to the surface and was in plain sight for a longer and longer period of time. Because the line was wrapped around the cleats, we could not pull the shark closer. The Commodore asked Steve, "Do you have a grappling hook?"

Steve disappeared and came back with two of them; each was attached to thirty feet of line. They each took one. Steve handed me the rifle. Steven got on one side of the boat and the Commodore on the other, and I pointed the rifle where I thought the shark would appear.

The Commodore shouted up to Trina, "When I say stop...stop the boat, but be ready to start up again when I tell you to." We were all set, and the command came: "Stop." Trina stopped the boat, and the shark came within five feet of the rear of the boat. Both men threw their hooks and both of them dug deeply into the shark. The shark was thrashing about, but he could not go anywhere, for he was being pulled from both sides. "Go...Go..." the Commodore yelled, and Trina started the boat moving again and at a faster rate of speed than before. The Commodore tied his line down and Steve did the same. The boat was now towing the shark. The Commodore added, "This will drown him, and we can pick him up with one of your winches, or better yet, Trina, head for your berth; we will do it there in grand style."

Steve went up to the bridge to bring us home while the Commodore unhitched me from the chair. He asked, 'Why didn't you shoot him?"

All I could say was, "I forgot."

When we got back to the dock, word spread about our catch and everyone came to see it. He was still squirming, but that soon stopped. The shark was hoisted up on to the dock by his tail, and all his statistics were recorded: height, weight, size, and angulation of his bite. Chad was there, writing all the information down as well as taking a picture of the shark hanging by its tail with Steve on one side and Trina on the other. The Commodore and I just sat on the sidelines with the other spectators. My arms, legs, and even the soles of my feet hurt from fighting that shark. I couldn't even applaud when everyone else did. The doctor gave me some oil to rub on my sore muscles.

No one could figure out what the shark was doing in the waters off The Cove.

Chapter Fourteen

I was going to go home but I had to delay my trip for a few days as I went to a spa twice a day for a whirl pool treatment and massage. Sue Ann would come and visit me at the Commodore's store to check on my progress. Trina told her mother about me filling the fuel tank on the boat. Sue Ann wasn't impressed until Trina told her what it cost…she made a special trip to tell how nice that was of me. When I told Russ of my shark adventure he added the part of me paying for the fuel, "They are hooking you as surely as you hooked Jaws." The last part made him laugh so much that he had to hang up. I was wondering how he found out about the fuel. I just chalked it up as another Russ mystery.

The town was just starting to settle down when there was an announcement or leak that there was no conclusive evidence that the explosion at the airport was caused by a bomb. The chief was really upset for he said, "That information should have never been given out. That was police business and its exclusive property."

A councilman took issue with him. He said at the town meeting, "When our dear chief is spending town money, whatever he is doing is town business…he doesn't own anything…he is our employee…not our boss."

The speech was received with a round of applause. The chief stormed out of the meeting. Mildred stayed behind to answer any questions. The chief was so upset that he came to the store to tell the Commodore and me. He sought my advice. I told him, "The council wants you out…start looking for another job or retirement." My words hit him hard. The Commodore added, "Listen to him…he's a smart man."

I went home the following morning, for my children had

called me to see when I would be around for a family dinner. I told myself, "That is the nicest part of The Cove; it is only a six-hour, pleasant drive away."

The problem of Sue Ann, no matter how I tried to forget it, was a constant companion. It was always with me, even on my pleasant drives to and from The Cove. I knew I had to act, for it was not going away. I visited again with Russ and his Skull group, but they had nothing new to add except to say, "Now is the time, for the chief is going to be preoccupied with his own problems." I waited a week before I again went to The Cove. I was of a single mind…Sue Ann had to go. The time I spent with my family convinced me that they shouldn't be forced to deal with a family they never knew they had or to find out that they had a different type of father than they thought they had. The more I thought about it, the wider the span of people that would be affected by my Sue Ann secret. That part bothered me the most. Sue Ann wasn't worth that much; she was only one against all the others.

When I got home, I immediately made arrangements to go back to The Cove. This time the trip wasn't a pleasure, for I was on a mission. I called ahead to the Commodore, who immediately had my room readied for me. When I got there, we went through the normal greeting process, except that the Commodore knew there was something different about me. "I don't know what it is, but you are definitely different."

"That shark ordeal took a lot out of me." We both laughed at my response."

"Come on; get ready. I called the ladies and we are taking them for dinner. Ruth wanted us to go to her house, but I told her "no." Tonight is an occasion: my friend George is in town." Pushing my protest aside, we were on our way.

The night passed without any incident until Ruth said, "You know, George, you can at least make believe you're having a good time."

"Why is it so hard for you people to believe I am still very sore? I had to go home in excruciating pain and then I drove back, just to be near you, and all you can do is complain? WOW, that is heavy."

No one believed me, but at least it stopped the complaining about my behavior; for that I was thankful. The evening finally ended, and we drove the ladies home. I leaned over for Ruth wanted to kiss me good night, but when she saw me wince, she said, "You're really not kidding, are you?" I just let the question hang in the air.

The next morning, after the sunrise special, I went for a ride to a neighboring town. I was told they were having a street fair. I parked the car and started to walk around and look at the junk that other people were trying to sell. I saw an andiron set that looked very familiar to me. It was very annoying, for it is not the sort of thing that normally would attract me. I walked away, annoyed at myself for having such a trivial thing bother me. After I had walked the whole fair, I went back to my car. I settled in for the ride back to the store when a call came in; it was Sue Ann. As soon as I said "Hello," she said, "Why don't you come over for dinner tonight? Maybe you can help me with a courtship problem. Is seven okay? I'm going to cook, so you go get a good bottle of white wine, unless you want to make that sangria again. All I got was a sip; when I went to get my own glass, it was gone, apples and all."

I laughed before I said, "It's a date." On the way back, I went to the grocery and liquor store and bought all the ingredients. I got to Sue Ann's about 6:30, and while she finished up dinner, I made my now infamous sangria. As we sat down to eat and sample the wine, I looked at her as I said, "Alright, what's bugging you?"

"It's this town. Chad asked me to go away with him, just over night to a convention of some sort. It was a dinner for newspaper people; some friend of his was getting an award.

127

Stupidly, I said 'yes', and why shouldn't I go? I mean…well, you know what I mean. I made the mistake of going to the local store and buying a negligee. I never go shopping locally, but I was working on a decision, so I went to the local store. I was having my nails done, and the girl doing them asked if I liked my purchase. I didn't say a word but sat mute until she was done. When I left, I was so mad; I know there is nothing I can do about it, but I can't believe I go shopping and I'm the talk of the town. It is times like this when I think you're right and I should move out of this gossip mill I call my hometown. "

I just smiled to see the great judge Sue Ann be so distressed with a little gossip. 'Well, you got to know you are a main item in town. You are "Numero Uno." Instead of being mad, you should be proud. Now come on; don't let it spoil a perfect dinner. Here have some more wine before you miss out again."

Suddenly I could no longer hear her. I was off in space somewhere, thinking back to the first time I'd met Joann. I was sitting in the chair but completely oblivious to what was going on around me. My meetings with Joann started reappearing in my mind as though they were a movie. As each episode flipped by, I was reliving the sights and smells of our meetings. Her perfume would drive me nuts. When she walked in to the room, the room was turned into a stage, and Joann played all the parts of the play. There was no beginning or end…there was no dialogue…there was just Joann. The more I tried to put her out of my mind, the worse the scene got. I was with Joann… someone who had ruined my life and made me in to what I was. The trouble was that I didn't know what I was. I stood up and looked around at my surroundings, but all I could see was the little examination room. I sniffed the air, and all I could smell was the perfume that Joann wore. I moved my arms about, but I could feel nothing, nor could I sense anything. I went to the door that led to the outside patio, and in my mind I was walking to the door that led out of the examination room. In the distance

I could hear my name being called and someone's asking, "Well, what do you think?" I walked towards the voice and found myself in the living room, standing before the coffee table with the curved legs and the fireplace. I looked and there were the andirons. On the side was the stand that held the long handled brush for sweeping out the fireplace, the shovel for picking up the ashes and the tongs for turning the logs. I couldn't understand what they were doing in an examination room. I heard the voice again, and before I knew it, the voice was coming from the person before me. It was Joann, wearing a loosely fitted black dress or gown, not a white coat over a white dress. The difference startled me. I had to go to the bathroom. The voice was coming from in front of me saying, "What do you think?" This time I knew it wasn't Joann but Sue Ann. We brushed up against each other as I was moving towards the bathroom and she was twirling to show me the dress. As we touched each other, she was not wearing any undergarments, just as her mother hadn't. The room went blank; I was in a trance. I do not know what happened. I went to the bathroom. When I came out after washing my face three times and making sure I was fully cognizant of my surroundings, I came out and was mortified by what I saw. Sue Ann, dressed in a black negligee, was on the floor. It looked like her gown had caught on the curved leg of the coffee table and she'd fallen. When she fell, she hit her head on the elaborate andiron, and I could see was dead. She was not breathing; she was chalk white, and there was blood oozing out of a terrible gash on the side of her head. There was no doubt in my mind that she was dead. Dead...the word went spinning around in my head; the question of whether or not I'd done it didn't fully settle in, only that she still hadn't moved and my opinion that she was dead hadn't changed. I felt like a heavy weight had been lifted off of me, and yet I felt sorry that a beautiful, educated woman that nobody wanted was dead. I thought for a moment as to what I should do and came to the conclusion...nothing. By now the blood had soaked the rug where it abutted up to the tile by the fireplace. I turned and left. As I went out the door, I said, "Good bye, Sue Ann." I went to my car and went to the store. The Commodore was closing up, so I gave him a hand, and afterwards we sat down and had a nightcap from his private stock. He concluded that we could hobble on one leg, so we had another. The combination of the wine and the two drinks were perfect for me to forget what I had witnessed and allowed me to have a restful sleep.

I was awakened by all the noise that was coming from the store. I showered to clear my head. There was a banging at the door. I shouted that I was getting dressed. The banging stopped. When I was done getting dressed and I had taken all the pills I am required to take in the morning, I walked into the bright sunlight. At first, it hurt my eyes, and I stood in the doorway that leads into the restaurant area. It was an anthill and a beehive of activity. People were running in and out, telling the Commodore things and listening to what he had to say before leaving. I could tell something big was happening for the Commodore was in his glory. He was the traffic director of information. He was the main man and his glowing face paid tribute to that fact. I went over by him and was quickly served the early-bird breakfast with coffee. As I was picking up the cup, he could be silent no more. "Sue Ann is dead! Tisha, you know the housecleaning lady, went there this morning and found her in a big puddle of blood...dead. The chief is there now and an ambulance, but she is dead. They don't know yet if she bled to death or if she broke her neck when she fell. It looks like she tripped over the coffee table and hit her head, but no one knows for sure. Mildred, the new detective, is in her glory; she and the chief are doing the investigating. The county was called in...no one knows who did that... but the chief is out there now, yelling that this is his town and the death occurred here and that he is in charge."

One of the deputies came over and said, "The chief wants to see you. "

"Were you the one banging on my door this morning?" By his silence it was easy to see that he was. "You go tell your chief that when he wants to see me, he knows where I am. I will not see him alone. I want a stenographer present to record what he says."

The Commodore was just itching to say something, so he added, "You tell him that I am a witness to what George said."

"Why did you say that?"

"I don't know. I just want him to know that he can't push my guest around."

Within a few minutes, the chief was in the store and very irritated. "He was supposed to arrest you." As he spoke he was spitting.

He was followed by the town council president, who was also overwrought, "On what basis are you arresting this man? We don't want any lawsuit for false arrest. Do you have an arrest warrant? Who signed it?"

I stood up between them with my hands up saying, "Gentleman, can't we discuss this like adults? Now, Chief, you have a warrant...well?" His silence was his answer.

"You were the last person to see Sue Ann alive and that makes you my prime suspect. Are you going to assume the position or..."

The Commodore stood up and in a defiant tone said, "No, he is doing no such thing unless you have a valid arrest warrant. Have you gone nuts?" Mildred and one of the deputies arrived on the scene, and the town council president was telling them to restrain the chief until …

Tempers were flaring and no one was making any sense. "Chief, now really...you know you need a warrant or at least probable cause. Go get a warrant. I promise I will be right here;

in fact, if you call me, I will come to the station house myself. Don't let this situation get out of hand; a lot of people will get upset…just go do things right."

The chief left after ordering the deputy to stay with me. Mildred walked out with the chief, giving him advice as they went.

"There is a town council meeting tonight, and I'm going to get that idiot fired." After his speech he left.

"Where is Trina? She must need some help with things. I mean, she just lost her mother." No one could answer me. "Does she know what happened? Commodore, call her."

As I sat at the table, I could not really define my own feelings. I wasn't sure if I was a murderer or what. The thought went through my mind that if I had called for an ambulance, would she still be alive? If that is true, what does that make me? As these thoughts raced through my mind, I could feel myself becoming very remorseful, yet I knew I better keep my composure for the chief was sure to come back with something, or he would just hold me for questioning. I knew there was no way I was walking out of this situation; the chief was holding all the cards.

Trina walked into the store hysterical. Ruth and two other women were with her. Each one was offering her suggestion that she should settle down. Steve was out on an overnight trip and was expected back within the hour. Trina didn't want him called; she wanted to tell him herself. While everyone was milling about, Steve pulled into the harbor, and Trina went down to meet him. The Commodore turned and half shouting said to Ruth and her group, "All of you stay here! Let them alone to work this out for themselves."

The phone rang and it was the chief; he had gone to the county judge, who had been temporally assigned to handle Sue Ann's cases, and he signed an arrest warrant. The warrant was defective, but I was not about to argue. I told the deputy. "Let's go."

As soon as we got to the station house, the chief and Mildred were waiting. I was led to a questioning room, which had been obviously set up to intimidate a suspect. It looked like something from a movie. On one wall was a one-way mirror. There was only one light in the room, and it hung over a table that was bolted to the floor, and attached to it was a set of handcuffs for restraining a suspect. Other chairs were brought in as needed. When we got in the room, there was only one chair for the chief; Mildred had to go get her own. I sat down and looked at the chief, who looked more nervous than I did. I sat there and waited until the chief walked around the room two times. Finally, he stared at me with a stern look on his face, and Mildred spoiled the whole scene by asking the first question: "Were you with Sue Ann last night?" The chief was obviously annoyed by her taking the leadership of the questioning. Mildred continued, "We have witnesses who can put you at the house last night."

I looked at her as I answered, "You must know that I have no obligation to talk to you. I also was not read my rights; therefore, I have nothing to say and so that we both don't waste each other's time, I have no intention of answering any questions at any time. No, my dear lady and gentleman, you will have to prove this case without my help, and be assured I will sue both of you and the town as well as bring criminal charges against both of you."

The chief yelled, "Put him in a cell; I can hold him for questioning. Get him out of here."

I got up and followed the deputy to one of the cells. Once inside, I made myself as comfortable as possible and waited for the chief's next move. The day became night and proceeded back to day. Because of my medical condition, the Commodore brought me my medical supplies as well as dinner and breakfast. He informed the deputy that he would be back with lunch.

About mid-morning I was released without a word's being said. I went to the store, just as Russ was setting up two speakers. When he saw me, he said, "I know what I'm doing here. Lila called me before they came and got you. Sit down; you're just in time for the show."

The speakers let out a few squawks and the words: "This meeting will come to order. Now, as you all know, our dear chief is about to make a mountain out of nothing."

Different people were shouting, and finally the president had to regain order. "Please, one at a time. We all know each other here, so please..." The voices started. "There was a murder committed in our town..." Before the speaker could finish the statement, another voice yelled, "We don't know if it was a murder or just an accident. Let's not start rumors like the airport thing: a bombing turned out to be an accident or at least no one knows what happened. We had armed troops in our town questioning everyone and scaring everyone into thinking we were under attack. We hired another detective to ward off the increased crime wave, and all we did was spend money for no good reason. A bombing, and now you add to that a murder! Who is going to come to this hell hole of crime?" The speech was greeted with applause. Another person spoke, "A person was killed!" The voice was interrupted by another who said, "A person died--that's all we know." Then many people started yelling at once: "She was a judge who thought she was Mary Poppins, riding her little bike and ringing that damn bell."

"Should we just forget about it?"

"It would be a lot better than having a big to do over it. What do you think that will do to property values? After the airport incident, do you know how many inquiries I got about buying property here? None! I would get one or two a day, but after the bomb scare...none. It is just starting to come back now. Do you know my own son thought that planes were flying over us and dropping bombs on us? He was having nightmares."

"What are we going to do about the chief? He's dying to play detective, especially since he now has a specialist to help him."

"All she can do is wear a dress two sizes too small for her; I thought it was going to rip! "So did I," another voice added. "Who is going to control the chief?" "Are we going to have another "Rambo" mess?" "Yeah, remember the whole town was blown up and all because of a loud-mouth sheriff. We don't have a sheriff, but we sure have a chief." The last remark was followed by laughter. When it quieted down again, a new voice was heard: "A chief who has sent out resumes all over the state and the whole East Coast; he's looking for a new and bigger job. He would just love to make this case a big one and make himself look good at our expense."

The voice of the president was again heard, "It seems we all agree that the whole situation should be downed played until we know for sure what we are dealing with, and in any case, it still should be kept quiet least we all be ruined. Who's going to keep tabs on the chief?"

"I will." There was a lot of noise as everyone was mumbling something about the speaker. It was Ruth. "I never wanted to hire the new detective, but you all yelled at me."

Someone else yelled out, "We just didn't want to be robbed by a crook!"

"At least a crook only takes what you got on you; the tax collector takes that and then some; he doesn't stop. I never heard of a crook's selling a house to get money. But the tax collector will."

There was a loud burst of laughter and foot stomping until the president called for order and moved on to new business.

By now the store was jammed, and business was booming. The Commodore turned to Russ and said, "Thank you, my friend, I think I'm going to do this on a regular basis."

Russ took down the equipment, and he and I retired to my favorite bench by the water to discuss our plans. Once we sat down on the bench and the sea air started to bathe us in its clean smell and dampness, I realized that I couldn't or wouldn't want to live as an adulterer but had no problem living as a possible murderer. I marveled at myself for having a sense of values that allowed such a condition. I just resolved that the brain is a wondrous thing. Russ sat for a long time, staring at the water. This strange silence between us just got louder as it lasted longer. Finally, Russ broke through the silence barrier by saying, "What's your next move? If you believe Sue Ann that she never told Trina, it seems to me you're done with this situation. If the death is ruled as an accident, you can live in peace; if you don't believe Sue Ann, you will have one more open item. Other than just asking Trina what her mother told her, what else could you do to find out?"

"Right now I think my best move is to do nothing. Even if they don't rule Sue Ann's death an accident, I don't think that they have enough evidence to bring a charge against me. The chief is not that stupid, but in any event I best just wait. The coroner's report is due in a few days; that ought to settle the matter."

I smiled as I said, "The chief is in a strange situation here; the town doesn't want him, and yet he has (at least in his mind) two open cases. Whether you like him or not, he has been a professional law enforcer for a long time. I really don't think he is going to drop either one of them. No, I believe he is going to try to go out of this town in a blaze of glory. Imagine if he can clear up both matters before he leaves?"

Russ added, "You mean before he is thrown out. With Ruth on his case, he better watch his step. According to Lila, Ruth is no fool, and she could never understand why the town paid him as much as they did. She just plain hates him."

The sun's setting, although a beautiful sight, made long shadows appear that put an ominous look on the water. The wind now felt much colder, so Russ and I abandoned the bench and walked back to the store.

"Russ, where are you staying?"

"Lila and I are going out to dinner. She set that room up for me. Well, you know she is the best source of information I have in this town; she is better than Face Book."

On that note Russ went to his car and drove off, and I went into the store where Ruth and her friend were helping the Commodore close up. I was informed that we were going to dinner.

When we got to the restaurant the chief was there with the investigator who handled the airport incident. Ruth became infuriated. "He's not supposed to be doing that! Does he think we are going to pay him to dig up a mess that could sink this town? What is the matter with him? Doesn't he realize what he is doing?"

Ruth left the room in a fury. The three of us sat down and ordered drinks, for we didn't know what Ruth was up to. In a few minutes, she came back, still infuriated with the chief. "I called the president of the council and told him he better get out here and put an end to the meeting that is going on over there. That chief will think nothing of sinking this town, just to spite us. He will hide behind some veil of doing his civic as well as his sworn duty." The waitress came over to get our order, and Ruth, attracting everyone's attention in the restaurant, yelled out, "How can you eat at a time like this? We're paying someone to bury us! Why doesn't he just leave?"

The chief got up from his table and started to walk over to us but changed his mind and left with the investigator. As they were walking out, the president was walking in. They stopped and looked at each other; angry stares were exchanged, but no words were spoken. Ruth called the president over to our table, and the five of us had a horrible dinner where Ruth re-hashed everything that went on at the town meeting, in addition to planning the agenda for the next meeting. Surprisingly, no one left but instead took an active part in planning the next meeting. Finally, we were done eating and we left. I looked at Ruth and said, "Thank you for an enjoyable evening."

She looked at me and started to say something, hesitated, and finally said, "I promise I'll get better."

When we got back to the store, the Commodore took out his private stock, and we toasted our good fortune for knowing a person like Ruth. The Commodore held up his glass as he proposed a toast. "She may be loud...she may be crude...but she can make a night pass. Did you take notice that no one left? In fact, they not only enjoyed her performance; they encouraged her. I'm going to apologize three times to her tomorrow, just in case I ever do something wrong. I don't want that lady hating me...no way. Good night, my friend." On that note we parted company.

The following morning I decided to go home. I called Russ, but he and Lila were out for the day, so I just left a message and started my ride home. Just as I was about to leave, the coroner came into the store. The Commodore was right on him and under a vow of secrecy, he stated, "She was dead before she hit the floor. When she hit her head, that blow broke her neck; that's what killed her."

That statement made me feel very good, for I didn't want to believe that I could have done something to save her and I didn't. I decided at that point that I didn't push her; she must have tripped over that long nightgown she had on. I felt good about the falling, but I wasn't still too sure I didn't push her. I decided right on the spot that I didn't. In addition, he stated, "I'm going to release the body today. I'll call Trina for her to make arrangements for her burial."

The Commodore said, "You can't go now."

I parked my car and brought my suitcase back inside. I called Russ and told him to forget the previous message; I was still in town and he should call me.

Chapter Fifteen

Trina came to the store with Steven to ask for our help in making the arrangements for her mother's funeral. The Commodore and I agreed to take care of everything. When Sue Ann's husband showed up, the first thing he tried to do was to establish himself as the man in charge. He was all set to make a speech, when Russ walked in the store. He grabbed the doctor by the scuff of his neck and the seat of his pants and threw him out of the store. Russ said, "Excuse me, Trina, but I didn't think you wanted to hear anything he had to say." Trina went over to Russ and kissed him.

The arrangements were made at the local funeral parlor. It was located two miles from the center of The Cove. Her will stated that she wanted to be cremated and to have her ashes thrown in the bay. There was an ordinance against doing that, but no one paid any attention to it. Steve and Trina said they would take care of that. Everyone in town showed up, as well as a large group of lawyers and judges from around the state. One lady who was standing on the side next to me and the Commodore said it best: "More people loved her in death than ever loved her in life." Her friend responded, "That's always the way."

The whole affair went off without a hitch, and afterwards a goodly number of people went to the restaurant for some refreshments after a mass was said in her honor at the same church her daughter got married. At the end of the mass, the Commodore stood in front of the church and said, "Amen."

Russ and Lila were the notable couple throughout the whole affair. As they were walking away from the restaurant, the chief walked up to Russ, and in a loud voice that was obviously calculated so I would hear it said, "Hold on; I want to have a talk with you."

Russ turned and faced him with an outraged look on his face. I quickened my pace so that I was next to Russ before he could do anything. I grabbed his arm and responded, "About what?"

"Do you think I believed that bull about the airport incident being an accident? Now we've just buried another accident. You two men seem to be around whenever there is an accident. I want to clarify these events for my own edification." As he spoke, he put his hand on his gun, and from behind him the president of the council yelled, "You idiot, you do that stuff somewhere else. If you have evidence of any wrong doing, you go get a warrant. If not, leave these men alone."

The chief became annoyed as now a crowd had gathered around, and everyone was chastising the chief for what he was doing. The judge from the county, who'd been assigned to take over Sue Ann's cases, walked over and in an authoritative, bombastic voice said, "He's right. Do you have any such evidence?"

The chief lowered his head and walked away. Russ was still infuriated. As an aside he said, "I'm going to find out when he'll retire, and that is one accident that is going to happen."

I quickly looked around to see if anyone had heard him and said, "Shut up; you don't need this."

Everyone went about his business as winter started to settle in. It came in overnight. One day, it was fifty to sixty degrees; the next morning, it was freezing. When the weather turns cold, The Cove just shuts down. The only place open is the store owned and operated by the Commodore. He would explain, "I'm too stupid to leave. Anyway, where would I go?" One gas station remained open, as well as the bank with its two employees and a minimal staff in the public services department. There was one department/grocery store that braved the cold. It got a delivery once a week. "The town has gone into hibernation" was a much-used phrase.

I said good-bye to the Commodore and was getting ready to leave. He looked so forlorn, standing in the doorway. Just then, the chief pulled up in his official car with the lights and siren going. He got out of the car and walked over to me. "You are under arrest for the murder of Sue Ann. Put your hands behind you." I was handcuffed and put into his car and driven to the station house for processing. I was finger printed, photographed, and put into a cell. The guard as he walked away said, "You will be arraigned tomorrow morning. I'm sorry."

The Commodore brought me my meals and medical supplies. While delivering them he said, "I called Russ. He will be here. When he comes, I would not want to be the chief or his fireball assistant, Mildred."

At nine o'clock, I was arraigned before the judge, which meant that the charges against me were read. When I heard "First Degree Murder", I was stunned. "Do you wish to enter a plea at this time?" the judge asked.

"Not guilty."

The judge replied, "A not-guilty plea has been entered; the trial will be held in two weeks."

The short trial date was a shock to everyone in court. Russ was standing behind me and said, "Get their evidence."

"Are you an attorney, sir?"

Russ just shook his head, "No, I am his investigator."

"Do you wish to have an attorney appointed, as is your right?" As the judge spoke, he looked down from his seat behind the bench as though he were looking at a strange animal. The look on his face was strange, but I couldn't understand it.

"No."

"You have, of course, heard the phrase 'The man who acts as his own attorney has a fool for a client'?"

"And I am positive you have heard it's better to have a fool as a client than a fool as a lawyer." The judge's smile confirmed he had heard the phrase before.

By now the courtroom was packed. The whispers and comments included everything from, "He should be hanged for killing such a nice lady"...to... "Do you know what this trial is going to cost us"...to... "That chief isn't that smart that I want to have him spend my money."

Russ received all the state's evidence, and it was all hearsay and innuendo. The only question for the jury to decide was: "Did I push Sue Ann to her death or did she truly trip?"

A special prosecutor was sent in to try the case. Because I was defending myself, Russ was allowed to confer with me on a more liberal schedule than would normally be allowed. The Commodore supplied me with everything else I needed as I developed my defense. The state had a lot of opportunity evidence; I had the capability that was necessary; the one big thing was motive...they had none.

One day the chief and Mildred came to the store and were being overly nice to the Commodore. While Mildred beguiled him, the chief put a bug by the table where the Commodore usually sat and in his office. They were illegal, but the chief was hoping for a lead as to a motive. When Russ left me for the day and the Commodore told him of his visitors, Russ immediately suspected foul play, and within minutes he had found both bugs. The Commodore went wild, but Russ quieted him down. Russ came back to the jail to inform me and to give me as much detail of the incident as he could. What he left out, the Commodore embellished upon when he gave me his version. It was obvious what the intent was; now all I had to do was use it to my advantage.

"Russ, do nothing; let me think about this. Is the chief still threatening you about the airport thing?"

"Yes, every time he's near me, he drops a little hint like, "Don't think the problem is going to go away; it took me a while, but I got your friend, and I'll get you.""

143

"What about the prosecutor? What do we know about her? Do you think Ruth and Lila will help me? How about the maid of honor?"

"Just tell me what you want them to say, and I'll…"

I waved my hands and pointed to my ears, for I had a feeling we were being listened to. I showed Russ a note I had written, and he nodded his head that he understood. Russ left and quickly prepared a write-up about the prosecutor. He had been working on one as soon as he found out who it was, so he didn't have too much more to do. The following day he brought it to the jail and had lunch with the Commodore and me.

She was a young lady who was very impressed with Sue Ann. On many occasions she had met with Sue Ann and was a great admirer of hers. Russ got a hold of the picture Chad had taken of the funeral, and sure enough she was in them. She graduated at the top of every class she ever took. Based on these facts, it was easy to conclude that she would grasp at anything that would tend to prove me guilty.

On the other hand, her boss was an experienced trial man. He saw the flaws in the state's case. He was pushing for a reduction of the charge so that it would be easier to prove. He called for a meeting between himself, her, and me. It was disastrous, for he was willing to drop the charge to involuntary manslaughter, which amounted to a slap on the wrist, but the prosecutor would not hear of it.

"You're going to give this animal…" as she spoke she pointed to me, "a free walk rather than do the work necessary to convict him? I will not be a part of any such deal. I'll go to the papers with this before I'll agree. I'll do the work, even if I have to do it on my own time. I intend to stay with this case right to the end." With those words, she stomped out of the room.

I quietly got up and left without saying anything. The way I saw it was that I had a hysterical young lady who'd forgotten her professionalism and was out for blood…namely mine. That sort of attitude, I knew, would be dangerous.

By the next day I had written out my plan. I wrote everything down to the last detail and gave it to the Commodore to give to Russ, for I knew they would search Russ when he came and left. I was told that there was a change in policy, and if I didn't like it, I should take it up with the judge. They were shocked when I didn't.

Following my instructions, Russ went to Ruth, Lila, and the maid of honor independently and asked for their support. "I will not lie," Ruth announced. Lila was less vociferous but repeated the same words. Russ quickly responded, "Oh no, I don't want you to lie. I just want you to go to the prosecutor and tell her the way George treated Sue Ann. Just tell the truth. Did he hug her? Did he kiss her? Was he attentive to her daughter?" They agreed.

Next, he went to the gas dock and asked the attendant if he remembered my paying to fill the tank of the boat. The attendant replied, "Sure, I remember. I don't get too many orders like that. I still have the charge."

"Well, you should tell the chief about that."

"I'll go. I liked Sue Ann; she always gave me a tip any time I did anything for her," the attendant responded enthusiastically.

Finally, Russ went to the chief and very coldly asked, "What would it take for you to get off my back about the airport mishap?" The chief was elated. "You know I can't testify against George, but is there anything else I can do?"

"You bet. Give me a motive for the killing so I can use it at the trial. The prosecutor says that is the weakest part of the case."

Russ just laughed. "He was banging her. Why else would he pay for the daughter's wedding and stay over at the house? They must have had a lovers' quarrel. Just ask Ruth and Lila about their impression of George's relationship with Sue Ann. They both saw them together many times…just ask them."

The chief could not wait to go see the prosecutor with the news. As the trial date drew near, the state gave me the rest of the discovery I was entitled to. On the list of witnesses was Ruth, Lila, and the gas dock attendant. Russ had followed my instructions.

Russ met with the maid of honor separately, for he did not want her to be called as a witness. He just wanted her to be in the courtroom at the appropriate time and to follow his instructions. "Now please, I do not want you to lie, understand?" She agreed.

The town's people were in a festive mood, just thinking about their chances of being picked as jurors. The state asked the court to move the trial to another venue for a bigger selection from which to pick a jury. "There are very few permanent residents who live in The Cove. It will be very hard to pick a jury, for everyone knows George and the Commodore and everyone knows that he and the Commodore are great friends."

The judge agreed, and the trial was moved to a town twenty-five miles away. The residents of The Cove were infuriated because, after all, this was their judge who'd been killed, and it happened in their town, and this judge was nothing to them. All to no avail, it delayed the trial one week, but the trial was moved.

The new facilities were much like the old ones, only twenty-five miles away. This meant that the Commodore had to travel further to bring me my supplies and food. 'I don't mind; I love the change of scenery," he mused.

The new venue for the trial displeased many people. The new town didn't want their town associated with a murder trial. The town had an inhabitance of twenty-five thousand people. It was in no way considered a big city, but it was six times the size of The Cove. Russ was quick to give me the statistics of the two towns on a chart. Most of the people worked somewhere else and came home at night and were home on the weekends, I just knew they weren't going to be happy about giving up their time to sit on a jury and listen to a lot of testimony on how one individual killed another.

The jail was attached to the courthouse, so once inside, I would never see the town. The only sighting of it was when I was transported from The Cove. It had a main street, which was the shopping area, civic center, and town hall. The courthouse was next to the town hall with the jail and police headquarters sharing the basement of both buildings. I was the first murderer to occupy the cells. The local police who were to guard me became the town celebrities, according to my jailer. "This is the first time the people of the town even know I exist. People stop me on the street and ask how I am, and you didn't even get here yet." My guard was just beaming when he told me his experiences.

The guards were very apprehensive about the Commodore's bringing me food. He asked them, "What do you think--I baked a file in the cake?" They didn't mind so much after it was explained to them that it didn't cost them anything to feed me; the Commodore bore the full expense. One guard, after inspecting the food, said, "You eat better than I do." Two other guards looked and agreed with him. I ended the meeting with, "May I now eat?"

The guards laughed, but they insisted on cutting everything up before he could give it to me. Russ could still confer with me, but he had to stay on one side of the table and I on the other. My one leg was chained to the chair, which was fastened to the floor. The room, however, was well lit, not like the room in The Cove that only had one light in it, but as Russ laughingly said, "A jail is a jail is a jail."

I was taken on a tour of the courtroom. I had to leave my cell, walk down a corridor for twenty feet, and go up a flight of steps into an anteroom. From the anteroom, I was brought into the courtroom. There was a railing about thirty inches high, separating the judge and council from the spectators' section. The judge's chambers had a door that led from his chambers directly behind his bench, which was two feet higher than the rest of the court. There were two tables in front of the bench about ten feet from it and about fifteen feet apart. The jury box was on my left with the jury assembly room directly behind it. The room was also the deliberation room. There were four windows that let a lot of light into the room. They were up high. There were seats for one hundred spectators. Admittance to the trial was by passes only that had to be obtained from the court clerk every morning before trial. This posed a problem for the maid of honor, who had to be in the courtroom at the right time. The Commodore was put in charge of taking care of it. At first, there was a fear that the whole town of The Cove would come, but surprisingly, only ten or twelve people showed up. When I was told this by the guard, I responded, "I thought I would draw a bigger crowd than that." In total, there were only forty some people in the room during the trial. However, there were four guards ordered to be there to protect everyone from me. They were told not to wear their uniforms for fear of prejudicing the jury against me.

The jury notices were sent out, and the trial was scheduled to start. The first order of business was the jury selection. The first panel consisted of fifty people. Over half of them were absent from the first roll call. The judge became so irate he ordered the police to go and arrest those who did not comply with the notice to be in the court.

"Your honor," I said, "everyone you arrest is going to hold me personally responsible for having to be here."

The judge rocked in his chair and replied, "So what? Aren't you?"

The state attorney added, "Your Honor, that could be grounds for an appeal."

Again the judge said, "So what? I am positive there will be many more reasons for an appeal. That can't guide me. We will recess until one thirty, and at that time we will see how many potential jurors are here.

"All rise," the court clerk yelled, and everyone left. I went back to my cell. Russ showed up in a few minutes, but without the panel list of possible jurors. "The judge would not release the list until he sees how many show up this afternoon." This judge is going to be fun to work with."

As Russ spoke, the guard was called away, or he too had to make phone calls to those people who didn't show up. The message was, "You better come for jury duty, or you will be arrested and subject to a fine. If you want to be excused, you must make the application yourself to the judge...in person...in court."

The afternoon session proved to be more fruitful; everyone who'd been summoned for jury duty was there. One by one they came before the judge and asked to be excused. The excuses ranged from one young lady who looked as though she were going to have a baby right in the court room to one man who kept saying, "What did you say, your honor?" no matter what the judge said. The judge really became annoyed, for the sight in the courtroom was far from comical; it was a pathetic commentary on a citizen's willingness to do his civic duty. The entire afternoon produced only one juror, a woman in her fifties, who was wearing enough make up for two people. Finally, the judge got so upset that he was going to put one woman in jail because she kept saying, "I didn't ask to be here; I don't want to be here, and why would the police arrest him if he was innocent?"

The clerk yelled, "All Rise" as the judge got up and announced, "We will try again tomorrow; call in the next panel." That statement meant Russ would be working all night again to see whom we should accept and whom we should excuse.

The following day was much the same, but with a little more luck, we were now up to seven jurors…seven more to go. The judge wanted a group of fourteen jurors, although only twelve would be deciding the case. The two alternates would not be excused until after the verdict was in. That statement almost got one man put in jail as he yelled out, "You mean I have to sit here and listen to this stuff yet I might not get to decide the case! Are you kidding? What a waste of time."

The judge's face turned bright red as he sat on his throne and held his breath before saying, "Yes." The third day produced the next seven; the jury was now impaneled.

The judge looked at his watch and the calendar before saying, "It is too late to start now. Monday, I have a conference I must attend, so everyone be here Tuesday morning, and hopefully we can start the trial."

I stood up and asked, "Your honor, may I go back to The Cove for the four-day hiatus?" Before I could finish my statement, the judge said most emphatically, "No…but you can have twice the normal visiting hours to confer with your team."

"All rise."

The fourteen people we wound up with were analyzed to be an even array of hard-working people. All fourteen had jobs, which meant they were losing money sitting in here. Four were self-employed, while the others had different types of jobs. One of the self-employed men was known as a loud mouth. Russ was very surprised that he was so quiet during the jury selection.

"George," he said, "you convince him and you've got a winner. I just had to make one call on this guy and found out all about him. Everyone knows him. He runs a small trucking operation out of a depot two miles off the interstate. When he talks in a whisper, they can hear him on the interstate. He works very hard and long hours, keeping his trucks rolling. His wife volunteers for all the civic functions, and what is most important is that they go to church with their two girls every Sunday. He looks like a gorilla, but he has a heart of gold."

I added, "Don't we all?! I'm glad you didn't have to make two calls on him. Who knows what you would have come up with."

There were no professionals on the jury, and nine were women and five were men. Their ages ranged from a twenty-two-year-old single lady to a fifty-eight-year-old single mother. Russ, with the use of his wizardry, found out she was never married. She had two children...both girls...and they were both married. Russ summarized the panel by saying, "Fair--I think it is...impartial ...yes...brain power... sufficient; I'd have to say this is as good as it gets."

Tuesday finally came, and everyone filed into the court. To everyone's surprise, the court wasn't half full. The young lady who was representing the state showed up with two interns, whom she quickly introduced to the court. She looked at me and immediately wanted to know who Russ was. "He is my assistant. Since I am having trouble with my eyes, he does some reading for me and handles the paper work. As the court can see, the state has brought two people to help her; I've only got one." The jury filed in. They no sooner sat down according to their number when the fire alarm went off. The judge, while trying to keep his composure, said, "Now what? Are we ever going to get this trial underway? The jury will please exit through the main doors. Will one of you deputies please show the way? The state's entourage, please follow but do not talk to each other. Deputies, please escort the spectators out. I will follow. In the exodus, I was with Russ and the Commodore as we made our way out of the building. There wasn't a deputy in sight. Russ laughed as he said, "We can just leave if you want?"

The Commodore added, "My car is right over here; we can be out of here very quickly. We can go to Mexico and grow beards and dance with the senoritas or fight the bulls."

Russ added, "All we can do is shoot the breeze, not the bulls." We all laughed as I said, "No, gentlemen, we are not running. I want this over with. Here come the fire engines, but I don't see any smoke." I looked at Russ, who had an impish grin on his face. "I didn't; I swear I didn't," he said.

The side door to the building opened and out walked the judge. The four of us just looked at each other, too stunned to say anything. Russ broke the strange silence by saying, "Does this sort of thing happen a lot?"

The judge just shook his head. He hesitated as a sort of smile came across his face. He said, "Never but a lot of strange things are happening with this trial."

Within a half hour, the building was checked out, and we were allowed to return. The sheriff came over with a mortified look on his face. The judge said in a surly tone, "Don't worry; I have the defendant in custody."

In a sweeping motion of his arm, he opened the door and waved us in as he said, "Right this way, gentlemen." Russ, the Commodore, the sheriff, and finally the judge and I walked back into the courtroom. The sheriff started to say something, but the judge just waved him off: "Good thing this murderer isn't a murderer, or else I could have been murdered." We all laughed and went to our respective positions.

The emergency was over, but it was destined to be the talk of the town for days to come. The town had a voluntary fire department, and two of the volunteers were on the jury. The deputy who was with the jury refused to let them respond. A brief scuffle ensued, but cooler heads prevailed, and the two men remained with the group. It was during the brief altercation that everyone forgot about me, and that is how I wound up with my little group. The sheriff could be heard yelling at them: "No matter what happens, someone always has to stay with the defendant. What would we have done if he'd escaped? What you guys did was stupid and reflects on me, not you two." Everyone in the courtroom could hear the sheriff admonish his deputies for the doors had not been fully closed.

Everyone filed back into the courtroom and settled down. The courtroom still wasn't filled as expected, so there was no problem with everyone's finding a seat. The Commodore made the maid of honor sit in the first row on the side of the state. He sat behind Russ and me.

There was a lot of paper shuffling by the state, but she finally settled down. The judge looked around the courtroom, fixed some papers on his desk, and finally leaned back in his chair.

He looked at the state as he asked, "Ready for the prosecution?"

"Yes," she responded.

He looked at me as he asked, "Ready for the defense?"

"Yes," I responded.

He looked at the state as he said, "Opening statement, please."

The trial at long last was under way.

The last person to enter the courtroom was the chief of police from The Cove. He was listed as a witness, so I didn't understand why he was sitting in the back of the courtroom. No one paid him any mind, which just didn't sit right with me. The chief had an ego that wouldn't allow him to take a back seat like that. I felt something was wrong but decided that I best concentrate on the trial. I'd have to worry about him later; after all, I was on trial for my life. As far as I was concerned, I was ready. Russ had all the key players in place, and even the judge didn't think I was a murderer. What more could I ask for? I sat back in my chair and waited with bated breath for the lady from the state to give her opening statement. By her words, the format of the trial would be defined.

Chapter Sixteen

The state attorney got up from her seat at the council table, smoothed out her blue dress as she walked to the center of the room, and faced the jury. She reminded me of an actress' walking out on stage, about to deliver some heart rendering soliloquy in a drama. With her all-blue outfit on, she reminded me of Sue Ann's style of dressing. As I looked, even her stockings were blue, or at least had a blue tinge to them. Her shoes looked as though they were dyed to match her dress.

She didn't have any rings on, which I considered strange given the current fashion trend. There was a bracelet that looked like she'd seen it and put it on, for it didn't go with anything. In fact, from what I could see, it was the only non-blue item on her. She started to become very aware of Russ and my watching her rather than listening to her. We both were sitting at our table with our hands folded in front of us, watching her every move. She walked from one side of the room to the other, nervously tugging at her dress, fixing her hair, and shifting her weight from one foot to the other. Finally, she started repeating herself, and the judge looked at me, but I refused to say anything. The judge interrupted her by saying, "I think you have covered that area in great detail already; please move on."

Like a petulant child, she spun around on one foot and said, "Thank you for your attention," and sat down.

"Do you wish to give an opening statement now?" As he spoke, he was tapping the gavel. I looked at Russ and stood up as I said, "No," and sat down.

"We will have the first witness."

The first person to be called was the coroner. He testified how Sue Ann died. Again the state started to ask the same type of questions over and over again, changing them ever so slightly. She introduced picture after picture of the corpse…both in the house with blood all over it and in the morgue. She would first introduce the picture for identification, have the coroner identify what it was, and afterwards would move it into evidence. The clerk would put a number on it, and she would continue. After the twenty-first picture was offered, the judge called us to his bench. "I don't want to curtail your case, but don't you think we have enough pictures?"

She got annoyed and pleaded, "Okay, just one more."

The judge looked at me, but I said nothing. "Do you intend to say anything during this trial?"

"I will as soon as she introduces any evidence linking me to what happened."

We went back to our tables, and she showed the coroner one more picture, and when the procedure was completed, she said, "I have no more questions of this witness" and sat down.

Russ had all the pictures before him in numerical order. I picked them up as I said, "Sir, you have identified all these pictures…twenty-two in all. Which one of them shows how Sue Ann, the person I am accused of murdering, was murdered?"

He thought for a while before responding, "None."

"Why are they here?"

"The state told me to bring them."

"Which one of these pictures shows how I killed her, the crime I am being accused of?"

Again he pondered the question before answering, "None."

Did Sue Ann bleed to death? I mean, there is a lot of blood in these pictures?"

"No."

"Do you know how she died using these pictures?"

"No."

"Your honor, I ask that these pictures be stricken from the record, for all though they are very descriptive, they don't prove any element of the crime of murder. They are grotesque and very prejudicial but cannot be used to prove murder; they only prove Sue Ann is dead, a fact I have already agreed to."

The prosecutor jumped up, but before she could say anything, the judge asked, "What was the cause of death? Do you know?"

"Yes, sir, she tripped over the coffee table and hit her head on the andiron and broke her neck; she died instantly."

I interrupted the judge by asking, "Which one of the pictures shows that?"

"None."

There was a silence in the room that just got louder the longer it lasted. The judge was annoyed at me for interrupting him but continued his questioning. "Do you have a picture of the andiron on which she hit her head?"

"No…I was told not to bring them."

The state didn't know what to say. The stillness got louder.

"I will hear the state on this matter. First of all, were these pictures turned over to the defendant as part of the discovery in this case?"

The state's silence answered the question.

"I hereby rule that these pictures are inadmissible."

He looked at the state as he asked, "Any other questions of this witness?"

"You say the deceased tripped over the coffee table. Could she have been pushed?"

"The coroner looked bewildered and after some reflection responded, "I guess so. I don't know; I wasn't there."

"I have no more questions."

"Was there any proof that I was anywhere near the body. By that I mean, were my footprints in the blood?"

"No."

"Was any blood found on me?"

"No."

"I have no other questions."

The next witness the state called was Tisha. After she was sworn in, the state asked her how she found the body and what she did.

"I called the police, and I was told not to touch anything, so I went outside and sat on the front steps until the police came. They asked me a few questions, and I was sent home."

The state walked away as she said, "Your witness."

I got up and waited for Tisha to settle down, as she was obviously nervous. "Do you want a drink of water?"

She just shook her head, "No."

"Why did you go to the house that day?"

"I went there to clean. I clean her house; that's what I do."

"Were you scheduled to be there that day?"

"Well, I don't have a regular day or time. I use her house as a fill in when I am not busy."

"I've taken the liberty of drawing a diagram of the house. Would you please review it to see if it is accurate?" As I spoke, Russ set up an easel and put the sketch on it. He positioned it so that Tisha and the jury could see it.

She looked at it and said, "Yes, it looks like that."

"Would you please use this pointer and show where you entered and what you did when you went inside?"

Tisha got up and walked to the sketch as Russ handed her the pointer.

She hesitated for a moment and pointed to the front door as she said, "I went in the front door and went into the front hall closet and took out the supplies I keep there and then on to the kitchen to start there." As she spoke, she traced her movements with the pointer. "I started to clean the kitchen." She hesitated, and her face turned red as she was blushing and then she whispered something.

"I'm sorry, but I didn't hear you," the judge said.

"I had to go to the bathroom."

There were a few snickers from the audience, so the judge

just tapped his gavel and silence reigned again.

I asked, "Will you please show where you went in the house with the use of this pointer?"

I handed her the pointer, and she complied, tracing her path from the kitchen through the house towards the bathroom, located by the front door, and back towards the kitchen.

She was about to sit down when I said, "Please, just a few minutes more. Was Sue Ann a neat person as compared to your other clients?"

The state stood up, but before she could say anything, Tisha responded. "Oh yes, she was my cleanest customer. I was surprised to see the dirty dishes on the counter when I came in."

"From the front door, you can see the entire interior of the house?"

"Yes."

"Well, when did you call the police? Didn't you see all the blood as soon as you came in?"

Tisha was so nervous she just whispered, "No."

"No, wait," I added. I took an outline of a body and placed it on the diagram. I stepped back as I took the pointer from Tisha and had her stand next to me as I rehashed her testimony in a rapid-fire manner. "You came in the door...went to the closet... to the kitchen...to the bathroom...and back to the kitchen...yet you didn't see the bloody mess in a house which is usually the cleanest one you clean?"

"No...I...didn't."

"No further questions."

The state was on her feet yelling, "I object." She turned and faced me as she yelled, "What are you implying?"

"The pictures you are showing are of a staged setting; it was not taken as the scene existed but after it was tampered with."

The judge was hitting the bench with the gavel as he was saying, "All comments will be directed to the bench."

The state without hesitating said, "Your honor, the

defendant is trying to imply that the state photographer staged these pictures." As she spoke, she was waving one of the photos. "He is a trained professional." She had worked herself into such a frenzy that she had to stop talking and sit down.

The judge looked at me while the state was ranting; I sat down and quietly folded my hands before me and waited for her to be still. The judge was still looking at me as I stood up and said, "This really is summation, but since the state opened the topic, I should be allowed to respond. Rarely, in fact this is my first time, that there is a professional person who is well aware of the habits of a victim. She is trained to spot dirt and other things out of the ordinary when she walks into a home. She did not see the scene as it is depicted in the pictures we have been shown. The victim died instantly, which meant her heart was not pumping out all the blood as shone in these pictures."

The state was on her feet yelling again, "We don't know that…"

The judge hit the gavel again. "You can argue those points in summation. Are there any other questions of this witness?"

The judge waited for a few minutes. The state stood up as though she was going to re-examine Tisha again, but one of her assistants tugged at her dress, and she sat down and just shook her head, "No."

The judge said, "The witness is excused; we will adjourn until tomorrow at ten."

"All rise." Day one of the trial was over.

While the state was giving its opening, Russ had a recording made of it. That night when we had our meeting, he brought the text of it with him. He had the text condensed so it just contained what the state said it was going to prove. The testimony of the coroner proved nothing except that Sue Ann was dead. Cause of death…broken neck. The next item would be opportunity.

"You know, George, you conceded Sue Ann is dead. You

agreed you were with her. Where is she going to go today? She doesn't have anyone who saw you do it. All she has is a witness who saw you leaving the house. I showed her picture around, and she is a solid citizen. I don't think you should question her at all."

"Let's see what she says on the stand. If she saw me, the only thing we can get from her is whether or not she heard me say goodbye when I left."

The Commodore is positive that she came to the store when the two of you were having drinks. Do you want to put the Commodore on the stand?"

I thought for a moment before I said, "I don't think so. The Commodore doesn't know when to keep quiet. Let's see how far we get tomorrow; so far, I have witnesses saying "no" to everything I ask. That's a good thing."

We finished our meeting, and Russ left.

"All rise." The second day of the trial was beginning.

After everyone settled down, the judge looked at the state as he said, "Your next witness."

The state called the neighbor who was walking by the house while I was leaving. The neighbor testified to that fact and the state announced, "I'm through with this witness."

The judge looked at me, and as I started to get up, the Commodore was tugging at my jacket. "One minute please, your honor." I turned and walked to the Commodore, who very excitedly said, "I am positive she was in the store that night. She saw you with me drinking."

I left the Commodore, and I approached the witness, who was nervously squirming around in the witness box. I stopped and went back to the center of the room. "When you saw me leaving, did you hear me say anything?"

There was a long pause before she answered. She kept looking at the state attorney and back at me. Finally I said to the state, "Will you please tell her to answer?" I looked at the judge who was about to say something, and I said to him, "Will you please instruct the witness to answer?"

Before anyone said anything, the witness said in a loud voice, "Yes."

"What did I say?"

"Good bye."

"Did you see any blood on me?"

"Well, no, it was dark, and I wasn't that close to you."

"What was I wearing? Did you hear anyone screaming?"

"No, I was at the far end of the property...I..."

"Did you actually see me?"

"I heard you...yes, I heard you."

Now wait, did you see me or did you just hear me or did you hear someone else who sounds like me?"

The state saw what I was doing and rose as she said, "I..."

I interrupted as I said, "Okay."

"Did you see me later on that night?"

The judge banged the gavel. "If there is an objection, you will give the state an opportunity to finish its objection and the court the opportunity to rule on the objection before you continue. I'll run the trial, not you."

He looked at the state, but before he could say anything, the state said, "I withdraw my objection." The judge, by his facial expression, was getting very annoyed. He looked at me again, "Continue."

I repeated the question, "Did you see me later on that night?"

"Yes."

"Where?"

"In the store. You were having a drink with the Commodore."

"Did you see any blood on me there?"

"No."

"Did I look upset or nervous?"

"No."

The state stood up, but before she could speak, I turned my back on her and walked to my seat as I said, "This witness is excused."

The judge really got upset as he said, "I am the only one who can excuse witnesses, not you. You're excused, Miss."

By the time he got done with his little temper tantrum, I was seated at my table with my hands folded before me.

The judge said, "I will see council in my chambers. We will recess now until two o'clock."

The judge rose as the clerk said, "All rise."

I waited until the jury left before I went in to see the judge. The deputy that was assigned to watch me followed me, as did the courtroom guard and the state attorney. Once inside, I sat down in a chair furthest from the judge. He took off his robe and turned to face us as he said, "I am getting the impression that you are trying to run this trial instead of me." I said nothing but continued to sit and stare at him. He looked at me and continued, "I will do all the rulings in this case."

I did not respond at all. The state attorney was confused by what was going on. She was still standing but looked very nervous.

"How many witnesses do you intend to call?"

"May I ask what they will be testifying to? So far she has not produced one witness that ties me to this crime."

The judge really got mad as he said, "The jury and I will be the judge of that, not you."

I did not respond. There was a strange sort of silence in the room as it was obvious to me that no one knew what to say. The judge was a young man who'd been on the bench for three years. I felt like telling him that I had underwear older than he but thought better of it. I was rapidly losing whatever respect I should have had for the judge, for it seemed to me he wanted to be in charge but didn't know how. I just smiled inwardly as I waited for him to say or do something. Finally he said, "I'll see you at two."

Everyone left. My deputy and I went back to my cell, where the Commodore and Russ were waiting to have lunch. My deputy just looked at what the Commodore had made and said, "I better go eat my lousy sandwich."

"Join us," Russ said.

"I can't; the boss will yell," he said as he walked over to his table.

"Well, gentlemen, what do you think she has in store for me next?"

Russ smiled as he said, "She's going to call Ruth and Lila to testify about all the affection you showered on Sue Ann. She wants to show that you two were lovers and that in a fit of rage, you pushed her down and that is how she died. You went to the house that night to kill her. That gives her a motive and opportunity and, because you're so big and strong, capability. She will argue that since you're an accomplished author and lawyer, you knew exactly how to hide your crime, and after your performance today, she will add that you know how to confuse and intimidate witnesses. That's her case. She knows she is weak in the physical evidence area, but you look like a gorilla, so she just may be able to sway the jury. But look at the bright side; you're ninety percent dead now. I don't think they will fry you; it would cost too much." The last phrase had the Commodore and him in tears because they were laughing so hard. I just smiled.

"Face it, you will have to take the stand. I have the maid of honor all set and primed," the Commodore added.

"You don't think the judge will throw the case out?"

"How does that work?" the Commodore asked. "I've heard of it but never understood it."

I looked at him and could see he wasn't kidding. "At the end of the state's case, I make a motion for a direct verdict; the judge reviews the evidence, giving all the full weight of it to the state, and if he doesn't think the state proved its case beyond a reasonable doubt, he can dismiss the case."

Russ waited until I finished before he immediately added, "No way! That judge isn't going out on a limb for you. He would gladly throw the switch if they decided to fry you. No, you better take the stand; then at least you can deny everything. It's better than what you've got. Make the motion to dismiss, and when he denies it, take the stand. Face it-- you'll be great, or better yet confess; they'll pay for your medical needs and they will put you in one of those classy prisons. You'll have it made; the Commodore and I will visit you. I'll ask Steve and Trina and maybe even Tisha will show up. Add in Ruth and Lila, and what else is there? WOW, ain't life in prison great?"

Russ, we have a little time before we have to go back. Go see if you can find the chief and find out why our chief is here. He wasn't on her witness list. I wonder if she is going to pull a surprise witness trick; you can never tell."

The Commodore with a surprised look on his face said, "She won't do something like that; you two guys are nuts,"

Russ got up and left. He was gone for a few minutes when the deputy said, "Let's go," and the three of us made our way back to the courtroom.

As we walked in, I looked around, but I did not see Russ or the chief. I was sorry I'd sent him, for he was a great comfort to me when he was at the council table with me.

The state's attorney walked in with her entourage. Today was a gray day from the little ribbon in her hair to her gray low-heeled shoes. She told everyone where to sit at the council table and started taking out her papers. In the midst of all this activity, we heard: "All rise," and the two o'clock session was underway.

The state called Ruth to the stand as their first witness. Her testimony went exactly as Russ had predicted. The last question by the state was, "Because of the way he showed affection for Sue Ann, did you think that they were lovers?" Because of the way that the question was asked and the speed in which it was answered, I knew it had been well rehearsed.

"Definitely," Ruth quickly responded.

With a sheepish grin on her face, she said, "Your witness."

I got right up and asked, "Will you please define what the word "lover" means to you?"

The judge interrupted, "The jury will disregard the last question and answer by the state and the question by the defendant; now move on."

I walked back to the council table to get my notes on Ruth's testimony as the Commodore leaned over the railing and asked Russ, "How can they disregard?"

Russ replied, "They can't" and waved the Commodore back to his seat.

I was annoyed at the judge, but I faced Lila and continued questioning her with, "Did you ever see Sue Ann and me together, other than in a crowded room with your being present?"

"No."

"I have no further questions." I sat down and waited for the state to call its next witness.

Russ came to the table and handed me a note; the state wanted to call the gas dock attendant to testify about your paying the bill for Steve's boat, you know as a present to Sue Ann's daughter, but the attendant has disappeared and can't be found and they can't find the bill. Steve and Trina are off on a charter, and no one knows where. Forget them and the chief; he's mad because he wasn't even asked to sit at their table.

I put the note into my pocket as I heard the state say:

"The state calls Lila Henderson." The state asked the same type of questions as she had asked Ruth. She was obviously leading the jury to the same conclusion; only this time both the judge and I interrupted before she got to it.

The judge said, "You are not going to ask the witness for the same conclusion as you did before that I ruled out are you?" I had stood up; but after hearing what he said; I sat back down.

The state hesitated and started to say something but stopped. She did this twice and finally said, "Your witness."

I looked at Lila from my seat and asked, "Did you ever see Sue Ann and me together except in a crowded room with your being present?"

"No, we were always all together."

"No other questions."

The judge leaned over and said, "You are excused; please be careful getting out of the jury box."

Russ leaned over to me and whispered, "That's funny; he never said that before; he must like her." I did not respond.

"Does the state have any other witnesses?"

A quick conference was held at the state's table. From the rear of the room, the sheriff was beckoned to, and he came up and joined the conference. The judge waited, but after a few minutes, he became impatient and tapped the gavel. Finally the state said, "The state rests."

He looked down at me and held his hand up, which I interpreted as he wanted me to wait. He turned to the jury, "The jury is excused; we will reconvene at ten o'clock tomorrow morning, when I hope we will be able to finish this trial. Please do not discuss this matter with anyone. Thank you for your patience. The jury can leave now until tomorrow at ten. Bailiff, please escort the jury out."

The jury stood up and was escorted out of the courtroom. The judge turned to me, "Do you have a motion?"

"Yes, your honor. It is the state's obligation to first prove that a crime has been committed; that they haven't done. They haven't offered any proof that Sue Ann's death was anything but an accident. All the pictures they showed displayed nothing but a messy house, and even that is in question. There is proof through the testimony of the house cleaning lady that brings the authenticity of the scene in to question. The only other proof of a motive to commit a crime is the testimony of two other citizens of The Cove. Their contention was that I showed affection for the victim; any affection I showed was in a crowded room with the witnesses present. All of this evidence taken together doesn't come near to proving a crime or that I did it. I move that the case be dismissed and I be allowed to go home. Thank you."

The state got up and after shuffling her papers about said, "All this is true, but this is what a jury is supposed to do--find the truth. The jury has to take into consideration the circumstances under which these events occurred. We have shown a string of events that reasonable people could agree that, in fact, the crime was committed and that he committed it. We can only prove a case with the facts we have, and if those facts lead us to the conclusion that a crime was committed, we must bring those facts to the attention of the jury. We are asking the jury to decide if the defendant, with malice aforethought, did in fact push the victim to her death, rather than her falling. We have shown opportunity, capability, and motive: a scorned, aged lover. Thank you.

"I will take these arguments under advisement. Please be here at nine-thirty tomorrow and be prepared to give your summations. I will give you my decision on your motion at that time."

"All rise."

That night at dinner, I sat down with my two assistants and wrote out what the prosecutor was going to say. When we were done, we found me guilty.

Russ stated the situation best when he said, "It's purely a circumstantial case, but circumstances can kill you, too. It will be reversed, for it is too thin, as the evidence could find anyone guilty. In fact, the only witness who puts you near the scene is the neighbor who didn't see you; she only heard you."

"I agree, but the question still is: how do I convince the jury I didn't push her? That judge should have dismissed the case; the only reason he didn't is that he wants me to take the stand. He is going to reserve decision on the motion to dismiss and see what kind of defense I offer. He can grant my motion at any time; he's just trying to be cute and aggravate me."

The Commodore, who had been quiet until then, said, "Well, my friend, if he is trying to upset you, I would have to say he is doing a fine job, for he has you upset. I think you better stop being cute and take the stand and deny the charges."

"But what can I deny? I was at her house. I left, and as I left, I said 'goodbye.' She will ask me about the kissing; she'll ask me about the gas bill, and I will be saying 'yes' to everything, so how do I turn the tide?"

Russ interrupted with, "I'm positive you will think of something."

On that note we quit and they left, and I went to sleep, not too restfully, but I tried.

The next morning at the 9:30 "All rise," the public was not allowed in; only the attorneys were present. The judge wasted no time in proving me right when with no fanfare, he said, "I have considered the oral arguments offered, and I have reviewed my notes, and although the defendant has offered sound and compelling arguments, I am going to reserve my decision on the motion and allow the case to go to the jury. Bailiff, let the spectators in."

The Commodore took the maid of honor by the hand and put her in the front row behind the state. Afterwards, he came and sat by Russ and me. "There is a bigger than usual crowd in court today." Russ commented, "They can always smell blood."

The judge turned to the jury and said, "The state has rested its case; the defendant has no obligation to put forth a defense;

and you cannot infer anything from the fact that he presents no witnesses or that he says nothing in his own defense. He may choose to testify or he doesn't have to; the decision is entirely his, and ..." He stopped talking at this point and turned his attention to me.

I looked at Russ, "I think that after that speech, I better say something."

"This judge is a son-of-a-bitch; watch out!" After Russ spoke, he made the sign of the cross and sat back in his chair and said, "Dear Lord, make us worthy for what we are about to hear."

I stood up. "After that introduction I will take the stand as my own witness."

I walked up to the witness stand and sat down. I had to move the chair around, but finally I was comfortable.

The state was busy shuffling her papers about and getting notes from her assistants. She straightened her green dress and approached the witness stand. She asked me a few questions about my age, occupation, and when I'd first come to The Cove. "What made you come to The Cove...was it to see Sue Ann?"

"Yes."

Were you communicating with each other?"

"What do you mean by communicating? I don't know what you mean."

"Well, did you write back and forth, you know, letters or e-mails?"

"Yes."

"How many and what were they?"

"Two e-mails."

Based on two emails, you came to The Cove to see her?"

"Yes."

"Where did you stay?"

"Lila has a spare set of rooms; I stayed there."

"Did you ever stay at Sue Ann's house?"

"Yes."

"How many nights?"

"Three or four, I don't remember."

"Did you go to dinner?"

"Yes."

"How many times?"

"Three or four."

"On every occasion when you saw her in public, did you kiss her?"

I hesitated for a moment as I thought about all our meetings before I answered, "No."

"Most of the time, did you?"

"Do what?'

She yelled, "Kiss her. You know perfectly well what I mean."

"I am under oath to tell the truth; I'm not here to try to figure out what you mean or don't mean…"

The judge hit the gavel. "The witness will not argue with council, and council will ask direct questions that do not have any ambiguity in them."

The state was visibly shaken by the judge's comment. She walked back to her table and, when she'd composed herself, faced me and said in a conversational tone, "On most occasions…I mean, more than half the time that you were with her, did you kiss her?"

"Yes."

Russ tuned to the Commodore and said, "He's got her."

"What do you mean?" the Commodore replied.

"You'll see. Get the maid of honor ready. Here we go…he's leading her right down the primrose path."

The state had a pile of slips in her hand that she kept referring to. It was obvious to me that they contained questions that she would be asking in a rapid-fire manner. I took a deep breath and got ready for the onslaught. I was right.

"Do you know Steve?"

She fired the question at me as though she were firing a gun. I responded in the same manner, "Yes."

"Do you know Trina, his wife?"

"Yes."

"Did you purchase a large amount of fuel for his boat?"

"Yes."

The state turned and faced her table, for she felt she had made a victory by getting that information in since they couldn't find the purchase slip, the attendant, Steve, or Trina. The people at her table gave her a thumbs up.

Russ again turned to the Commodore as he said, "He's got her...he's got her."

"Did you pay for part of the wedding because of Sue Ann?'

"Yes."

"Did you walk Trina down the aisle for her wedding because of Sue Ann?"

"Yes."

"Were you at Sue Ann's house the night she died?"

"Yes."

"Were you Sue Ann's lover?"

As she asked each question, she kept raising her voice, both in pitch and volume. Her last question was at the highest and loudest of them all. As she asked the question, she was waving her finger at me, so it was a perfect setting for my answer. While she was building up the tension for the finality of her last question, I saw Russ tap the Commodore, who looked over at the maid of honor, and when I felt all was ready, I said, "Are you nuts? Sue Ann was my daughter and Trina is my granddaughter."

The maid of honor stood up and said, "I heard her thank you. I wondered why she called you "Grand dad.""

Immediately I added, "You heard that?" I turned to the judge and said, "I will have another witness."

Dear Dad

The judge sat dumbfounded as a cold, silent chill fell on the courtroom. The air became so thick that it became hard to breathe. The state attorney returned to her table and sat down; she looked as though someone had just hit her. Silence was supreme.

The judge tapped the gavel a few times. There was no need for it, since the dead silence was still there. It was like having another person in the room.

Finally, he said in a whisper that could just about be heard, "The bailiff will remove the jury from the courtroom."

Everyone looked around, for no one knew what to say. The jurors all stood up and walked out of the room. On the way out, everyone could hear the vociferous juror complaining. His words were not distinguishable, but his voice had a certain resonance that filled the courtroom. The judge looked at the two of us and finally at the maid of honor as he asked, "Why did you yell out like that and why did you sit where you were sitting?"

The Commodore stood up and said, "Your honor, I did that. She told me she had heard the defendant's granddaughter call him granddad or pa, and I told her she should tell the state. Did I do something wrong?"

The judge never answered him. The maid of honor added, "When I came to court, the session was starting, and the attorney for the state was very busy with all her papers, so I didn't know what to do, but after I heard what you said and the defendant's saying that Sue Ann was his daughter...well, I just thought I should say something. I'm sorry if I did something wrong...I didn't mean to."

The judge never responded to her question either. He sat for what seemed like a long time but finally said, "I reserved decision on the defendant's motion; I will now rule on it; the motion is granted."

Without saying a word, I got up and walked over to the

council table. By the time I got there, Russ and the Commodore had picked up our papers, and we went to the back of the room, where the maid of honor was waiting; the four of us left.

We drove back to The Cove in silence. I was glad it was over, and I remembered the priest who'd told me that one day I would have to admit Sue Ann was my daughter; he was right, but I don't think he would have guessed under what circumstances I would be forced to do it.

We got to the store, and Ruth and Lila were waiting along with the chief. The chief had been fired and still had not found a new job. He sat slumped in a chair on the far side of the room, trying not to be too obvious. The Commodore went and got him and had him join our celebration. Once we were all assembled, Russ took over. One thing that Russ does better than anybody else I know is to throw a party at my expense.

Ruth was the first to come over, and she was about to kiss me when Russ said, "Don't do that. If anything happens to you, what is he going to use as a defense?"

"George," she said in an apologetic tone, "what could I do? The chief told them about me, and I had to tell the truth about what I saw. I hope you're not too mad."

Lila continued right after her. "The chief went to the state, and that lady prosecutor just hounded me until I agreed to testify. I hope…"

The chief interrupted her as he pointed at Russ, "You set this up."

It was now my turn to put things to rest. "One thing I learned as an attorney was to recognize when a case is over. It's over; we all did what we had to do, and now it's over, so let's sing songs or something. Here's a toast…"

Russ continued with, "To the chief and his new career. We all wish you well."

The waitress was bringing over finger type food that Russ had ordered and told the chief how to make, and the man from the liquor store brought over chilled bottles of champagne. The rest of the time was spent in idle chatter until the food was gone and the champagne was gone. I left to go to the bed provided for me by the Commodore. After being in jail, it felt very comfortable.

It was late in the day when I finally got up. Even though it was past the early-bird special time, the Commodore made me a special case. As I was about to enjoy a second cup of coffee, from outside of the store I heard my name. "George, is that you?"

I remembered the voice; it was the loud juror. He came walking into the store with a swagger that I would generally attribute to a sailor. "May I talk to you?" The Commodore heard him too, so he came over.

"My name is Peter. My mother was religious. I was on the jury, and today one of my trucks broke down in this area and, well, I wanted to talk to you anyway." When this man talked, the chandelier overhead rattled. I had no trouble hearing him, nor did anyone else in the place. It's been normally a quiet day, he was providing the entertainment that would make it into a notable day.

"I wanted to know what happened. One of the other jurors whose daughter is a legal secretary told me that the judge threw the case out. Can he do that? I don't understand how the case was started in the first place. Did he throw it out? I mean, he had me sit there and lose money, and I didn't even get to decide anything! I didn't think you were guilty of anything. I didn't think that girl with her tight dresses proved anything. I want to write a letter to whomever and complain about that bitch's wasting my money. I…

"Wait, "I shouted, "lower your voice and don't curse, and I'll answer all your questions." The Commodore by now was seated at our table.

After he quieted down and said he did not want anything to

eat or drink, I explained, "The judge heard the case and decided that there was not enough evidence."

"It took him that long? What I want to know is how I can write a letter, complaining about the state. Other than trying to put on a fashion show, what the hell was she doing…and on my dime…just tell me whom do I write to?"

"You do that, and that lady's career is going to take…"

"Good! She didn't care about me, and that judge came in to see us and started to give us a talk that we were a necessary part of the system. Did they teach him that in judge school? I was told that if I want to write a letter, I should write it to the chief justice of the courts. Is that true?"

"Well, that should do something, but why don't you cool down for a day or two. You say our system is bad, but can you think of a better one?"

Peter stood up, shifted his weight about, and said, "Thank you." He left as abruptly as he'd come.

The Commodore commented, "When he got up, I didn't know whether he was going to hit you or what; he didn't even say good bye to me."

I stayed the night, but the next morning I was packed and ready to go. I thought the Commodore was going to cry when I shook his hand goodbye.

"Please don't forget me; your room is always ready for you…Come visit me whenever you want. Here's our special picnic basket treat for your trip home." As he spoke, he handed me a little picnic basket with a light lunch in it. He stayed in the doorway until I was out of sight. I felt a strange pang of loneliness as I pulled away. I also felt very stupid for feeling that way. I thought to myself, "It was a job, and the job is over." It is always easy to say something like that, but it is hard to believe it.

When I got home, I called to see where Russ was (he had gone home also). His secretary replied, "He's on the grounds;

hold on and I'll page him if you want?"

"No; please; I just wanted to make sure he made it home okay. Tell him to call me next week for lunch."

My next order of business was my children. What to tell them was going round and round in my mind. I came to the conclusion I would just tell them...nothing; it was a sad set of circumstances, and I would appreciate it if it were not mentioned again. After we met and had dinner together, I knew they didn't like my explanation, but they were caring enough not to press the issue. I heard them talking in the other room, and they agreed that, "When he's ready to tell us, he will." That ended the topic, or so I thought.

The following week Russ called me, and we had dinner at his club. There was a dance club affair that night, and all of us (including me) were enjoying ourselves, when out of the blue Russ said, "You really aren't naive enough to think this is just going to die. Remember when you would get drunk, you always told the story of a pebble falling in the water; you would say in a very pompous tone: 'The ripples go everywhere, even in places you never thought they would.' I can't wait to hear where these ripples hit." As soon as he said the words, he was off dancing around the place, playing the host with the most.

I spent two days with him, and then I decided to take a drive through the New Hampshire Mountains before I headed home. For some reason I didn't want to return; I felt stupid for feeling that way. With a resolute voice, I said out loud, "If something is going to hit the fan, I'm better off being there than here in these stupid mountains." Toward home I went, but all the way home, I kept telling myself: "It's over...get on with your life." For the next week, I was proud of myself for not thinking about the trial, Joann, or Sue Ann.

The call came from the Commodore. "George, the lady from the state has been hanging around town, shooting off her mouth about the fraud you think you pulled on the state. She hounded the chief so much that he doesn't even come out of his house. All he does is smoke one cigarette after another and drink scotch all the time. I don't even recognize him when I bring him his food supply. I have never seen a man come apart as fast as he has; for the life of me, I don't know why he is acting like he is. Why don't you come down and talk to him. Come on, you can't be that busy."

I felt like the fly being invited into the web of a ferocious spider. In the old days, I would enjoy the challenge, but I just wasn't feeling as adventurous as I did before.

The Commodore continued, "Remember Peter...you know the loud mouth...he didn't write a letter to the chief justice; he went to see him. He caused such a scene that he was put in jail. Finally, he was given an audience with the almighty chief justice, and when he was done, the matter was turned over to an investigation team, who got all over the attorney who had handled the matter and the judge who heard the case. Of course, you understand that everything I am telling you I am getting in bits and pieces from everyone. It's the hottest topic down here. The prosecutor even accused Ruth of exaggerating her testimony. Ruth got so mad that she smacked her. Our new chief of police...Mildred...Oh yes, after they fired the chief, they hired Mildred as the temporary acting chief until a replacement can be found. She quieted everything down. Come on down."

After listening to the Commodore's ranting, I finally said, "I'll be down in two days. Set up a meeting with Lila, Ruth, and the chief; not Mildred, but the old chief." I hung up the phone and realized that I didn't even know his name, since I and everyone else around him always called him "Chief."

Two days later, I told everyone I was going to visit my friend the Commodore. Russ called, "If you need me, just call."

I didn't know exactly what I was going to do or if I should do anything at all. I just knew I was tired of the whole mess and I just wanted it to go away...and go away it would...of that I was sure. I pulled into town and went directly to see the Commodore. He greeted me with open arms and even carried my bag to my room; resting after my drive, I sat in the store directly across the room from the prosecutor. Up to now I didn't even want to know her name, but now things were different. When she walked over to me, the first thing I said was, "What's your name?"

She responded, "Hilda. Do you want me to sit down? I want to get…"

"Hilda, shut up and get away from me, and don't ever come by me again…ever."

She fell back as though I had hit her. She was still in a state of shock as she turned around and walked back across the room, picked up her bag, and walked out of the store. The waitress ran after her, saying, "Miss, your bill." Hilda stopped and gave the girl some money, turned, and kept walking.

The Commodore, who was watching everything, asked, "Is that what is meant when they say, 'He threw down his gauntlet'?" "Yes, I replied."

"What about Ruth, Lila and the chief? Can we get the three of them together for a meeting? I've got to know what she said to them and have all of them sign affidavits to get a restraining order on dear Hilda."

The Commodore shook his head, "No, it's not that she says anything to them; instead, she went to their hair dresser and started asking questions about if they ever discussed your trial with her; the hair dresser didn't know anything about your trial. When the hairdresser said she knew nothing about it, dear Hilda told everyone in the shop that Lila and Ruth testified and that they said…well, you know she embarrassed them by the stories she said; she has become a one-person rumor mill. Ruth and Lila can't go anywhere without everyone's pointing a finger at them. They don't even like to come to town. As I told you, the chief doesn't even come out of his house anymore."

"What do we know about Hilda? I better call Russ and have him do a little digging. I will go see her boss and the judge and see what they think I should do."

The next day I drove to the prosecutor's office and was summarily refused a meeting with him. His secretary said, "He doesn't have time to waste on a closed case. Hilda doesn't work here anymore, so whatever she does, she is doing it as a private citizen."

When she stopped talking, I said into my tape recorder, "That was the voice of… What's your name, miss, and you are the secretary to…?"

She ran into the office, and before I could do anything, the prosecutor walked out. "Just what do you think you're doing?"

"I'm trying to save a bright young lady's legal career. I don't want to bring formal charges against her. I was hoping you would help me, but if you don't want to, that is your prerogative…just tell me and not have your secretary do it."

"Alright, come in…'

As we walked past his secretary, she was crying and very upset. I just said, "Miss, please, there is no need for that." I went into the prosecutor's office and we sat down. As he sat behind his desk, he rocked back in his chair and started saying, "This office doesn't take lightly a…"

"Wait," I said. "I came here as a friend, not an adversary. Call Hilda and tell her to stop harassing her own witnesses. She is going around town…"

It was the prosecutor's turn to interrupt me. He sat straight up in the chair as he said. "Yes, I know. Ruth and Lila both called me. Ruth called and told me what Hilda is doing. I've called her but she refuses my calls. I guess you will have to bring formal charges against her. She idolized Sue Ann; she went to law school to be just like her. She blames herself for your being able to walk away from killing her. She blames the chief for giving her misinformation, and she blames herself for doing a bad job."

"Can't she just accept the fact that I'm innocent of any wrong doing? What about the judge? Do you think he can help? She is driving everyone nuts in The Cove with her war stories. I mean…Oh, I don't know what I mean."

The prosecutor wrung his hands as he stood up, "I don't know if I should personally get involved, and if I act as an officer of the court…give me a few days and then give me a call. Let me see what I can do unofficially."

I got up and shook his hand. "That would be great; there has been enough harm done. Thanks again, and I'll be in touch, and if there is anything I can do to help, just let me know…she's a nice young lady." I walked out of his office, and as I walked past his secretary who had quieted down, I said, "Please don't be annoyed at me." I left and went back to The Cove. On the way I stopped at the home of a friend of the Commodore. He was a legal stenographer. I had asked the Commodore if he knew anyone who could transcribe a tape. He was the same one who had taped Hilda's opening statement at the trial. I asked him to transcribe the tape I had just recorded. "You never know when something like this will be needed." He understood. I drove back to the store where the Commodore was waiting with baited breath to get the news. I didn't disappoint him.

That night Ruth, Lila, the Commodore, and I had dinner. No matter what I said to them, I just couldn't get out of my mind the mess that had been started by that first email that started off, "Dear Dad."

Something must have happened, for I stayed around for three days and heard nothing more about Hilda. Everyone in town was convinced she was a nut, and things started to get back to normal. Russ found out that Hilda was an only child, and her parents worshipped her. While Hilda was in high school, Sue Ann had gone there for a law day seminar. From that day forth, all Hilda would talk about was being just like

Sue Ann. She took the news of Sue Ann's death very personally. In his report Russ added the phrase. "She should have never been allowed to handle this case; the ripples of the water splashed all over her." I could just imagine Russ' laughing as he wrote the last phrase. I got the transcript of the tape and kept it with my file of the trial. I knew this was the end of it, or so I told myself at least twice a day.

Chapter Seventeen

I came back from The Cove, saying a prayer all the way home that the end I sought...I'd finally found. As soon as I got home, the phone rang; it was Russ. I asked, "Do you have radar? I just got in the door...I haven't even taken my coat off yet."

"You are always on my mind," he sang to me. I was wondering if the information I sent you about Hilda was of any use?"

"Of course, it showed me the difference between an attorney and a trial attorney."

"How? She impressed me as a bright young lady. Her grades were good, and she got good references for her job. Where did she falter?"

"She forgot that the case isn't won or lost by what the attorney says, but the witnesses."

"Is she still mad at the chief?"

"I don't know, but the case is over, so let's just let it die a natural death."

With that being said, Russ hung up after I promised I would call him the next week for dinner. He explained to me that he was hosting an "old fogy" night, and he was running out of old fogies.

I settled back into my normal routines. I was going to write a book about the case but decided against it, for writing about it would just prolong the memory of what had happened, and I really wanted to forget the whole affair. My children never questioned me about it, so it was dead, or at least that's what I wished in my heart of hearts.

The very next day, I got a call from Trina. She and her husband had returned to The Cove, and she was ready to take her place in the community, or at least that's what she said. "Can I call you, George, or should I call…" I interrupted her and said, "George will be fine."

"Well, I am just now starting to realize what being my mother's sole heir is all about. My father called me but, frankly, I don't trust him. He and my mother…oh, never mind, I don't want to go into that… but between her insurance and the house, I am a millionaire, but with the expenses I won't be a millionaire for long. The banker wants me to go to a financial adviser. Some of the other people in town are coming to me with propositions…"

At this point I could hear her crying. Before I could say anything she said, "Please help me. I have to pay someone, and the Commodore told me to call you; he thinks very highly of you, and he is the only businessman I know. The local attorney who is handling the house sounds like he is taking over…and well… I don't know if I want him to. I mean he's a lawyer, but… I just don't know what to do. I went to the Commodore when I found out I was pregnant…"

She was crying too hard to continue. I asked her, "Where are you right now?"

"I'm in the store; I am using the Commodore's phone."

"You do nothing…don't sign anything…just get a box and put all the papers you've got, or what they want you to sign, and put them in there. I will be down there in the next day or two; tell everyone they will have to wait until that time. If anyone puts any pressure on you, give him or her my number and have him or her call me. Now put the Commodore on. I waited for what seemed an eternity. Finally I could hear the Commodore wheezing as he said, "Yes."

"When I get down there, I am going to kill you. What is wrong with you? I wanted the Sue Ann affair thing to go away. I don't want to be reminded of it by anyone." I said the words and tried to convey the message that I wanted out.

The Commodore replied, "Shame on you! I'll clean your room...bye." I sat in my chair, staring at a dead phone. I cursed; I complained to myself; I swore that I wasn't going...I did all these things as I packed my things and cleaned all the paper off my desk, for I didn't know how long I would be away. All the way from my house until I pulled into The Cove, I was going to turn around and go home. I was hoping that the Commodore would be in the street to greet me so I could run him over.

"See, Trina, I told you he would come. He loves you. He won't leave you in a lurch like this. I mean, after all he is going to be..."

By that time I was out of the car and standing next to the Commodore. I grabbed him as I whispered, "You say it and I will kill you here and now."

Trina came over to me and kissed me hello. "Thank you for coming, and I want you to charge me the same as these others want to."

"Less a family discount of twenty percent, of course." The Commodore added the words as he took my bag to my room.

Trina left the room but was back carrying a box; she had done what I'd told her to do. The Commodore walked back after taking my bag to my room. He heard what Trina was saying and pointed to his office, which was in the basement of the building. Trina and I went into it, and as soon as we sat down, she started crying. "Why are you crying now?" I asked in my most sympathetic tone.

"I don't know...it's just that my mother worked her whole life for me, and here I am, going through her life like it is nothing...I don't know."

"Well, you have to stop, for if you don't, I'll start, and we will get nothing done." I took the papers out of the box and assembled them into different categories: house, life insurance, and taxes. When I came to a folder titled "Business," I stopped. "What's this?"

"Steve and I are setting up a fishing service right here in The Cove. We are going to rent pier space, and that's the lease for the spot. I put everything concerning the business in there."

I opened the folder, and I was impressed at the way she had everything organized. "I took a business bookkeeping course in school," she said as I went through the folder. The next folder I opened had the house papers in it. It included the deed to the house. Sue Ann had bought mortgage insurance, and when the insurance company paid it off, Trina would own the house free and clear of any mortgage. Those were the papers the local attorney wanted her to sign. I put them on the side as I said, "Tomorrow, we will go see the attorney, and you can sign them. Piece by piece, I took out each paper and explained it to her, and we made a decision as to what was to be done with it. It took us three hours to get done with everything, but when we were done, Trina thanked me. "I now feel as though I know what is going on."

From upstairs, I could hear chairs being thrown about, people yelling, and above all, "How can you people harbor a murderer?" It was Hilda, back again and creating a problem. "Don't tell me he isn't here; his car is parked in the back. Where is he?" I told Trina to stay put as I climbed the stairs to the main floor. Hilda was in the center of the room, dressed in some sort of jeans and blouse set with her hair all disheveled. She was waving a gun about while yelling, "Where are you keeping him?"

I was on the opposite side of the room from the Commodore, who was trying to talk to her. "Hilda, please, why are you doing this? Why do you think we would help him? We all knew Sue Ann longer and better than you. How can you even think of killing him; he didn't do anything."

While he had her undivided attention, I walked around her so that I was directly behind her. I was looking for something to shield myself while I got the gun off of her. There were about ten people in the room who'd been shopping or enjoying the early-bird dinner menu. Another man picked up a chair, and with eye contact we were both going to charge her at the same time. Suddenly we heard Mildred yell out, "Drop that gun."

Hilda turned and fired at Mildred, hitting her in the shoulder. Mildred fired, hitting Hilda right in the forehead. Hilda fell to the floor; she was dead instantly. The Commodore went to Hilda and I ran to Mildred. The blood was spurting out of the bullet hole with each beat of her heart. One of the customers grabbed a tablecloth and came to Mildred's aid. He tied the tablecloth around the wound to try to stop the bleeding. The two deputies came running in, and one of them called for an ambulance while the other grabbed Mildred. He tried to applied pressure to the wound to stop the flow of blood. Mildred was going in and out of consciousness, mumbling something, but I couldn't understand her. I was resting her head on my lap while I was in a state of shock myself. All this was happening because of …I could not find any reason that I could live with. While in a daze and covered with Mildred's blood, I was helped away from the scene by the Commodore, while the ambulance crew called the hospital, seeking instructions while tending to Mildred's wound. The last I heard was the wail of a siren and the last thing I felt was a cold wet towel over my face as someone was washing my face. I slumped down in a chair in a daze. I heard Trina saying, "He came here to help me… now look at him."

The Commodore responded, "Relax, he's not dying. These Italians are tough."

The rest of the day was spent in a daze while I was forced into a shower with my clothes still on while the blood was being rinsed off of me. I got undressed, and the Commodore wrapped me in his bathrobe as I was shoved into bed, and someone was telling me to take two pills to relax me. Another person was taking my pulse as I drifted off. It was sometime later that I was able to appreciate my surroundings. I lay in bed, shaking my head in disbelief. After a few attempts, I was able to stand up; it was early in the morning of the next day. I came out of my room, still wrapped in the Commodore's robe, and I met the chef, coming to work. He sat me down as he made the coffee for the morning rush.

He brought me a cup of coffee and toast as he said, "After yesterday, we will be busy this morning. I must have gotten ten calls from people, telling me what happened here. Everyone will want to see where the shootout took place. The Commodore will have to rename the place the 'O.K. Corral'." He thought his last remark was funny. I went back to my room and took another shower before I got dressed. By the time I came back into the store, the chef's prediction about the crowd was right, for the place was packed. I even helped out by washing the dishes. The Commodore walked in, carrying a tray full of dirty dishes. As he put them in the sink, he said, "One of the customers called the hospital, and the report is that Mildred is in guarded condition. I don't know what that means, but we'll go see her later." No matter what I tried to tell myself, I felt personally responsible for what had happened. Right at that moment, I felt my best therapy was washing the dishes. A deputy walked in and told me I would have to give a statement. I nodded and washed some more dishes before I said, "I'll come over as soon as I can." I realized it was not the answer he wanted, but I just wanted to wash the dishes before I had to relive what had happened because of me. A guilty feeling is something I just couldn't shake, no matter how many dishes I washed.

The rush finally ended, and the Commodore and I went to police headquarters and gave our statements. From there we went to the hospital, but Mildred was under heavy sedation. The bullet had hit an artery, and she had lost a lot of blood. We were allowed to look into the room, but all I could see were tubes running all over, ant all I heard was the beeping of a monitor. The Commodore and I returned to the store for the normal dinner crowd rush that, like the morning rush, was overwhelming. Neither one of us could think of anything to say, so he went back to clearing tables while I went back to my dishes. Hours later, still with a heavy heart, I went to bed, but the guilt lamp was still burning. I was so mad at Joann and Sue Ann for getting me involved in this horror story that I thought of going and desecrating their graves. I didn't know where Joann was buried, and then I remembered Sue Ann had been cremated and her ashes thrown in the bay. I kept praying for peace of mind, but that prayer wasn't being answered either. I sat up in bed and silently said, "Maybe tomorrow I will find peace again"; at least it was something to look forward to.

In the morning I was having the early-bird special with the Commodore, when an elderly couple walked in. They looked like tourists who were having a bad day. The woman just looked drained of all feeling. Her complexion was a pasty white. She was hanging onto her husband's arm for strength as they navigated the tables and chairs. They walked over to us and before they said anything, I just knew that they were Hilda's parents.

"Are you the Commodore?" the man spoke as he was choking back tears. "We are Hilda's parents." The Commodore got up and got a chair for the woman, for she looked like she was going to fall. The man took a chair from the next table and sat down. The waitress came over with a cup of coffee for both of them. They sat at the table, sipping their coffee, as they tried to think of what they should say. It was a strange silence that shrouded the table. When I could bear the silence no more, I said, "We know what you are going through. How can we help?" The woman finally spoke. "You must be George. Can you give us back our daughter?"

I felt sorry for the woman, but I felt affronted by her

comment. "Do you know your daughter came in here with a gun to shoot me? I feel sorry for you, but I'll be damned if you're going to try to blame her death on me. What do you want?"

The husband tried to quiet his wife, but she just kept crying as she said, "Where did it happen?"

"Right there," I replied as I pointed to the center of the room. "The lady who was defending me from your daughter was shot and is in the hospital. She is fighting for her life. Did you know your daughter owned a gun? Where would she have learned to use it? I don't believe it was just a lucky shot she got off. She knew how to use that thing." I'd felt sorry for the lady when she came in, but after she made the remark about getting her daughter back, whatever sorrow I was feeling was gone. I just felt tired of being the target of everyone's hatred. The Commodore could see how upset I was getting, so he asked, "Would you like something to eat?"

"No," they both said. The husband paused for a few minutes before he asked in a sheepish tone. "Where does Lila live? Does she have rooms for rent?"

The Commodore wrote down the directions to her house, but before he would give the directions to them, he said, "Wait, I will call her first; she is still shaken up over what happened." He left and came back very quickly. "She said she would rent you the rooms, but she was very insistent about the fact that she does not want to discuss your daughter at all. Do you understand…not at all…do you still want the address?"

The husband looked at his wife, who was still trying to regain her composure. She shook her head "No."

The Commodore had anticipated their next question, so before they could say anything, he said, "Here are the directions to a nice motel on the highway. They will be able to accommodate you, but you still didn't answer George's question. Where did she get and learn to use a gun?"

The man said, "When she was in New York City, going to

189

law school, she joined the Italian Gun Club." His wife interrupted, "And you bought her a gun." Those words drained the last bit of energy from the lady as the couple left for the motel. I found out later, when the funeral director came in for dinner, that they asked him to make arrangements to send their daughter's body home when the police released it. He smiled as he said, "Commodore, your guest is sure great for business."

I heard the comment but refused to acknowledge it. I went to bed, for I had resolved to go home in the morning and forget all about The Cove ...forever.

The morning came none too soon. I packed my clothes, had the early-bird breakfast with the Commodore and chef, drove past the dock Trina and Steve had rented, and aimed my car for home. The further from The Cove I drove, the better I felt, for I was done with it and everyone there. I kept telling myself that all the way home. I resolved that in time, memories of what happened there would fade, and like all bad experiences, I would shed myself of the unwanted memories. I kept saying that they would fade, but they weren't. I was still upset with myself, for I didn't know what had happened to Sue Ann: did she fall or did I push her? The question never left me. I tried rationalizing what happened in terms of "so what." I'd been accused, tried, and found ...there was never a verdict by my peers but a decision by one man...the judge. He'd said the state didn't prove their case, so I was not guilty, but that decision wasn't good enough for me."

I decided to forget my dilemma and visit with Russ for a while. There was something always going on at the club, and the diversion would do me good.

As soon as I got out of the car, Russ took one look at me and instead of the normal greeting between two friends, I was greeted with, "You look like hell; you obviously aren't sleeping. It's that Sue Ann thing! I'm glad you came. Come on; we'll get you settled for tomorrow; we are going fishing with another member of the club. We are going on a quiet little lake where the fish jump right in the boat. One of the chefs from the club is coming, so we will eat well and we can get back to nature…you know, all the buddy-buddy stuff."

I spent the rest of the day preparing for the trip. Russ had made up a list of equipment we would need because we would be staying in a log cabin owned by another member. The only problem was that the other member was a true outdoors man, not a group of city slickers who were going to rough it for a few days. I packed the truck Russ borrowed, and the four of us met at the club and we were off. The drive to the cabin took five hours, so it was late afternoon by the time we got there. Everyone helped; we swept out the place and brought in some fire wood while the chef, Tony, made us a fireside dinner, which was augmented with great wine. It was at this time that Russ told me the other guest's occupation. Eugene was a psychiatrist who was good at hypnosis.

In the morning, Tony and Russ went in one rowboat and Eugene and I went in the other. Just trying to get the rowboat, equipped with an outboard motor, away from the dock without falling in the water took both of our combined talents. We finally mastered the art of rowing, and we went out into the lake. We decided to use the outboard motor later. The combination of the wine at dinner the night before and the hot sun made for an ideal setting for napping and talking.

Before I knew it, I had told Eugene the entire Sue Ann story. He was a master at getting me to talk, or as he explained it, "People want to be punished if they feel they've done something wrong. It doesn't matter what other people say; it is their own conscience that they have to deal with. You're no different from soldiers who go to war and kill other human beings. Some get medals for bravery and for doing their duty for their country, but they can't accept the fact that they did something wrong by their own standards of right and wrong, and in your case, you don't know what happened. It can be that you do know but your sub-conscious has blocked it from your conscious, so my friend, to break down that wall you've built, maybe hypnosis is the answer...or said another way...it can't hurt."

"Are you telling me that beneath this happy facade I've created may be the mind and soul of a monster?"

"Do you think you would be the first one? Many people do things they shouldn't, and because they can't deal with what they've done, they carry around the guilt their whole lives. Many of us have memories of things we wish we hadn't done; some things are very trivial by other people's standards but are monumental by our own. The big difference is knowing something is easier to deal with than not knowing; in your case it's not knowing that is bothering you...you're not used to not knowing."

By now we had drifted way out into the lake and had not even gotten our poles wet. The discussion stopped as we attended to the task at hand, namely fishing and then figuring out how to get back to the dock--once we figured out where it was. We heard the roar of a motor, and Russ' friend, who'd loaned us the cabin, had decided to visit us; when Russ told him we had drifted out into the lake, he decided to come to our rescue before we got into trouble. Eugene and I both thanked him. We came back fishless.

That night the five of us had a truly fine dinner with great wine that allowed me to get a good night's sleep for once.

The following day Eugene and I went out in the same boat again to try to fish, but as the sun beat down on me, I became very relaxed, and Eugene, being the professional that he was, got me talking about Joann, Sue Ann, Trina, and the rest of the people in The Cove. He always stopped the conversation or twisted it so that I wasn't talking about the night Sue Ann died. I asked him why.

He smiled as he said, "Russ told me you were bright and would take notice of ploys. I don't think you are ready. Right now the only thing you would say is that you don't know because that wall you've built is still very strong. No, my friend, when you want to know what happened, we will do it in my office where, if anything goes wrong, I have the facilities to help you. Here on this lake is not the right place."

"Are you telling me hypnosis can be dangerous?"

Sometimes, people never come back from where hypnosis takes them…you know…shit happens."

We both laughed and once again tried our hand at fishing with the same results. Thank God we'd bought our own food supply and didn't have to depend on nature's bountifulness. It was another peaceful night, and when the morning sun woke us, we packed our things and headed for home.

That night there was a big party at the club. Russ had a policy that if a couple met at one of his parties, they got a twenty percent discount on their engagement and wedding receptions.

"How do you know where they met?" I asked the question, even though I knew the answer.

"At the prices I charge, who cares?" was his immediate response.

I was introduced to everyone as an old friend of the family …the bride's side or the groom's side--depending who was doing the introduction.

The next day I called Eugene and asked when we could meet. He put me on hold but within a few minutes, which seemed like hours to me, he responded, "How about next Tuesday? I'll meet you at my home. It's twenty miles from the club. I'll email you the address. We'll do it at one o'clock…okay?"

"Alright, let me give you my…"

He interrupted me by saying, "Did you forget? You put your

email address in your new books. I'll see you on Tuesday at one."

I didn't understand the reason for the delay, but I decided he's the doctor, so I should just do what he says. I started to leave when Russ came running out. "Wait, he shouted; here is a tape recorder. Say the time when you turn it on and when you shut it off. It will record everything you say while you are hypnotized. I know Eugene, but I don't know him that well."

I thanked him and went back home. I didn't realize it, but I had been away more often than not. I called my family group up and took them all out to dinner. They all appreciated my gesture of good faith. Over the next few days, I got caught up on the pile of mail that had accumulated and, unfortunately, answered a call from the Commodore.

He started off with, "I know you're too busy to call me, but I didn't want you to think that we don't think of you." He started to give me a rundown on everyone, but I cut him short by saying, "How's Trina?"

"We have started a pool as to whether she is going to give birth to a child or a tank; she got big fast. Lila and Ruth have been her constant companions. Everyone is excited, especially Steve, who is handing out cigars with the label, "Whatever." The one who is really hitting it hard is the chief. He won't listen to any one. All he does is smoke, something I never remember his doing, and drink. He is suffering from depression, and no one knows what to do for him. I was going to ask the doctor to commit him to a hospital, but I just don't think I should do that. Oh, by the way there were two investigators coming around and asking a lot of questions about you and Hilda. Her parents think you killed her. I told them what happened, but I don't think it did any good, for they went to everyone who was here that day and questioned them anyway. They also questioned the people at the airport as to what happened out there. The owner of the airport really got mad and called the aeronautic board and refused to answer any more questions. He said all those questions are hurting his business. The town fathers made Mike, the deputy, the temporary chief, in lieu of Mildred. She's recovering, but it is a slow process because of all the blood she lost. She is in therapy right now. They had to teach her to walk again…poor lady. Mike's fiancé is afraid that the same thing will happen to him."

I thanked him for the update and tried to say good-bye, but he wouldn't let me off the phone until I promised I would visit him. I received an email from Eugene, reminding me of my appointment and giving me directions to his home. The day for me to visit Eugene finally came, and in the morning, with a grim determination and armed with my tape recorder, I drove to his office that he had in his home. I waved as I passed the club.

His home was located on the outskirts of a small town. It was at the end of the main street. The house was an old structure that looked like it'd been built in the 20's. There was a three-foot high fence that went around the property. It had two entrances for the ingress and egress to the house via the circular driveway that was in the front. The driveway was paved with colored paving stones that were put down in some sort of pattern that I couldn't make out. There was a row of hedges that went around the center of the circle with a marble statue in the middle of it. The statue looked like some goddess, holding a water jug. It was not to my taste, but I imagined he loved it. There were two big columns in the front, and a wrap-around porch that was magnificent. There were plenty of rocking chairs for a small party. There was a portable bar along with a portable serving tray on wheels. The set up was ideal for looking at the stars on a summer evening. There were four steps on the staircase from the driveway to the porch. The two massive doors with their etched, stained glass, countryside scene inserts were quite beautiful. A doorbell that played a tune and ended with a voice saying, 'Welcome' set off this entrance.

Chapter Eighteen

Within a few minutes of my ringing the bell, Eugene answered the door.

"Welcome to my home." As I entered the foyer, there were doors on either side with a staircase that went to the second floor. On the side of the staircase was a walkway that led to the back of the house He closed the door, and I followed him to the rear of his house. As we went back, I could not help but notice the antique table, upholstered chairs, pictures, and lamps that lined both sides. On the right was an old-fashioned kitchen, which I took a quick look at as he opened the door to his office. When I walked in there, I was awe struck. The office was made of a deep-colored mahogany wood that just glistened from the light shining through the large glass wall. The walls of the rest of the room were made from the same color wood as the floor and desk. The ceiling was white, which reflected the outside light. His desk was made of mahogany planks with a glass top, which allowed the wood to still be seen. With pride he pointed to it as he said, "I made that." The wood was too hard to write on, so I had a glazer make a glass top for it. I had a problem, though, for the glass kept sliding around. He came back and put a few drops of glue down and that solved that problem.

He pointed to the two red leather chairs and told me to sit down. There were four other chairs around the room up against the wall. There was a large lounge chair done in the same red leather pattern as the upright chairs. The small tables around the room all had Tiffany lamps on them plus figurines of all sorts. It was obvious that someone spent a lot of time shopping to find the right thing for each place in the room. Eugene saw me taking a great interest in the decor of the room and said, "My wife is a flea market, house sale, and estate sale junkie; there isn't one that she misses, no matter where we are or whatever else we have planned. I bought her a bumper sticker for her car that says, 'Caution…this car stops at all sales'."

A striking woman walked into the room. She was of slight build but walked with a certain graceful gait that looked as though she was floating. She was carrying a tray with three cups on it. She handed me one, gave another to Eugene, and put the tray down as she took the third. There was milk, lemon, sugar and honey on the tray. She put down the tray and asked how I drank my tea. "Nothing--I drink it the way it is." She and Eugene mixed honey with theirs.

Eugene looked at me as he said, "You never met my wife, did you? This is Mary. Mary, this is the infamous George that Russ always talks about."

"Russ is your best promoter. When things get dull at the club, we always call upon him for a "George" story, and he never lets us down. He is a delight."

"Your home is beautiful; the decorations must have taken a great deal of time."

"Oh yes, shopping is my passion, my hobby, and my vice… my only vice."

I looked around the room again, and without realizing it, I must have stared at the red leather lounge too long. Eugene saw it too for he said, "I bought that." I looked at Mary and back at the lounge as I said, "I can see why."

Mary got up with a coy look on her face, took the tray and the empty cups, turned and said as she walked to the door, "I know you men must have important things to talk about. George, I hope to see you before you leave."

Eugene pressed a button and drapes were closed over the window. He pressed another, and the lights dimmed in the room. I was starting to feel a little woozy, and Eugene got up and helped me to the lounge. As I lay back, I took out the tape recorder, looked at my watch and said the time as I turned it on.

Eugene said, "We are going to have a taped session?"

"Yes," I replied. "I hope you don't mind?"

"Not at all, but remember you will be baring your soul."

"A priest told me that once. You two must be in the same business."

"We are, only I get paid more. Self-confession is one of my best tools to help people to help themselves."

"Did you drug me?"

"Yes, it was in the tea. On the rowboat, we had the wine and sun. In my office I use a 'wine and sun pill' with the same results. Now relax. I'm going to start a statement, and I want you to say it with me, but I want you to finish it. "I got in my car and headed for a town called…""

That's all I remembered. I was drifting off into a different dimension…a different time and place. I was out for over an hour, for the next thing I heard was, "Here drink this juice; it will help to clear your head. You can shut your recorder off now; it is…" and he said the time.

"You can go in the sunroom on the porch and listen to your tape. When you are done, we can discuss it if you want. I think we were successful at breaking down the wall that has been disturbing you. Only you will know if we did after you have heard the tape." He pointed to a door that lead out of his office to the wrap-around porch. He had built a sunroom by just putting up glass storm windows; it was perfect. I took my glass of juice that he had refilled and bravely walked out on to the porch and into the sunroom. For the first time, I wondered if I really wanted to hear what had happened. I argued with myself, but I knew I had to know if I was going to get on with my life. I rewound the tape, sat in a comfortable reading chair and started the recorder and mouthed the words, "I got in my car and headed for a town called The Cove. It was the town Sue Ann told me she lived in."

In minute detail I recited everything I'd done and where I'd gone up until the eventful night. She had invited me over to her house for dinner. After we ate, we sat in front of the fireplace, and she told me about her intended plan of going away with Chad. She was very excited, for she'd even bought a new nightgown type ensemble; she was very anxious to show it to me. She got up and went into another room to change. Before I could see her, I could smell her perfume; suddenly I wasn't in her house; I was in the last examination room with Joann. The room was different in that it was the last one down the hallway, where all the examinations rooms were. I didn't understand why the change, but I didn't question the reason for the change. Joann/Sue Ann walked in and came toward me. I noticed that Joann/Sue Ann wasn't wearing her usual white pants suit with a white lab coat but rather a white flowing dress. As Sue Ann came near me, I saw Joann. The effects of the wine started to take over, and I had to go to the bathroom. I turned away and went to the bathroom by the front door of the house. When I came out I walked out the door, saying good-bye as I left. I went back to the store and had a drink with the Commodore and went to bed. The following morning is when I found out Sue Ann was dead."

By the time the tape was done, I had finished the juice and was ready to discuss the session with Eugene. I went back into his office and sat in the chair before him like a naughty little boy, sitting before the principal at school. "Well, what do you think really happened?"

"George, you relived your experience with Joann, but this time you were with Sue Ann, and you did to her what Joann had done to you: Joann just walked out of the examination room, said goodbye, and left. You did the same thing: you said good-bye and left. Whatever Sue Ann did had nothing to do with you. I doubt very much if you would have had the presence of mind to appreciate what happened to her. From the time you smelled the perfume, for the sense of smell is a powerful thing, you were not with Sue Ann but with Joann, only this time you were the one to walk away."

I sat back in the chair and let out a sigh of relief. "Other than paying your bill, I don't know how to thank you."

The door to the office opened, and Mary made a grand entrance into the room as she said, "I hope you'll come with us tonight. There is an appreciation dinner at the club, and I told the ladies of my group that I would bring you along so that for once they could hear a "George" story right from the author's own lips."

"No, you said you could hear a story right from the horse's mouth." On that note we left and headed for the club. I rode with Eugene, while Mary drove my car. Eugene wanted to make sure the effect of the drug had worn off. As we pulled up to the club, "Wait," I said, "I don't have a reservation."

Eugene laughed, "I think Russ can squeeze you in somewhere." He did.

The people were just starting to arrive for the gala affair. I always kept a change of clothes in Russ' office for such occasions. Eugene and Mary started to mingle with the guests to help Russ "Meet and greet", while I went to his office to change into something more appropriate. Russ' office was located on the third floor of the clubhouse. It was built like a tower, so he had a three-hundred-and-sixty-degree view of the facilities. It had television screens so the he could scan many different areas at a time. There was one for the front door, bar area, kitchen, and (most importantly) for the back door, where all the deliveries were made. "This one pays the bills," he would brag. There were also cameras located around the property for security purposes.

Also in the office was a twenty-four-foot closet where he kept his different ensembles. He had a fetish for jackets. He had them in every color and design. For the affair tonight, he had chosen an electric blue number with white pants. He had an array of ties and shirts that any haberdashery store would be envious of. He had a bathroom with a walk-in shower. His desk was of a semi-circular design that really didn't serve any purpose except to be different. On another wall was a large screen that projected the images on his computer.

The computer was the heart of his operation. The lady in charge of it was Nancy. Nancy's job was to keep all the information current. The information included the final records, which Russ wasn't really interested in, and the guest list. The government assigns social security numbers, but Nancy assigns social numbers. She classifies people as to age, weight, race, height, occupation, income, looks, location, and marital status. When Russ wanted to have a party like this evening's, he would tell her it's a three-hundred-guest, general-mixer party. Nancy would sit down with her social number register and start filling in table numbers. Each table would have eight to ten people. Next, she would sort by occupation. Eugene and Mary are professionals, married, with a high income, so she would seat six or eight other similar people with them. Singles would be put at other tables, and the process would go on. Invitations would be sent and responses recorded. Where there was a gap because someone couldn't come, she would go to that grouping and call if she had any substitutes. She knew everyone in town, and everyone knew her.

Russ put a party together like a general plans a major battle. If given the opportunity, Russ would expound on his theory. Pointing a finger at the sky, he would declare, "War is hell, and so are parties. You have to man them both so the whole group moves as one." Since he was very successful at it, no one argued. I had brought the tape recording with me. I wanted it transcribed. Nancy went to the machine, and in a few seconds told me at what table a certified court reporter was seated. I thanked her and finished getting dressed. I was to sit with Russ at the VIP table. She gave me a quick run-down of the other guests seated there. She, of course, armed with her singles' list, made it a point to go to those tables and make sure everyone met each other. Since there had just been a wedding of two people who'd met at the club, this section would be the busiest.

Eugene sometimes helped out with the classifications; because of this, Mary knew of Nancy's existence and job. Mary just called ahead and had her group seated by her. Mary came and got me, and the group heard a "George" story first hand.

As expected, the party was a great success. Russ was elated when he got up and announced a new engagement, but he wouldn't tell. "I'm no busy body or snoop; that's not my job; when they are ready, they will make their own announcement." Everyone just laughed.

After the party was over, I spent the night at Russ' house. The next morning I had my coffee and I was ready to leave. I told him I had given the tape to the court reporter, and it was to be given to him. Russ walked me to my car, and just as I was about to leave, I had to ask, "Who got engaged?" With an impish smile, he replied, "I don't know." "You mean you lied?" I'm not running for Pope...I'm running a club." With that thought in mind, I drove home. The drive home was peaceful and for the first time in a long time, I enjoyed the scenery and the peacefulness of a clear conscience. The feeling was great.

Chapter Nineteen

As I kept pondering where the line should be drawn that would separate me from this curse of Joann, the thought of what I had gone through was maddening. No matter how many times I spoke to Russ about it and regardless of how many names he called me in the still of the night, when everyone was asleep, I was visited by the thoughts of what had happened and what might happen.

I usually worked at an office I had built in my home. I had a large front room, which I'd divided by a bookcase with a glass back. I had the bookcase built by the front door so that when the door was opened, the bookcase protected me from the elements. Instead of books on the shelves, I had souvenirs from different trips I had taken. The items looked foolish to everyone else, but to me they were a trip down memory lane every time I looked at them. I had put the picture of me holding the twins on it, but I soon realized that the picture was defeating the chances of my forgetting about them. The picture came down and went into the bottom drawer of the case.

In the rest of the room, I had a large television set and in front of that, I had a large easy chair. On the side of the room from the front door, I had an eight-foot alcove built, in which I had a desk with two leather upholstered upright chairs for visitors and a large black swivel chair for myself. The arrangement worked well. The other rooms on the first floor were a formal dining room, which I kept for it had been my wife's dream to have one, and I could not bear to get rid of it. Next came the cooking area of the kitchen, and after that a fifty-foot-long kitchen that was used for all family functions. It was in the big back room that I built a secretary station that worked very well, for it answered my needs. Upstairs in the house were three large bedrooms and two full bathrooms.

The front wall of the room where I had my office was a large window from where I could see the entire street. On the window was a vertical blind that I could adjust, depending on how much sunlight I wanted to let in. Over my desk I had a large light, and in the room there were three lamps that when lit, gave the room an ominous look. I would sit at my desk and open the blinds and greet each day as the traffic would increase as my neighbors scurried to work. If I was at my desk with my desk lamp on, everyone knew I was working.

From the front door of my house down to the street were two flights of stairs; the first section from the street had eight steps and a five-foot landing, and after that, five more steps lead to my front door. From my vantage point, I could see all my visitors long before they could see me.

One day as I sat at my desk, a cab pulled up, and a tall slender man got out. He was well dressed in a suit with a vest. He paid the cabbie and turned to walk up the steps to my house/office. He looked to be about my age, but I did not recognize him. On this day I'd had to bring in a part-time secretary that I used to clean up some correspondence and to sift through the mail that had accumulated. The stranger rang the doorbell just as my secretary was bringing me some papers to sign. She answered the door and looked at me, for neither she nor I had expected anyone. After she opened the door, the stranger stepped into the little foyer behind the bookcase. My secretary looked at me with a puzzled look on her face, for she didn't know what to say or do. I motioned to her to bring the man in. She brought the paper to me to sign as I motioned to the man to sit in one of the chairs in front of my desk. I quickly signed what I had to sign, and she was gone. I turned my attention to the stranger and asked, "You'll have to excuse me, but I don't remember having an appointment today."

A warm smile came across his face as he said, "You didn't. I am being very rude by barging in on you. I am Dr. Lloyd Stein."

When he said those words, my blood ran cold. I didn't know whether to throw him out or just sit and listen to what he had to say. I chose the latter. I meekly said, "How can I help you?'

"As you know, my wife, Joann, worked up here after medical school. " He kept talking of the past and how he was up here to attend a convention of some sort, but after hearing his name, my mind was a million miles away. The one person in the world I didn't want to meet was he. I kept looking at him, trying to look like I was listening, but all I could think of was that he'd come to my home/office to do me bodily harm. What other reason could he possibly have? Although I saw his lips moving, because of my mental attitude, I could not distinguish what he was saying. As he spoke, I could see his facial expressions change from a smile to a stern look. At first, I thought that I had to be wrong, but the lingering thought of self-preservation was still paramount in my mind. In my left-hand drawer that I always kept locked, I had a gun. I always had one, for some of the people I had represented in the past really frightened me. As I watched him, he kept shifting his weight from one side of the chair to the other, and all I could think about was how I could, without raising any suspicion, unlock the drawer. Thankfully, my secretary came in with a tray with two cups of coffee with milk and sugar on it. This diverted Lloyd's attention, while I unlocked the drawer.

"Would you like some cookies?" she asked as she pulled out an extension I had on the desk for visitors to put their papers on, which also served as a little table for times like this.

"Oh, no," he replied. "This coffee is fine. I like it black."

As soon as she left the room, he continued talking in between sips of coffee. I quickly opened the drawer and put my hand inside and placed my hand on the gun. All I could think about is when I'd first bought the gun. The big discussion was if I should get an automatic or a revolver. I was convinced that if the gun would sit around for a long period of time, I was better off with a revolver, for automatics tend to have more problems and might jam when I needed it most. To prove his point, the man I'd bought the gun from told me to go to the local gun range and see what type of guns gave the most problems. That visit convinced me a revolver was the type of gun to buy.

Lloyd was still talking and I heard him say, "I don't have any animosity towards anyone; it is just that, well, you know I paid for Sue Ann's education and wedding."

I lost my concentration on what he was saying because I started thinking about the conversations I'd had with the chief of police on many occasions about the wisdom of the mandatory registration of all firearms. We'd have a sharp disagreement, for I would always say, "Registration is one day before confiscation." That always annoyed him, and his final argument was, "What do you need a gun for?"

My quick response would be, "To shoot you when you stop being a servant of the people and want to become the ruler of them."

My mind went back to Lloyd who was now saying, "You know, what happened so upset me and destroyed my faith in women that I never remarried after Joann died."

I was going to ask if he had ever gotten a divorce from her and that I'd thought he had died, but I decided against it. I just wanted to get rid of him. When I had my desk built, I had two buttons installed to contact my secretary: one was just to signal that I wanted her, and the other was for "Emergency...come get me"; that is the one I pressed.

Within seconds, she was in the front room saying, "There is a call for you on the other phone; I know you should take it."

I took my hand off my gun and left to go into the back room. I waited a few minutes before I walked back into the front and announced, "I'm sorry, Lloyd, but I must leave now. Please give your information to my secretary, and I will contact you. I am sorry but I have to leave." I turned, and as I was leaving, I heard, "I live in Fairfax, Virginia; stop and see me on your way to The Cove."

As I was leaving, I thought what a dumb thing I'd done. I'd moved away from my gun. He could have shot me in the back. Now the drawer was open and I was at a grave disadvantage. I went out the back door and left. I went down the street and waited; in a few minutes, a cab pulled up and took Lloyd away. I returned to the office and was greeted by, "Thanks a lot; you leave and left me with him."

My weak response was, "I knew you could handle the situation better than I and you did."

"Here's the information he gave me. Sign the last items on your desk. I'll mail everything and then I'm going home."

I did what she said, locked my gun drawer, and called Russ. As he picked up the phone and before he could say anything witty, I said, "Lloyd Stein just left my office; he is alive and well, and for a dead man, which is what you told me, he moves around pretty well."

There was a long pause on the phone, for Russ' weak point was that he could not take any criticism, no matter how well deserved. Finally, in a weak voice he replied, "I try my best; that is all I can do. Go do something else, and let me see if I can find out what happened. Do you have anything on him?"

I read him the information I had received. "I would like to make a trip and go see him; he paid me a visit, so I'm going to go see him. Give me a call as soon as you find out anything. Stay well while I go chase a ghost." The phone went dead. I spent the rest of the day clearing my calendar for a quick trip to Fairfax, Virginia. It was about a five-hour drive from my home, so I made plans to stay a day or two.

In the morning I finished packing and got in my car and was ready to go when Russ called. In my car I have a speakerphone, so I just kept driving. He started off with, "You know what happened?"

I interrupted him with, "No, whatever happened is the past; just tell me what I need to know right now. Is Lloyd Stein alive?"

"Oh, yeah,…after his internship up here, he and Joann went back to The Cove area. He was a gifted surgeon, so The Cove was too small a town for a man of his talents. He got a great job in a hospital in Fairfax. Their first house was located about a half-hour out of town. Joann restricted her practice while she was pregnant. After the birth of Sue Ann, she became more active, not only in her profession, but also in community affairs. Something happened, and no one knows what it was, but Lloyd found out that Sue Ann couldn't be his child. Her blood type wasn't right, I'm guessing, but it makes no difference. He beat the hell out of Joann, but she wasn't talking; no charges were brought and Lloyd moved. That's why we thought he died. Nevertheless, he still contributed to Sue Ann's support and education; we thought it was coming from an insurance policy, but we were wrong. Joann and Lloyd separated, but they never divorced. They both signed an agreement that neither one would make a claim on the other's assets. No one seems to know if it would hold up in court, but since it was never challenged, the whole issue became moot.

When Sue Ann graduated from law school, she was offered a few jobs, one of which was being a clerk in a judge's office. Lloyd just stayed away from her. Anytime he wanted to do anything, he did it through Joann. When the judge died, Sue Ann was given the job as judge. Her appointment got quite a few people mad, but politics being what they are, they couldn't do anything. She was judge and that ended that story. She was considered by many to be absolutely brilliant.

Lloyd practiced medicine in Fairfax, and Sue Ann was a judge in The Cove. Whether she knew the whole story about Lloyd, no one knows, but she never tried to find out what had happened, or if she did, she never spoke about it to anyone. Lloyd never hooked up with anyone; in fact, some think that he is homosexual because when seen outside of the hospital, he is always seen alone."

While Russ was talking, I kept driving across the state to get on the turnpike going south. The story of Lloyd kept my attention, but what really bothered me was that after all these years, why start anything now...and why with me; it made no sense. A few honks of the horn made me pay more attention to the road and put Lloyd out of my mind, at least for a while.

I estimated the drive down to Fairfax, Virginia, to be about four hours. As I was driving down, I kept questioning why I was going. I just could not understand Lloyd's seeking me out, and here I was doing the same thing he did. There was a bond between us; one that neither one of us wanted. I pulled into a rest area and just sat for a long time as I tried to make some sort of sense out of what I was doing. I started the car, resolved that I was going to go back home but I just knew that I had to go see where Lloyd lived and worked. I found it hard to believe that his wife's unfaithfulness would destroy his life. Russ had said that he never remarried and that he never got a divorce. Finally I just yelled out, "Why the hell did you have to bother me?"

I stayed in a motel outside of the city of Fairfax. As soon as I got settled in the room, I called Eugene; Mary answered the phone. I asked for Eugene, but she had to tell me about Russ' new brainchild: "Big Rib Night." "Oh, George, you have to come one night. It's on Wednesday nights. The limit is three hundred people. He makes the guests wait in the lobby, and while there, the hostesses (which includes Nancy) run around giving everyone who forgot to bring their name tag a new one. They also serve drinks and finger food. At seven, the doors to the main dining room open, and everyone marches in to the tune of "When the Saints Come Marching In." There are no assigned seats, so the seating is random as everyone marches in. Nancy runs all around introducing everyone to each other. Russ takes the center stage and announces, 'If you have a problem with someone at your table...kiss and make up or just leave...you are all my family, so don't ask me to pick and choose.' The process probably sounds awkward to you, but he has everyone seated in fifteen minutes. There are bottles of wine on the table and, of course, waiters and waitresses' waiting to take drink orders. Russ leaves center stage, and in a few minutes he marches back in, banging a big bass drum followed by the chefs' pushing carts on which he has these large roasts...prime rib. They immediately go from table to table, carving the size rib you want, followed by another cart with all the trimmings. The band is playing...the people are serving...and everyone is talking; it is just great. You must come with us. You wanted to talk to Eugene; I'll get him."

I thought to myself, "I love Mary, but..."

Finally I heard, "George...what can I do for you?" In the background I heard Mary yelling, "Tell him about the cake; he'll love it."

"Tell me about the cake first before she has a fit."

"They wheel this big cake out on a cart. On the cake is a picture of a girl standing and a boy down on one knee, saying 'Please.' This is all done with whip creams and fruit placed in the right places...it is very artistic. I don't know where your friend finds these people, but he keeps coming up with great ideas. He gets everyone quieted down; he grabs the mike, and he announces who has to come up and cut the first piece. I must say that Russ, whatever else he may be, is first and foremost a showman with Nancy by his side. Now why did you call? I don't think it was to hear about the Wednesday night bash."

"I was visited by Lloyd; he was Joann's husband. Russ had told me he had died, but obviously Russ was wrong, for he is alive and kicking. I can't figure out why he would even come. He lives in Fairfax, Virginia, and I am now in Fairfax, going to see him. I don't know why I'm doing what I'm doing, and I can't figure out why he came to see me. At first, I thought he came to see me to shoot me. He has me going in circles. I hoped you might be able to give me some insight because I am at a loss."

"I would have to know more about him because right now, it sounds like you have hurt his pride, and he just wants to see the man that made his wife feel like she wanted to betray his trust."

"Wait a minute! I didn't do anything. I don't know where this idea came from that has you thinking that I am some kind of great lover or something. When I knew her, I was not seeing her to have an affair."

"Well, maybe you weren't, but she was, and she picked you, and he probably just wanted to see what you look like. So go see him…have fun…let me know what happens."

"I asked Russ to find out about Lloyd. He has more about him, so call him and have him fill you in with more details."

"I will. We are having dinner with him tonight. After the second bottle, I'll ask about Lloyd. You stay in touch."

I wasn't thrilled with his comments or help, but it was better than nothing. I resolved that I would go see Lloyd.

The next morning I went to the hospital where he worked; it was the biggest in Fairfax. I just rode around because I didn't have enough nerve to walk in and start asking questions about Lloyd. Also, I didn't know what kind of reception I would receive. Lloyd had given me his home address, so I took a ride to his home. It was in the fashionable part of the suburbs; it was exactly what I had expected. It was located on a cul-de-sac. The house had a circular driveway in front. From the circular driveway, you had to make a sharp right turn to get to the three-car detached garage. The house itself was enormous; it looked as though it had ten rooms at least. It was two stories high with a small balcony across the entire front, which over looked the driveway.

The landscaping was impeccable with weirdly shaped bushes in abundance. In the back was a large pool that was barely visible through the hedges that surrounded it.

Looking at the house, I just couldn't imagine one person living in it all by himself. The more I looked at it, the more it looked like a monument to a man's stupidity. I kept asking myself, *What is he trying to prove and to whom is he trying to prove it?* The house with its surroundings for only one person took the word "ostentatious" to its full meaning.

I started to turn around to head back to my hotel when a sports car cut me off. I had to jam on my brakes or I would have hit the car. Before he got out of the car, I just knew it was Lloyd. I was right. Lloyd got out and came over to me as he said, "I can't believe you would come here and not come in for a drink. Please park in the driveway. Don't be so anti-social."

I just smiled and nodded. I had to backup before I could make the turn into the driveway. He went in first and pulled into one of the garages. By the time I got out of the car and went to the front door, he had it opened and was waving me in. I immediately envisioned the story of the spider's inviting the fly into its web. Being of stout heart, I entered.

In the foyer was a large chandelier that just overpowered the room. It looked as though it was the size of the room. It was not lit, but my imagination could just envision what it would look like if it were on. I followed him through the house as he gave a running commentary about it. We walked right through and out onto the back porch of the house. From this vantage point, I could see the entire back yard. It had a hedge all around it. There was a pool in the middle with a cabana on the far side. There was a large brick barbecue that looked like it belonged in a large restaurant rather than in someone's back yard. It reminded me of the back porch of Sue Ann's house overlooking the marina and the bay. On one side was a wet bar. Lloyd was jabbering away, but I was so preoccupied with looking around that I didn't hear him at first until I heard, "George…George… what would you like?"

"Just something cold."

"Here sit at the table." The table had a glass top and four chairs. The afternoon sun was shining on it, so Lloyd went over and pressed a button, and an awning came out from the house and shaded it. He came to the table, carrying two glasses filled with lemonade and sat on the opposite side of the table from me.

"When I was younger, I would have a glass of wine, but now I find that if I drink one now, I would be asleep before I finished it." I just nodded my head in agreement. He continued, "They really gave you a hard time about Sue Ann's untimely death, but you handled it well. A dismissal by a judge…that doesn't happen too often does it, especially in a criminal trial? I would have loved to have been there. I am pretty much retired now, but every so often the hospital asks me to teach a class or to consult on a few cases. Believe me I enjoy it; it keeps me from going nuts."

He kept talking about himself, but every so often, he mentioned something that had happened to me at the Cove. Finally I could stand no more of his chatter, so I interrupted him. "Lloyd, why don't you go to see Trina and her twins? You don't really sound like you enjoy living here in this mausoleum by yourself. What happened is done. I don't know why it happened, but there is nothing we can do about it now."

My words had a profound effect on him, for his facial expression changed from a soft smile to a solid stone expression.

There was a long pause before he responded, "You mean it really shows? You're right, of course, and maybe someday I will be able to; however, right now I don't know. I've gone to the Cove and have even gone to Sue Ann's house when she wasn't there, of course, but I never could bring myself to ring the bell. I saw Trina when she was waitressing, but again I just mingled with the other tourists and left. I usually have a late lunch or an early dinner about now. I find it easier to digest. There is a local restaurant that cooks for me and delivers. I wish you would stay and dine with me here or else we can go there."

His invitation caught me off guard, but before I knew it, I had accepted his invitation, and he called our order in. After that was done, he started telling me about Joann and him. He even told me about the night he came home after finding out that Sue Ann wasn't his child. "That was the worst time of my life." As he spoke, I could see tears' welling in his eyes. He continued, "You have no idea how many times I wish I could relive that day, but as you said, what happened is over. I can't erase it, even though I very much wanted to."

I could see he was starting to really lose his composure. I was really annoyed at myself for saying I would have dinner with him. Thankfully, the doorbell rang, and he had to leave to answer it. He came back with a young man, who quickly set the table and served the food. Lloyd refilled our glasses, and there was a strange sort of silence as we ate. I felt that silence was the third welcomed guest at the table. It acted as a buffer between Lloyd and me. Other than a few comments about the quality of the food, our meal was eaten in silence.

This strange threesome was broken by Lloyd's saying, "If you want, you can stay here. You'll have your own suite, and I would enjoy the company; as you can see, I have plenty of room."

I looked up at the house as I replied, "I can see that you do, but no thanks. I am comfortable where I am. Anyway, I want to get an early start tomorrow to go home; they are predicting bad weather of some sort." I got up and started to walk towards the front door. As I walked through the house, I took my time to inspect it more closely. My knowledge of housewares is limited, but even I could see that every item was expensive... from the lamps, to the dining room table and chairs. The list just went on and on. The Oriental rug under the dining room table looked like it cost a lot; it wasn't to my taste but WOW. I walked into the living room, which had three sofas set in a group with an Oriental style coffee table in the middle. When I saw the table, I had a flash back to Sue Ann's table. I abruptly turned and made my way to the door for fear that if something happened to him, I would really be in trouble. When I got to the door, without any delay, I opened it and walked outside as I said goodbye. As I got in my car, I waved to him and shouted out, "Go see Trina; you'll love the twins." I got in the car and drove to my hotel.

Chapter Twenty

Once in the safety of my room, I sat in the easy chair and let out a sigh of relief. I had a strange feeling that just made me feel cold, so cold that I just sat there and shivered. I couldn't make up my mind whether I felt sorry for him or if I hated him for making me mentally re-visit a place I didn't want to be. I thought that once Sue Ann was out of the picture and with the help of Eugene that I would rid myself of the feeling of wrongdoing, but sitting in a chair in a room by myself, I knew I was wrong. Whatever it was that was making me feel uneasy would be with me for the rest of my life. There was no getting away from it…whatever it is. When I saw Lloyd's coffee table, I relived my time with Sue Ann; when I saw his back yard, I was on the rear terrace with Sue Ann. As these thoughts went through my mind, I started to think I was going nuts. Thankfully, the phone rang. The ringing sounded so strange to me that it took me a long time before I answered it. By the time I did, the caller had hung up. I was thankful that the phone kept track of who had called, so I just had to push a button, and the calling party was called back. It was Eugene. I got a bittersweet feeling when I heard him say, "Hello."

"Russ gave me the full story on this Lloyd guy; you better watch yourself. He doesn't sound like he's dealing from a full deck. He never divorced her, but he never got over her unfaithfulness. That's weird, to say the least. Did you go see him? I mean, did you really see him?"

"I sat in the chair, not knowing whether or not I really wanted to talk about Lloyd, but I replied, "I went to his house. It looked like a mausoleum rather than a house. It's enormous and filled with expensive, beautiful things. I don't know if I should feel sorry for him or if I should pity him. He told me the whole sordid story about him and Joann. He scared the hell out of me."

"His pride was hurt. This is his way of showing everyone that he is better than anyone. He has lived a life of trying to prove to himself and those around him that he was not at fault for what happened...it must have been her...she did wrong, not him."

I heard the words, but I just could not believe them. I tried to say something, but before I could, Eugene continued with his analysis. "Contrary to many beliefs, the male ego is one of the most fragile things on Earth. There is no explaining it, and in most cases, it means little, for most males take disappointment in their stride. However, there have been cases where certain men can't deal with having their pride hurt; they have been known to do many strange things, things that defy logic and all rational thought. Your Mr. Lloyd sounds like one of those men, so be careful."

"I told him to go see Sue Ann's daughter, Trina, and her twins." Before I could finish the sentence, he interrupted me.

"You shouldn't have done that! He cannot forgive Joann, and Sue Ann is lost to him. Trina doesn't even know who he is, and now her children...that's adding insult to injury. All he is going to see is a life he should have had rather than the life he has; he couldn't deal with losing Joann, and now he is going to have to face losing Sue Ann and not being near Trina and her children. All that may be too much for him. When are you coming home? Your being down there is making Russ nuts."

"Do you really think he is a danger to himself and others?"

"There is no doubt in my mind that he is. As he gets older and out of his profession and away from people that he can show off to...he will be in his own little world that will be closing in on him. He will not have any way to release the pressure that he is putting on himself. I think coming to see you was just one more step away from reality. To answer your question, yes, I do believe he is a danger to himself."

"Is there anything I can do?"

"Yes, get out of there and get back here." I recognized it was Russ talking, not Eugene. He continued, "You're not going to be able to pull another Sue Ann defense out of your pocket."

"Okay, I'm leaving in the morning. I'll call you when I get home. Thank both of you for thinking of me; not many people have friends like I do." I hung up the phone and just sat for a long time before I got up and went to bed for a long night of twisting and turning, trying to find that one spot. I never did.

In the morning my plan was to leave early and get breakfast on my way home. I packed everything and turned on the T.V.; the news was showing a traffic jam on the highway; a tractor-trailer had turned over, and the morning rush-hour traffic was a mess. I turned the T.V. off and went to the dining room in the hotel and had breakfast there. I guess everyone else in the hotel had the same idea, for the room was packed. Finally, I was served. I went to my room and got my things and was on my way out the door when two men approached me. "Are you George?" By the way they looked with their short haircuts, frumpy suits, and the way that they acted; I knew they were the police. Before I could deny who I was, they showed me their badges and asked me to come to police headquarters because they had a few questions they wanted to ask me.

I stood in front of the hotel and looked at my two pursuers and was annoyed. My next thought was that they hadn't told me why they wanted to talk to me.

"What do you want of me? I am on my way home. If it wasn't for the traffic jam, I wouldn't even be here, so what do you want." It was easy to see that they were both annoyed that I took the belligerent attitude that I did.

"You were the last person to see Lloyd Stein alive. As he is now dead, we have some questions to ask you."

I was impressed by their speed and ability to track me down

so quickly, but that did not alter the fact that here I was being dragged into something I wanted no part of. I looked at them as I replied, "You know I have no obligation to talk to you. I really have to get home. Where is your station? I will follow you, so I can leave right from there. If you'll feel better about it, one of you can ride with me."

They looked at each other, for it was plain to see that they'd never had a request like that before. They nodded to each other and one of them said, "It's five minutes from here. If you want to bring your car, I'll show you where to go and I'll let you park in our garage."

We split up; my escort went in my car and the other officer went by himself. The station was literally right around the corner. I was allowed to park in the police garage, and we walked into the station through the back door. I was taken to the detective room and another detective joined us and sat at the computer, ready to type my statement.

After a series of general questions, they started to get into my relationship with Lloyd and Sue Ann. It was obvious that they had gotten the whole story on Sue Ann and were now trying to see if there was any connection between the two cases. They became very annoyed when I refused to talk about the Sue Ann situation. When they questioned me about her, I just replied, "That matter has been adjudicated and has no place here. I have no obligation to be here. I am here to try to help you out, so please just keep your questions limited to Lloyd. One officer jumped up and screamed. "You will not tell us how or what to ask! This is a murder investigation…there are no …"

I just interrupted him by standing up and saying. "When you conduct yourself as a professional, I will be glad to continue, but I will not stand for your trying to bully me."

The officer was led away by another officer. As soon as things quieted down, I started talking before any of them could. "I've come here and given you my statement. You have my address, so if there is anything else, you can contact me; if not, I thank you for your hospitality." I turned and walked toward the door.

"Wait," came a voice from the other side of the room. "This isn't The Cove…you don't tell us what to do…we will tell you when you can leave…now sit down before I throw you down."

"No, you do what you think best, but I am not going to take any such treatment from you."

The man started to make a move towards me, and by now there were many more officers in the room. Another officer restrained him. The tension in the room could be felt. No one made a move until finally one detective came over to me and said, "Thank you for your cooperation. If there is anything else, we will be in touch."

"Before I go, could I hear what happened to Lloyd?"

"He tied a rope around his neck and jumped off the front balcony of his home in front of a few of his neighbors. He died instantly; he broke his neck."

"Thank you," I said as I left the office. The detective who rode over with me came to me and said, "I don't know why they wanted to bring you in, but you know I only take orders."

"I know." I left and drove across the state line as soon as possible. The rest of the drive home was uneventful. Once in the safety of my home, I poured myself a glass of port and sat in the easy chair and tried to make sense out of everything that had happened, but I just couldn't. Another person was dead because of Joann's indiscretion. Finally sleep became my ally and my protector…at least for the night.

Epilogue

I followed up after a while to see what had happened to the rest of the people who were affected by what Joann had done. Sue Ann and Hilda were dead, but as I thought about it, there would have been no Sue Ann if it weren't for Joann.

No one heard anything else from Hilda's parents. The undertaker sent her body home, and that ended any further involvement with them. A hearing was held about the shooting, but nothing came of it.

Trina and Steve were the proud parents of twins: a boy named Steve, Jr., and a girl named Joann. Their business was thriving and they both became pillars of society.

Ruth and Lila were still Lila and Ruth; nothing really changed in their lives except they were very fond of taking the twins for a walk around town and being introduced as the twins' aunts.

Russ enjoyed the part he played in helping me out with the problem I had. His first love was helping me in my hours of need. He thoroughly enjoyed telling people that. The airport incident finally ended with the decision that it was an unforeseeable accident. That finding made the owner of the airport very happy. He expounded to all who would listen, "I run a clean operation here. I do no wrong, and the government agrees with me."

The chief finally drank and smoked himself to death. No matter what the Commodore said or did, he could not get the judge or the doctors to commit him to an institution. Although he felt badly for not being able to help the chief, he finally realized that being in an institution would be no kind of life for anyone. He resolved to be happy that he had failed. Ruth, Lila, Trina, and he were the only people at the funeral. That hurt the

Commodore more than anything. "He was not an animal," Trina heard him say while leaving the gravesite.

Mildred was never able to get full use of her arm, so her career as a police officer was over. She was awarded a citation for bravery for the shooting incident, but because it had ended her police career, it did not impress her. After the awards dinner, she moved from The Cove just as quickly as she had arrived. No one knew where she came from or where she'd gone.

Chad was still the editor of the local newspaper. The paper was regaining some of its former glory. The story he'd written about my trial was picked up by one of the major newspapers, but they never ran it. No one could figure out why. The story about the airport incident was also picked up, and they ran that, giving Chad full credit for writing it.

Still riding herd over the town is the Commodore. His life has changed very little, even though he is at the center of all activity and news. He runs his store and restaurant as he caters to the locals and the tourists. He tells and retells the story of the shootout in his store at the least provocation. While retelling it, he has added more details and even, on some occasions, has changed some of the facts to please his audiences.

Eugene and Mary still live up by the club, and Eugene still helps Nancy out with her personal list. Every so often when I go see Russ, they stop in to visit and join us for dinner. Mary still holds the record as being the best shopper in the area, a title that she cherishes.

I wrote this book as therapy for what happened to me. As I wrote it, I relived some of the sorrow and fear and finally relief. My friend the priest, whom I take out to dinner once in a while, told me that reliving the incidents would help to cleanse my soul. He just laughed when I told him that his advice came a lot cheaper than Eugene's.

I went back to The Cove when Trina had the twins. She was the one who brought me up to date on what everyone was up to.

She couldn't say enough about Lila and Ruth, who are both a great help to her. After listening to her, I didn't know whether or not to curse Joann or thank her for what she had done. When my picture was taken holding the twins, I was really challenged to control my emotions. How could I hate them for what their great-grandmother had done?

On my way back from The Cove, I was torn between the two greatest emotions...hate and love. Between the two, I found hate is easier because avoiding the person/thing will take care of it. Love takes a lot of giving and, therefore, is much harder but a lot more satisfying. When I got home, I resolved to forget about The Cove until the twins' first birthday when I'd promised I would go back, but what about Christmas?

I know I have to draw the line somewhere, but I just didn't know where or when I would do it.

The End

About the Author

George Delmarmo is a retired accountant and attorney living in Brick, New Jersey. He has traveled extensively while representing an international list of clientele. His experiences varied to all types of assignments that required his special mixture of talents. He started writing to fill the void in his life created by his retirement. He has written a series of books, which are a reflection of his travels and experiences. He is a member of the New Jersey as well as the New York bars and is a licensed accountant in the State of New Jersey.

Memoirs of a Retired Modern Day Mercenary, George.

George is a retired mercenary who at the end of his career started writing his memoirs.

To contact George please send an email to:

hogfarmer@aol.com

Books by George Delmarmo

A Heart Never Heals: The story of a girl George sees in a vision. She appeared to George while in Italy working on a case. She was walking out of the Mediterranean Sea. The vision is so vivid that he visits the Vatican to confer with a Cardinal seeking an explanation of what he saw. The Cardinal advises George to start from the very beginning of the events of what brought him to that spot at that time. George relates the details of his journey. When George returns home he finishes the case before he starts on his maddening quest to find his vision.

All About Mary: The story about the extent that the police will go to entrap someone. The tactics police use when used against them creates the backdrop of the story. Emotions such as love and affection are used like any other tool. The legality of an act is only a wisp of air and so many words when the party in charge tries to use them for their own benefit. The main character is an attorney in the prosecutor's office who changes her name and her persona in order to get her man. The results she achieves winds up being her own downfall.

Cooperstown Diamonds: The story of a man who lived his life to the fullest by manipulating everyone one around him. He was the kind of man who lived his life according to his rules and somehow everyone just let him do what he wanted. By using his personal charm and cunning built for himself his own World and loved every minute of it. He would be accused of many things but with the help of his friend was never found guilty of any wrong doing. He could play his life as one would play a fiddle, just for his pleasure.

The Darkest Day: Deals with a family's problems of Divorce and Abortion. It also deals with a woman who decides that she is going to become the matriarch of the family. Her domination destroys the family for no one in the family wants her to assume such a role. What the members of her family want are secondary to her unmerciful quest to become the dominant factor. She learns too late the folly of her choices. The financial viability and the stability of her family are destroyed before her very eyes but this does not deter her from her quest.

Deception by Marriage: The story of a man and woman who use marriages as a method of getting what they want out of life. They have no regard for the human tragedy they leave behind. They have no sympathy or concern for the people around them. Divorce and abandonment are used as tools and a convenient method of getting in and out of situations that no longer interest them. The children as well as spouses they leave behind are of no concern to them as they go through life searching for what they feel will satisfy them for the moment.

End of the Light: The story deals with one man's encounter with the supernatural. The love of one man is traced throughout his life and the life of the woman he loved. Their affection for each other lasted throughout both their lives. Although she died years before him he was still close to her until his death that occurred years later. After her death her spirit stayed in the lighthouse where they first met until he joined her. Try as he may he could not forget or get away from her. The story is sad for he never wanted to.

Hate Crimes: The story revolves around a group of people who use the acts of the police to create a resort type setting. People are invited to participate in some of the infamous shootouts. The story examines the actions of police and criminals alike. After studying them, the acts are used to train a group of people to enforce what should be done rather than what the law allows. The training of different groups of people blends in with the resort type atmosphere that the story is set in. The training is sometimes used to thwart the police's efforts to stop crimes.

It Begins... It Ends: The story of a murder case set in an actual setting. It shows the investigating and defending of a suspect while life still goes on. Although a lawyer takes on a case his on personal life as well of his associates still continues. Each element of the story is set in the middle of all the activities that take place as an ordinary part of living. The story also points out the errors that can be made in gathering evidence. These errors whether done by omission or commission can get a person convicted. The story stresses the defense attorney's job.

Last of the Last: The story of a man who pleaded guilty to a crime he didn't commit. At the time he did it was cheaper to do so than to go through a trial. After the plea is entered the government changes the terms of the plea. The change deals with the prison he will be sent to. The man decided to agree to the terms anyway. He contracts a fatal disease. The closer he gets to death's door the more he can't deal with his plea as a mark on his soul. George is hired to have the guilty plea set aside.

Mississippi After Dark: The story of a series of unexplained disappearances and deaths. The police feared that a serial killer might be responsible. He had to be stopped. The question was how. No outsider law enforcers were welcomed in the state least of all the FBI. The state was concerned with their public image if the story leaked out to the media. They did not want the federal government serial killer division officially involved. The State's concern was created by the popularity of the movie, Mississippi Burning. George was hired to quietly find the killer and to end the killings.

Outraged in Mexico: The story of a town and its people caught up in violence and manipulation of a system that was ruled by one man. When they could take no more they rebelled against the tyranny and recaptured their lives. The retribution they took against those who enslaved them and the effort the people put forth to rebuild their lives is what makes up the basis for the story. The people involved are constantly forced to decide what values they want to nurture and what to disregard. They are forced to change their values to rid themselves of their oppressors.

Rape: The story of a young man who is accused of Rape. The case causes the boy and girl to examine their own minds as to whether or not a rape occurred in the legal sense and in the moral sense. The state becomes so relentless in their quest to convict the boy that they forget that their job is also to protect the innocent. The ethnic and religious backgrounds of the two people is difficult to keep out of the case as they are both caught up in the whirlwind that is created whenever the crime of Rape is charged.

2.8 Seconds: The story of an alleged plot to assassinate the Pope during his visit to Venezuela. The people of the country were divided as to the value of having the Holy Father visit the country. George was hired to find the people involved as well as make sure that the assassination did not take place. Neither the church officials nor the authorities wanted to be connected to the investigation in anyway. His assignment also was to include developing an assassination plan that circumvented all the precautions taken by both the church as well as the government security forces.

When God Ain't Lookin': The story covers the life time of two people meeting, parting and reuniting again. The characters are from two different worlds. Ann is a nun who is not sure she wants to be a nun because of the hypocrisy she found in her order. Although twenty-five when she first meets George she looks much younger. George is a twenty year old young man when they meet and has no idea that he is dating an older woman who is a nun. Their meetings over the years cause much joy and sadness for both of them.

Yellow River: The story of the "Enforcers" leaving Hong Kong when it was returned to Chinese rule. They were the Chinese who helped the English control Hong Kong during England's rule. The "Enforcers" were hated by their own countrymen and feared by everyone else in the world. They feared nothing. They had no ties to any Faith, Family or Country. They were ruthless and yet well educated by watching the British. The "Enforcers" were allowed to leave Hong Kong and enter Canada and America as long as they were penniless. They had to find different ways to bring their wealth with them.

www.ingramcontent.com/pod-product-compliance
Lightning Source LLC
Chambersburg PA
CBHW032141020726

47496CB00003B/666